The Redemptive Chronicles:
Retribution

by
D.M. Kurtz

Cover art digitally painted by Sam White: Copyright © 2017 by Sam White

Cover formatted by Gaston Kurtz: Copyright © 2017 by Gaston Kurtz

Manuscript edited by Natasha A. Kurtz and Laura M. Kurtz

A special thanks to Alan Horton for his friendship and support during the early stages of writing and development.

ISBN-13: 978-1499146394
ISBN-10: 1499146396

DEDICATION

To my loving wife, who has always supported me through this venture, and to my sister, who has been a constant guide as the adventures contained within Retribution have unfolded, and to the numerous friends and family members who have given their encouragement.

CONTENTS

CHAPTER 1

TIES THAT BIND?

Lightning flashed dimly amid swirls of darkness to reveal a decayed land; bare soil broken only by the remnants of dead brush and trees. These crunched lightly under the feet of a young man, clutching tightly to his cloak as it rippled in the wind. Slowly he crept toward an object that stood out in sharp contrast to the surrounding wasteland. He was not sure why but he seemed drawn to it, as if it called out to him, beckoning for his approach. As he drew closer he began to relax the grip on his cloak, for the wind lessened, the lightning ceased and the clouds parted ever so slightly to cast a sudden dim ray of light onto the device which was now only a few paces away. It glittered under the rays of the sun, a metallic silver sheen, and the young man gasped when he took in its form and beauty, for he now realized that the strange item was in fact a sword, stuck into the ground at a slight angle. Marvelous he thought it to be; wonderfully crafted, though odd as well, for an unusual inscription could be seen etched into the length of the blade.

Its hilt was darkened silver, and it had the shape of two thin dragon wings spread out to grant the wielder protection from an enemy blade. The rest was like that of the upper body and head of a dragon, with the blade protruding from beneath a closed maw; two red rubies were its eyes. The creature's body twisted down and around the handle, with each coil spread apart just enough to create the perfect grip for the wielders fingers; the wicked spiked tip of a dragon's tail was the pommel. Filled with wonder and recognition the young man reached out with his fingers that stretched slowly toward the hilt before he took in a sharp breath and jerked back his hand, for blood began to pour out from the rubies like tears, spilling down the blade and staining the earth below...

... "Nnnh!" the young man rose from deep slumber with a grunt and a jerk while heaving deep gasping breaths as the images of his dream flashed through his mind. With a shake of his head he rubbed weary eyes, pushed up to his feet and squinted as he left the shade of the oak that had allowed him rest from his labor in the fields he'd been tending since early dawn. He frowned when his stomach growled angrily to make plain its irritation at its master's long labor without a meal since midday.

After pulling a canteen from a pouch on his belt, he removed its cap and took several deep swigs before he replaced the lid with a content sigh as the cool water touched his throat. Then, with a smile at the thought of whatever meal he knew awaited him back at home, he returned the water-skin to its pouch and moved over to the team of oxen he had been using to plow the fields. After wiping perspiration from his brow he retrieved and donned the cloak he had draped over the handles when a light, chill breeze suddenly blew his sandy brown, medium-length hair into his eyes for a moment before he brushed it away with some irritation; his cloak he pulled tightly around him and buttoned the three black pins near his right hip.

He had a handsome face, in its own way, for puberty had had little ill effect on it, though his rough life of near constant work had marred his otherwise pleasant features with a few light scars. A medium tan covered his skin as a sign of his hard work in the sun while well-built muscles that complemented his otherwise average and slender six-foot build could be seen rippling over his arms and shoulders. The cloak he wore was of a once-white fabric now faded, worn, and stained with years of sweat and dirt. It was laced with a deep red and black in a woven design that lined the front edges. His mother had made it herself for him as a gift on his fifteenth birthday, and it had served him faithfully in the four years since. His boots were of a dark black leather, cured from an old hog, and a belt of the same material as the boots was clasped round his waist, but the most curious and valuable object of all was the sword that hung by his side.

The magnificent weapon had been a gift from Kelmîn his father, signifying the boy's growing from youth into manhood at the age of fourteen. The blade was of truly marvelous craftsmanship, with a razor edge that seemed almost magical, for it never grew dull nor showed any sign of rust or wear from the ravages of time, and this was without requiring oil or polish. The scabbard was dark black, with pure silver adorning the top and bottom. Though large, it was lighter than most swords and was perfectly balanced; the blade itself was roughly four feet in length.

With a stretch and a yawn the young man bent down and secured the cleverly designed blades of the plow into their place above the wheels before he spurred the oxen out of the middle of the field and onto a well-worn road. With just weeks until the harvest his eyes took in the crops that he and his brother with their father had worked so hard to plant: rows and rows of corn and beans were to his right, with wheat and potatoes on his left. After heaving a content sigh he absently surveyed the vast countryside while he continued along the road; marveling as he often did at the great tree-covered passes and rolling hills of the Basilicus Mountains to his left. He grimaced suddenly, for images of a swirling darkness flashed through his mind as his eyes scanned a small clearing in the distance and his lips twitched while he recalled briefly snippets of the vivid dream that had held him captive earlier. Shaking somber thoughts from his head he pressed forward, and after several minutes he reached the halfway point, marked by two great oak trees standing side-by-side with a hammock between them. Here the path curved and he came to a vast field of oats to his right with a vegetable garden to his left. Immediately following those was a large pasture with a dozen or so cows; all grazing, lolling lazily about, or lying down enjoying the sun.

"Daedrin, dinner!" the voice of his mother rang out faintly as he came to a final curve and his farm, made up of the main house, a barn and a chicken coop, came into view. The home itself was a humble dwelling, made simply of logs with two bedrooms, a small kitchen, and a dining area that also served as the recreational area; it had three windows. Daedrin's father had begun to build the structure with his own hands just three years before his wife Seline had learned that she would soon bear their first child, and he had completed the construction only weeks before Daedrin's birth. Beside the house only a stone's throw away was the barn, which, while large enough to hold all of the livestock currently housed only their two horses and a single goat, while the back portion of the building stored what little was left from the last harvest; kept as food during the months of planting and for trading when merchants visited in early spring. Built onto the side of the barn was a pen that housed nearly twenty chickens and a single rooster, with a large yard right behind; barren from its constant toil under the animals' feet.

Smoke rose from the hardened clay chimney atop the roof of the house and, as Daedrin approached the dwelling the delicious smell of roast beef stew wafted into his nostrils. He breathed deeply and his belly growled once more with a hunger that served as another reminder that it had already been hours since his last meal. Quickly he steered the oxen into the barn, disconnected them from the plow and directed them each to their own stall where he filled their feeding trough with oats. He then moved to the front of the house and washed his hands and arms with water from a well beside the front door before wiping his shoes on a braided mat and stepping inside.

"Well, it's about time," Melkai, his younger brother of eight years said from his seat at a wooden table in the center of the room. The boy rose with a goofy and proceeded to gather the several books that were laid out around him before placing them on a shelf in one corner.

Daedrin smirked while he removed his sword-belt and hung it from a hook beside the door.

"You jest now," he replied as he wiped his hands on a towel he had retrieved from a hook near the door. "But the day will soon come when you are finished with your studies and can tend to the farm just as long as I."

"Boys," the voice of Seline echoed from across the home, "help set the table, please."

Daedrin placed the towel back on its hook and walked through the door directly to his right where he entered the kitchen just in time to see his mother carrying a large pot full of beef stew to the dining room; she nearly spilled it all over her son when she ran into him.

"Whoa, mother, let me get that," Daedrin said as he took the pot from her and steered it to the table. He was quickly followed by his brother and mother; Melkai laden with bowls and spoons while Seline carried two more pans of food.

"Mmm, spinach and rolls," Daedrin's mouth watered while he beheld the feast as it was laid out on the table. "Where's father?" he asked.

"Finishing up on repairing a saddle," Seline told him while she filled four cups with water from a pitcher. "He'd better be in soon, or he jus' might miss dinner," she added with a laugh.

"All the more for us," Melkai quipped.

"That quick to eat your hard-working father's portion of the meal, eh?" Kelmîn's voice boomed suddenly from the front of the house as he entered.

Melkai smiled sheepishly. "Of course not father," he said. "Ah, it was *him* that wanted to eat all of it!" he added while pointing at his brother. "I was trying to stop him, honest." He put on his best poker face and Kelmîn laughed before he tossed over the back of a chair the small towel he had been using to wipe his hands as he approached the table.

"That certainly sounds like something your mother would allow," he said humorously; he received a playful glare from his wife as he moved to sit at the head of the table. "Now, I'm famished," he added. "Let's eat!" He was met by hearty agreement from the rest of the family while they took their seats; Seline to the right of her husband and Melkai to the left, with Daedrin beside his younger brother. They held hands and looked up as Kelmîn blessed the food.

"We thank you, Creator, for this wondrous meal," he declared solemnly. "We know that we are very blessed to have so much, when there are many who have nothing. I thank you for keeping my family safe from harm, and I ask that we continue to have your protection. Give us strength to face each day, for you certainly know we need it, and," he added with a smile, "perhaps grant Melkai a strong stomachache for his selfishness; amen." They all laughed after he had finished and began passing the food around the table.

"We're going to have quite a harvest this year," Daedrin commented absently once all had bowls filled with stew.

"Yes," Kelmîn agreed between mouthfuls. "It's going to be a difficult season, but we will manage. Your brother here is strong," he added with a smile as he ruffled Melkai's hair. Daedrin smirked while his mother frowned.

"I sure worry about all of you, when it comes time for the harvest," she said pensively. Kelmîn took her hand and smiled while he brought it to his lips.

"I know, love," he said reassuringly as he let their hands part, "but we'll be fine; we always are. You need not worry." Seline smiled weakly.

"Uh-hum," Daedrin cleared his throat, causing Kelmîn and Seline to turn to face him; he had one eyebrow raised at their intimacy. Seline turned a bright shade of pink, while Kelmîn grinned and winked at his son.

"Not to spoil the evening," Daedrin said, "but you'll likely need to hire someone from the village after this season." Kelmîn's face hardened suddenly at this declaration, while Seline looked downcast.

"Daedrin," Kelmîn said roughly, "I thought we told you; you're not leaving."

Daedrin's jaw tightened. "I thought I'd gotten it into your thick head that there's nothing you can do to stop me. I'm already a man, free to go where I wish!" With a crash Kelmîn slammed his fist onto the table and cursed.

Seline gasped. "Kelmîn, watch your tongue!" she exclaimed. He ignored her.

"Are we seriously having this discussion again?!" he said as his voice rose steadily. "The son I raised should know better than to go traipsing all throughout the land with a blacksmith and some village harlot!"

"How dare you?!" Daedrin declared as he shot up from his seat with fists clenched and shaking. (About this time Melkai silently slipped out of his seat and retreated to the room he shared with Daedrin.) Kelmîn sighed while he ground his teeth angrily.

"Daedrin," Seline interjected with a frown at her husband. "I know that you love Marin, and Skane is offering adventure but, you must realize that there is naught to be gained from exploring Silmaín."

Daedrin sighed and rubbed his jaw in frustration as he sank slowly back into his chair.

"I know you think that mum, but I disagree," he said. "Though that is hardly the issue here," he added with a glare at his father. "The traders have spoken often of opportunities for work out in the far reaches of the country. My place is not here," he waved his arm about in a grand gesture, "forever. I want more out of life than farming, for myself and for Marin." Silence ensued, and while Seline and Daedrin picked at their food Kelmîn only stared angrily at his plate. Finally, with a dark look in his eyes he spoke terrible words to his son.

"Daedrin, if you should indeed choose this path then know this: you will no longer be considered my son," he declared. "You will be as a stranger to me; never again will you be allowed to set foot in my house."

Seline gasped while her spoon fell from her grasp and clattered loudly on the table. Her eyes filled with fury when she beheld the crushed and enraged look on her son's face as he leaped from his chair and tore out of the house, pausing only to grab his sword-belt from the wall. With a swift stroke she slapped her husband hard across his face before rising quickly from her seat and running after Daedrin, but by the time she made it through the door his speed had already taken him far from their home.

He'd run for several minutes with hurt, furious tears filling his eyes before a stitch in his side forced him to stop and catch his breath; poisonous thoughts filled his heart as he paced angrily. *Ungrateful, worthless excuse for a father,* he thought. *To speak so cruelly of Marin... and to dare threaten me! Not his son... how can he say that? How can any father say such a terrible thing to his own son?* A single tear finally escaped and slid down his cheek before he brushed it away angrily. Slowly, as his thoughts calmed and his racing pulse slowed to a steadier rhythm he walked over to an oak at the edge of the grazing pastures and slumped to the ground with the tree at his back, feeling utterly defeated. Closing weary eyes he quietly muttered soft prayers before falling silent and, after a few moments he slipped into a light sleep.

The first rays of moonlight were just beginning to caress the land when Daedrin woke with a blink of momentary confusion before the previous encounter crashed hard through his mind. He grimaced and remained as he was for several minutes until finally, as the moon rose slightly higher to cast its rays more clearly on the grass of the fields he rose to his feet. After a few moments of silent pondering he decided that he was not yet ready to go home and so, with a stretch and a yawn he moved gradually down the path toward the nearby village of Linull.

The place was named after a rare healing herb, called Linellin, which grew among the fields that skirted one edge of the town. As far as anyone knew Linull was the only place in the entire world that the herb could be found, and so traders and common folk alike traveled from even the furthest corners of the realm of Silmain to buy or barter for the treasured plant. Linellin could cure a vast array of known ailments as well as rapidly heal many injuries and, needless to say its worth was unimaginable. The villagers however were kindly folk who followed the path of benevolence as laid out by the Creator, and so they sold the herb at a very low cost, or even gave it to those who had great need of it's remarkable powers, yet could not afford its already more than generous price.

The sound of crickets and frogs tickled Daedrin's ears from the dark of the surrounding fields; cheerful sounds, he realized, despite his somber mood. Absently he tugged at the hilt of his sword while he walked for nearly fifteen minutes before the village crept into view with its small, humble wooden buildings with thatch roofs that lined the street on either side. First to his right as he approached was the town smithy, followed by four homes before the street opened up into a sort of main village square; empty at this late hour, save for a few chickens scratching at the ground for food. Lamps were lit in homes, and raucous laughter could be heard from the tavern down the way.

"Oi, Daedrin!" a familiar voice, thick with a folkish accent touched his ears. Daedrin smiled weakly as he beheld his good friend Skane approaching him in all his massive six-foot-five, muscled form, for the sight of his companion brought some warmth to his troubled heart. When the distance between them had closed he greeted his friend with an outstretched arm and a fervent hand clasp that left his fingers filthy from the grime on the hands of the hard-working man.

"I saw ye from the window of my smithy," Skane told him, and then asked, "are ye alright, lad?" as he took in the forlorn look on the young man's face. Daedrin shrugged wearily and, after a few moments of silence Skane wrapped one of his barrel like arms around the shoulder of his friend.

"Well, ye look like one in need o' a pint of ale, eh?" the blacksmith asked with a grin.

Daedrin laughed and nodded. "Never have I needed a drink more than now, my friend," he replied.

"Well then, by all means let's travel to my home, shall we?" He gave a firm squeeze and a pat on Daedrin's shoulder before removing his arm. "Per'aps some ale and good company will lift yer spirits enough to speak of what ails ye," he added while the two companions strolled down the street and passed the village smithy before they approached a home that was placed near the edge of the main village square; it was four houses down from the beginning of the lane.

Skane opened the door and made a light motion for Daedrin to enter before following himself and sealing the home behind them. The young man then proceeded to light a small oil lamp that hung high by the entrance with a match from a box stored beneath before he passed the light to the blacksmith. After taking a step forward, they moved down a narrow, unfurnished hallway with plain wooden floors before entering a kitchen at the end of the hall. After centering the lamp on a round table surrounded by four chairs, Skane proceeded to remove two plain pewter cups from a shelf and drew a pint of ale for each of them from a small barrel on the counter. When each had mug in hand, they took a seat at the table and sat in silence for a few moments; Daedrin stared blankly at his mug while Skane observed the young man carefully and sipped from his own cup.

"That ale won't drink itself, m'boy," he mused with a slight smirk. Daedrin blinked, looked up at his friend and smiled weakly.

"I apologize," he said, "too much on my mind tonight, I'm afraid." After heaving a sigh the young man took a long swig from his mug, the swiftness of which caused ale to spill over the rim and down his cheek, which he swiftly wiped away.

When he looked up it was to Skane peering at him with a single raised eyebrow. Daedrin chuckled at the strange look on his friend's face and looked down sheepishly for a moment while the blacksmith took a sip from his own mug and simply waited. Finally Daedrin rolled his neck with a scowl, took another swig of ale and began to tell his friend what had transpired earlier that evening.

When the tale was relayed in full Skane looked on with narrowed eyes. "So then, are ye reconsiderin' our trip?" he asked cautiously.

Daedrin quickly shook his head. "Absolutely not," he said, and his friend let out a huge sigh of relief. "My father... well, in his eyes farming is all there is to life, because it's all he's ever known. But you know me, Skane," to which the blacksmith nodded his assent and smiled when he beheld a glimmer of joy return to the young man's eyes. "I've always wanted more… Marin certainly deserves much better than I can offer if we stay," he added with a smile as the image of her fair face flickered through his mind. "Every story from the traders of far off lands has ever increased my desire to rest my eyes on the marvels of the world. I wouldn't cancel our plans for anything…" he paused as his eyes narrowed. "Even if it means never laying eyes on home again," he concluded softly, and Skane winced.

"Well I… certainly hope it'll not come to that," he said quietly before taking another sip from his mug. "I can offer no good counsel to aid ye with yer father, I'm afraid," he added after a beat of silence. "Ye know that mine died when I was but a boy, so I… have no experience with such things." Daedrin smirked and downed the last of his ale in one long swig; Skane chuckled and did the same.

"As soon as Melkai's studies are finished," Daedrin declared as he placed his empty mug onto the table, "I can leave this place behind me."

Skane dipped his head. "Well as always, lad, ye are most welcome to stay here tonight, if ye wish. Guest bed is always yers."

Daedrin nodded gratefully while he yawned. "I think I shall take you up on that. I'm… not ready to go home just yet."

"Well, let's get some rest then, shall we?" Skane sighed and slapped his hands on his knees. "The sun casts its first rays early this time o' year!" After rising from his seat, Skane grabbed the lamp and motioned for Daedrin to exit. Leaving their mugs behind on the table they moved out of the kitchen, down the hallway and entered a small room plainly furnished by a small cot and nightstand with a single window overlooking the bed. After bidding his friend goodnight, Skane exited the room, letting it plunge into darkness penetrated only by weak moonlight that drifted into the room from the faded glass.

After removing his sword-belt and boots, Daedrin sank onto the thin mattress and shifted to his side to get more comfortable; yet despite his best efforts, sleep refused to come. His restless mind wandered, from the darkest depths of painful memory to the furthest reaches of imagination before ending in the faded flashes of brush and wilderness as he tried to recall the dream that had plagued his unconscious mind earlier that day. He tossed and turned over the next hour while the tumultuous sounds of the tavern next door touched his ears, and in the midst of his frustrated thought grew the gnawing sense that he was neglecting something important. With a frown at his inability to grasp whatever it was that eluded his mind he rolled to his side and breathed deeply until, at long last sleep slowly took hold.

CHAPTER 2

NASCI

Daedrin woke with a jerk and a gasp, pulled from his slumber by the sudden remembrance of a midnight meeting with Marin that he had forgotten in the midst of his turmoil over the words of his father. He blinked as his eyes adjusted to the darkness of the room under faint moonlight that was just as dull as when he had first laid down. Rising quickly he rolled off of the bed with a dull thump when his feet hit the floor before he pulled on his boots, grabbed his sword-belt from its place on the wall and strapped it on as he left the room, pausing only to shut the door quietly behind him.

A sudden piercing cry caused Daedrin's brow to furrow as he approached the front door of the dwelling, and he jumped in surprise when Skane burst through the door of his own room and rubbed bleary eyes while he stumbled into the hall.

"Ye heard that too, eh?" the blacksmith asked as he pulled on his boots and hurried to join his friend. Daedrin nodded with a worried look while he pulled the front door open and stepped outside where he stood for a moment and listened intently.

"Help me, please help me!" a frantic voice suddenly echoed through the village streets. The young man felt his heart skip a beat, for beneath the panic of the cry were the familiar tones of one whom he loved dearly.

"Marin!" he exclaimed softly when he suddenly turned and pressed through an alley to his left with Skane close behind. They ran through it as quickly as the little lane would allow and, after a few turns they came to one of the meadows where the valued Linellin grew. The land was covered in naught but the leafy green herbs with little yellow flowers, save for a single elm right in the middle. To his horror, Daedrin then beheld something that he had only imagined from stories of legends in distant parts of the country: a Nasci. It stood on its hind legs and left deep gouges in the base of the tree as it steadily climbed up the trunk.

Its appearance was like that of a great wolf, except in place of fur were dark black scales, and the creature would have been at least four foot tall were it to stand level on its thick, muscular legs. Its head was short and wide above broad shoulders, and it had a stout neck beneath a protruding maw filled with vicious teeth; on its hindquarters was a nub for a tail. For a few moments Daedrin merely stood there as he exchanged a shocked glance with his friend but, the uncertainty did not last long, for he caught a glimpse high up in the branches of the worn hem of a deep green dress that he knew well.

Sudden terror while his heart began to race loosed whatever inhibitions the young man had about confronting such a creature. Silently he drew his sword and crept up behind the Nasci, using such stealth as he did when hunting a doe, and all would have been well had the creature not been graced with a keen sense of smell, for when Daedrin closed the distance between them it suddenly turned with red eyes that gleamed in the moonlight as it charged with a roar. He had no time to react and it was upon him in but a moment; with a pounce it knocked him to the ground with a loud thump.

"Daedrin!" Skane cried in horror as he came to his senses and drew a knife from his belt before running to aid his friend. "Get off him, ye great lummox!" he yelled while waving his arms rather foolishly, but much to his surprise the Nasci did not move.

Cautiously he approached it with blade brandished before he slowly dared to press a hand against its side; it did not react. Emboldened, Skane placed both hands on the creature's scaly hide and pushed with all his might against the brute, causing it to roll to its side with a dull thud. Daedrin, to Skane's horror, lay limp and still where he had fallen; he was covered in blood. The blacksmith knelt down and gently touched his companion's shoulder when, with a gasp, Daedrin suddenly sprang up to his elbows and cried out in agony as he groped his left leg.

Skane nearly fell over in relief. "Praise the Creator, lad, ye live!" he cried.

Daedrin groaned, and they both focused their eyes on the creature now lying lifeless amid the herbs of the field. The hilt of the young man's sword could just be seen protruding from the monster's belly where it had slipped between a set of scales and pierced the creatures hide.

"The Creator must be watching out for me," Daedrin's face was pale with shock as the words shakily escaped his lips. He reached out to grasp his sword but fell quickly back and stifled a shout of pain.

"Don't move, lad!" Skane commanded as he moved to inspect Daedrin's leg. "That's quite the gash you've got there, and I think your leg is broken," and so it was. Blood slowly pumped from the tear in Daedrin's thigh just above the knee where the bone had ripped the skin when it snapped.

"Skane," Daedrin's voice was weak, "help me."

The blacksmith quickly removed the leather belt from his waist and wrapped it around Daedrin's leg just above the wound. He cinched it tight, causing the young man to flinch and groan as the blood flowing from his leg was slowed. He reached his arm out and Skane pulled him to his feet, all the while keeping a hand on his friends shoulder to steady him.

"We must get ye to the healer, quick," Skane said worriedly, but for a moment Daedrin just stood there in a daze while he stared down at the slain mythical creature at his feet. Finally, with Skane's help he bent down slowly, removed his sword from the creature's chest and wiped the blood from the blade off on a cloth he had withdrawn from his cloak. After rising, he sheathed it and, had the situation not been so dire he would perhaps have felt noble. As it was he could hardly control the shudders that began to course through his body while the pain threatened to numb his conscious mind. He took one step and would have surely fallen on his face had Skane not grabbed his arm.

"Don't try to walk on yer own," the blacksmith commanded. "Let me help ye," he added as he wrapped one of his barrel-like arms around Daedrin's shoulders. When they turned the young man grunted, for Marin's slender form suddenly collided with his own as she wrapped her arms around his waist.

"You're late," she choked while her body trembled and she held back sobs; her normally bright, fair words were now barely above a whisper. Daedrin held her tightly and opened his mouth to speak but, a weak groan was all that escaped his lips as his world spun, his vision faded and he stumbled.

"Marin, get 'old of yourself and help me!" Skane barked and Marin jumped with terror plain in her eyes. "C'mon!" Skane yelled again as he pulled Daedrin forward. She flinched again at the shout but turned swiftly, ducked and pulled Daedrin's right arm over her before she placed her own around his waist.

"What was that?" she asked softly while they stumbled forward.

Skane grimaced. "I have but one explanation, love, and it's not one I like," he said as he exchanged a dark look with Daedrin's heavy eyes. "That creature looks exactly as I pictured it from the stories we've 'eard told by the merchants."

His voice trembled slightly as he spoke aloud what they were all thinking. "It must be one of... the Nasci," he uttered the name with great reluctance. "And if tales be true, where there is one then doubtless more cannot be far behind." He glanced at Marin as what little color had remained drained from her face.

"We have to warn the village," she declared as she slowly

regained her senses, "we have to leave, now!"

Skane nodded slowly. "Ye may be right. Let's first get 'im to Tara, let 'er set that leg; then we shall decide what we must do."

Marin tightened her grip around Daedrin's waist as they all hobbled through the field, awkwardly pressed into the narrow alley and finally stumbled back into the main village square. They suddenly found that they all were the object of attention for nearly half the town, for many had left their homes to investigate the strange sounds that had reached their ears. A flurry of activity broke out as everyone began speaking at once while they crowded around Daedrin and shouted their concerns.

"For the love o' the Creator, be silent!" Skane roared over the tumult of the crowd, and all talk grew quiet before ceasing altogether as he added, "I swear if ye don't all move out o' our way I'll break the arm o' every one ye!" Without waiting for a response he pulled Daedrin and Marin forward and barreled his way through the crowd as all scurried to make way for the injured man.

The healer's home was a little ways down the lane at the opposite edge of the main square and across the street from the tavern. The wooden door creaked as the blacksmith entered first while nearly dragging Daedrin and Marin behind him.

"Tara," he called out frantically, "help!"

The sound of footsteps rushing across a wood floor greeted them right before a tall, beautiful young woman only a few years older than Daedrin appeared through a door stationed behind a wooden table at the back of the house. Her blonde hair flowed just over her shoulders while she moved, and her brilliant green eyes narrowed when she saw Daedrin.

"What happened?" she asked. "A rogue farm implement get you?" her slightly raspy voice resonated with elegance and grace as she knelt down to examine the wound in Daedrin's leg. Skane only shook his head slowly while the healer scowled.

"Lay him down here," she ordered with a lifted finger at the table she had passed earlier. Skane didn't hesitate, but picked Daedrin up like he weighed no more than a feather and placed him gently down. Already Tara had grabbed a jar of mashed Linellin leaves and was pouring the herb into a bowl before mixing it into a paste with some water.

"He will be alright, won't he?" Marin asked quietly while she brushed her long, dark hair away from her eyes and whispered fervent prayers.

Tara glanced up, startled, as if noticing her for the first time. Her lips remained tense while she continued to mix the herb and water with a plain wooden spoon and ignored Skane and Marin completely as she focused on her work.

"He'll be fine," she said when at last the mixture was thick. Quickly she set the vessel aside and pulled back Daedrin's cloak and tunic up above the break in the skin before selecting a small bottle of grain alcohol. With a grimace at the severity of the damage, she poured liberal amounts of the clear liquid into the wound; Daedrin groaned and clenched his teeth to keep from screaming while Marin and Skane shifted uncomfortably at their friend's pain.

"I'm sorry," Tara smiled sympathetically, "but this won't be the worst of the pain you'll feel." All of Daedrin's muscles were taut like a fiercely wound up spring as she next grabbed a rag and wiped away the blood and dirt that had worked its way into the gash.

"Lie still," Tara commanded after she threw the now filthy rag to the side. "I'm nearly finished." Finally she took the pot and spoon and poured some of the concoction into Daedrin's wound where she spread it evenly around and over the damage. The young man breathed deeply, for as the herb touched his torn skin it brought with it a cooling sensation that eased his pain. After setting the utensils to the side Tara's lips moved in silent prayer while she moved her hands slowly and carefully over his leg around the gash until, as if she had found something the others could not see she settled a hand on each side of the break.

"I know it hurts already," she said, "but this will be unlike anything you've ever felt."

She looked at Skane and Marin. "Hold him down," she commanded. "I don't care how strong he is; no man can take the pain he's about to receive without his muscles reacting on their own." When Skane had a firm hold on Daedrin's shoulders and Marin had grasped his legs, Tara took in a deep breath.

"Marin, grab that," she ordered with a nod to the side where the wooden spoon lay on the table.

"Put it in his mouth," she added once the object had been lifted. "Bite down hard," she told the young man as the utensil was placed between his teeth. Then, after taking a deep breath she pressed down hard and quick.

The sound of Daedrin's scream though muffled nearly drowned out the sickening crunch the bone made when it popped back into place. He thrashed about, for his body seized and it took nearly all the strength of his companions to hold him still. Marin whimpered at the sight and covered her mouth with her hand when Daedrin finally lay still. Hurriedly Tara dressed the wound by wrapping it tight with bandages that sealed the herb under the skin. She then removed a half cylinder fashioned from oak from a nearby shelf filled with various assorted sizes, placed it over the break and tied it securely in place.

"Peace," Tara spoke soothingly as she gently wiped Daedrin's now damp forehead with a cloth. "Peace. It is done, now. By morning the herb will have done its work, and as the Creator wills it you'll be good as ever, though the wound will leave some light scarring." She smiled at Daedrin sadly while a look of empathy coursed through her fair face. "Now," she continued as she moved back a step, "don't go acting like a man and try to walk on that leg 'til the morning, after it's had a full night to heal. I'll want to examine you as well before you put any weight on it, alright?" She peered fiercely into Daedrin's eyes until he nodded.

"No argument here," he said between gasps for breath.

Tara smiled. "Good," she said before her face turned hard. "Now, get out of here," she added; her grayish green cloak shifted while she moved around the table. "I've a cold supper to enjoy after tonight's interruption…" Her voice trailed off as she moved through the door she had entered previously, letting it slam shut behind her.

"Well," Daedrin began as he took in deep, shaky breaths and looked at his two friends. "Thank you both. I would certainly have perished out in that field without your help." Skane looked embarrassed while Marin smiled sheepishly and swallowed hard as she reached for Daedrin's hand.

"It is I who owe you the thanks," she said. "Both of you," she added with a glance at the blacksmith.

"Ah, it was nothing," Skane said sheepishly. "Certainly nothing ye wouldn't've done for me, in a pinch."

Daedrin laughed weakly. "You may be right."

"Well, we should get ye back to my home," he told the young man. "Let ye rest that leg. I only hope that the village is still 'ere when ye wake..." His voice trailed off as he remembered the danger their home could now be facing.

Daedrin shook his head. "I cannot stay here, not with such looming danger while my family remains unaware."

Skane placed a reassuring hand on Daedrin's shoulder. "Don't ye worry about them. I will see that they are warned and ready."

After a brief pause Daedrin nodded. "If there is any I can trust with this, it is you," he declared. "I only hope that we are not in any real danger," he added with a grunt that was followed by a blinking grimace when he swung his legs over the side of the table and battled a wave of nausea for his sudden movement.

"Careful," Marin warned with a grimace while she reached out a hand to steady him. "You've lost a lot of blood..."

Daedrin nodded slowly and gave her a weak smile. "I'll be alright."

"We need to move quickly," Skane interjected as he wrapped an arm around his friend's shoulders and helped to hoist him off of the table. Marin quickly did the same and, when Daedrin was steady on his one good leg they helped him move back through the door and onto the street.

They ignored the chattering of the villagers as they made their way through the main square before coming to the door of Skane's home. The blacksmith pulled the door open with his free hand when they approached and the three pressed awkwardly sideways through the threshold and moved down the hallway to the same guest room that Daedrin had stayed in earlier.

"Lie down," Marin ordered as she helped him unclasp his sword from his waist with a weak smile when their eyes met. "We will see to it that the village is prepared for whatever may come, and we will make certain that your family is brought here safely."

"Aye, don't ye worry, lad," Skane told him. "I shall see to it myself."

Daedrin nodded as he lay down on the bed, still in his boots. Marin reached out to brush the hair from his face before leaning in to kiss him gently on the lips.

"We will be alright, won't we?" she asked after she had pulled away. Her deep blue eyes begged for some reassurance so Daedrin, searching for words but finding none to be fitting smiled weakly and nodded as he took her hand, lifted it to his lips and kissed it gently.

"We need to go, Marin," Skane interrupted solemnly. She glanced back at the blacksmith, nodded and rose to her feet before she pulled away and let Daedrin's hand fall to the bed. Sleep took hold of the young man before his companions had even left the room…

… A melodic scream pulled Daedrin out of a deep, dreamless slumber while the first light of dawn was just caressing his face through the glass of the window. *Have they come?* he wondered as he shot up and his pulse quickened. He strained his ears but after a few moments silence was the only thing to meet his senses and he sighed, thinking it must have been only a dream. Slowly he sat up and pulled back his cloak and tunic before carefully removing the splint and gently unraveling the bandage underneath. The wound tingled still with a light pain, for though the herb had dissolved into the skin to leave little trace of its previous thick paste it also had not been allowed quite enough time to fully do its work; light scarring now marred the previously smooth flesh on his thigh.

He sat for a few moments more when suddenly a chorus of screams rang out, followed by crashing and the shattering of glass. Strange sounds met his ears, also; shrieks unlike anything he had ever heard. Deep and dark they were to his ears, as if filled with some cruel malice. Without another thought Daedrin bolted off the bed and nearly flew out of his room; he buckled his sword-belt to his waist as he went down the hall and burst through the front door of the home. The sight that greeted him nearly froze the very blood in his veins.

Nasci were tearing through the village as they slaughtered every living thing in their path. Some people ran in a panic while others tried to resist and successfully slayed a beast here and there but all were inevitably cut down; crimson blood flowed freely through the streets.

"Noo!" Daedrin cried as grief that quickly turned to a boiling rage racked his heart. Five of the creatures heard his cry and turned to quickly thunder toward him with their own wretched howl. The sound of metal on metal rang out when Daedrin let his sword loose from its sheath; ruby eyes gleamed in the sunlight beneath a blade that glimmered with a metallic silver sheen. Time seemed to slow as he charged while a strength he had never known before surfaced from deep within and, after a few moments the two lines collided.

The first Nasci went down easily enough, for Daedrin sidestepped with a furious swing and its head was severed when it came into contact with his naked blade. The silver suddenly burned ever so slightly as the strange inscription etched into its length lit up with a faint orange glow that caused the creatures to pause briefly before converging on Daedrin with a vengeance. He roared with a cry of righteous fury while he swung his sword like a madman and wounded two more of the creatures when they lunged. Parry, thrust, parry swing; he fought with a skill he had never known until that moment.

After a few seconds that seemed to span hours in Daedrin's mind the Nasci began circling him. With a furious cry he lunged at the nearest creature and cut out its eyes with a quick swipe. It screeched and lunged blindly back at him, so he jumped to the side and cut off its head with a mighty blow. Quickly he followed through with a thrust of his sword in the opposite direction and clove another through the middle of its skull. The two remaining Nasci, having already been injured both lunged at him together and Daedrin leaped into the air, sailed over the heads of the brutes as they thumped into one another.

The young man thrust his sword beneath him when he came down and plunged it straight through one of the beasts as he landed. The move threw him off balance and he fell to a crash hard on his side before quickly rolling to barely dodge a swipe of lethal claws. Letting slip a grunt he jumped to his feet with an upward swing of his blade at the final Nasci; the creature roared when the razor-like edge sliced through its snout and left it's jaw split into four dangling pieces. Two quick steps closed the distance between them where Daedrin plunged his sword deep through the throat of the beast via its open mouth. Heaving labored, gasping breaths while his sword dripped with fresh blood Daedrin took no time to marvel at his accomplishment as he stumbled and surveyed the carnage within the village.

Everywhere he looked bodies littered the streets, both of Nasci cut and sliced and humans mauled and torn to shreds. He coughed and blinked when the scent of blood filled his nostrils before a sickening fear suddenly overtook his heart as two thoughts crashed through his mind. The first was that neither Skane nor Marin had awakened him, and this could only mean that they were either out on the road or else somewhere in the village fighting for their lives, if they indeed were not already laid out in the street with the rest of the dead. The second was of a horrifying image of his family being overwhelmed and slaughtered, with potentially no warning of what was coming.

For a brief moment he struggled before bolting off with a dash through a side alley while muttering fervent prayers for Marin and Skane as he ran away from the heart of the village. He stumbled and slid to a halt when he exited the narrow lane, for he beheld Tara with her back to a wall to his right where she wielded a knife threateningly at a Nasci while it moved toward her.

"Stay back!" she cried, but the creature stepped forward menacingly with fresh blood dripping from its open maw as it snarled. Daedrin's jaw tightened and he moved quickly; he approached the creature from the side and took full advantage of its focus on Tara. With a grunt and a quick slice he brought his blade upward to cut cleanly through the jaw of the brute, leaving the front half of its head severed as the monster collapsed.

Breathing heavily he yelled, "Run!" to Tara before sheathing his sword and taking off himself. After sprinting through a field of Linellin he crashed through the woods while he used the sun's dull rays through the trees as his guide. His lungs began to burn but he pressed forward and, as he emerged from the brush his foot caught a root that caused him to stumble and crash hard onto the ground with a grunt. He groaned, and his heart skipped a beat when he looked up, for just over a hill only a stone's throw away a billowing pillar of smoke could be seen.

"No… No, no no no no no…" Daedrin fought to breathe as he pushed himself to his feet and stumbled forward. When he crested the hill he choked and fell to his knees, for his home was utterly in ruins. The barn was completely engulfed in flames, and the front door of the house could be seen lying out in the front yard, having been clearly ripped from its hinges. Daedrin cried out in anguish, stumbled to his feet and rushed forward; he called out the names of his family frantically while he approached. He cringed and coughed when he passed the barn, for the smell of burning flesh filled his nostrils while the screams of the animals filled the air. After rushing to the front of his home he flew through the open front door.

"Mum, dad!" he screamed, "Melkai!" Dishes were shattered everywhere; deep gashes were in the floor, walls and furniture, all of which were coated in the blood of a single Nasci lying dead at his feet as he entered. Breathing furiously Daedrin fled through the home and plunged into the open air as he crashed through the rear door of the house. He spotted a set of human tracks leading away toward the mountains, and his heart was filled with hope. Rushing he followed them, all the while dodging scattered farm implements and swatting away tall grass and reeds. His heart began to beat harder in his chest, for as he moved further from the house the tracks became mixed with those of the heavy, brutish paw prints of large creatures. He nearly stumbled over the body of a slain Nasci while he crashed through the brush, and he swallowed hard when he passed the remains of several more. Then, as he rounded a tree just paces away

37

from the base of the mountains, his eyes took in a sight that would be forever scarred into his memory.

Four bodies lay on the grass before him; the first three were that of a small child, a man and a woman all close together; mauled, torn and left where they had fallen. The other was of a single Nasci, gashed and sliced in several places just a few paces from where the bodies lay. Daedrin stopped dead in his tracks, and time seemed to crawl to a halt. He blinked and choked as started to move toward them when Nasci, too numerous to count, suddenly crashed through the brush behind him; they let loose a wretched howl when they spotted him. With a spring away Daedrin ran with a surge of horrified grief as he passed the remains of his family before he plunged into the forest. Roars and thudding behind spurred him on while his two legs carried him speedily through the thick brush; trees crashed by, clawing at him, as if trying to slow his effort to escape certain death.

As the burning in his lungs became nearly unbearable he stumbled and crashed hard to the ground with a grunt when pain shot through his chest. Lifting his head he searched desperately for some way of escape, and his eyes were drawn to a large oak to his left with great roots that looked to be washed out and hollow. With the shrieks of the Nasci drawing nearer he stumbled up to his knees and half walked, half crawled over to the base of the tree and slid down under the cover of the roots before turning over and raking in a pile of leaves behind him until all but his nose and eyes were covered.

The ground began to tremble beneath the heavy footfalls of the

Nasci as dozens of the creatures bounded up the mountain and barreled past the oak that had become Daedrin's shelter without so much as a pause to indicate that they had caught his scent. He watched with wide eyes and struggled to control his breathing while the monsters flew past and quickly faded from view. Slowly his muscles began to relax as the thundering faded into the distance and, with heart still pounding he slid down deeper into the leaves for a few moments before swiping them away from eyes that now filled with tears.

CHAPTER 3

SURPRISE!

Daedrin's body trembled as he lay sideways on the ground beneath the shelter of the roots and clutched his knees to his chest. His breath was shaky and labored, for his whole body felt numb and the color had all but drained from his face. His chest felt tight, as if he had been laid in a vice and pressed just shy of being altogether crushed. He tried closing his eyes but, when he did so the torn and bloodied image of his family was all that he could see.

Why... he nearly choked at the single thought when it formed, for it brought a near complete shock of all his senses and overwhelmed his mind. Finally, after what must have been several hours he slowly shifted his weight and crawled out from under the tree before rolling so that he was sitting upright while still clutching his knees.

He felt his eyes widen slightly when he surveyed his surroundings and blinked with the realization that he was roughly three miles from the farm. With a sharp breath at the thought of his home he closed his eyes and let the dark images flash through his mind's eye. *I can't leave them like that,* he thought, *it will not take long for wild animals to…* his thoughts trailed off and he swallowed with much difficulty, for his throat was taut and dry. Gathering his strength he placed his two hands onto the ground at his sides and pushed up to his feet before, with a deep intake of air he began to move slowly down the rolling pass under the now bright light of the sun as it hung overhead.

It took him nearly two hours to make it down the mountain, for weary though he was he moved with great caution while he eyed the forest warily for any sign that the Nasci might be close. The journey however was uneventful, and when at last he approached the edge of the tree line and caught a glimpse of what lay beyond his stride slowed and he stopped as he placed one hand on a nearby tree to steady his weight. He ground his teeth together and, with much effort, he dispelled all thought, took in a deep breath and exited the forest; his eyes he averted with a deep pang of grief when they caught a glimpse of the remains of his family to his left.

Quickly he moved across the field, passed his home and paused briefly with a grimace as he took in the sight of what had only yesterday been a barn filled with life. Warily he dared to approach the rubble, smoking ever so slightly, and swallowed hard when he beheld the charred remains of the animals that had been trapped inside. His nostrils were filled with the foul stench of burnt flesh so strong that he coughed and cringed; heat still radiated from the burnt embers.

After closing his eyes for a moment he took in a shaky breath and stepped through the threshold, and though his heart screamed at him to move quickly he cautiously stepped around debris and nails while he peered into the rubble for any tool left intact. To his surprise he saw near the back an area left mostly untouched by the fire with a handful of farming tools leaning in the corner that were only slightly blackened by the smoke and heat. He moved across the barn, retrieved a shovel with a wince at its warm handle and quickly exited the building over the now collapsed back wall where he let loose a deep sigh of relief as his lungs were once again filled with fresh air.

Daedrin then strolled with a frown to the well near the front of his home, for his eyes took in deep cracks all throughout its wooden basin. Gently he grasped the still intact handle and gave it a few pumps before breathing a quiet sigh of relief when fresh water poured from the spout. With one hand he splashed his face and took in a sharp breath as the cool liquid touched his skin before he stooped low and drank deeply. When his parched throat was satisfied he lifted his head and wiped his face with the sleeve of his cloak before withdrawing his canteen and proceeding to fill the leather bottle. While he returned the water-skin to its place on his belt he left the well and moved around the corner to an open area just behind the house.

He felt his lips curl as he smiled ever so lightly, for his eyes came to rest on a stake in the ground that brought to his mind a now cherished memory of throwing old horseshoes with his father and brother while his mother looked on with a smile, cheer or a playful boo. His joy, however, faded with the recollection and his grip tightened around the wooden handle as he strolled forward a few steps and plunged the shovel into the dirt.

The sun had begun to hide its face below the horizon as it gave way for the moon to appear before he had completed the brutal task of digging three holes in the earth. Torturous work it was; long and interrupted by many outbursts of sorrow and rage. When at last it was done he crept slowly over to where his family lay, surrounded by brush completely that was trampled under heavy tracks that were too numerous to count. With eyes red and wide he crept over to the body of his mother and swallowed hard when his eyes took in her broken and bloodied form. She lay on her back with head turned toward her husband who laid just a pace away; deep gashes were carved into her belly, and one leg was torn and crossed over the other at a twisted angle.

"Oh, mum," he muttered weakly as he fell to his knees at her side, gently placed a hand on her forehead and brushed back her disheveled hair before closing her wide eyes. His own lids slowly shut while he fought for a few moments the tears that threatened to burst forth before allowing the grief to wash over him; his whole body shook with the force of his weeping. After several minutes he struggled to contain the choking sobs that racked his chest beneath hunched shoulders until finally, ever so slowly the wells in his eyes ran dry and he lifted his gaze to look once more upon Seline. With great sorrow he beheld a kitchen knife, stained with blood, clenched tightly between the fingers of her right hand.

Pain that formed suddenly in his temple caused Daedrin to take in a sharp breath as his mind was filled by a brief flash of his mother while she flailed the blade wildly around her. With a blink he shook off the image and looked up to see a sword at his father's side, and a few paces away was a small dagger; both were dark with crimson stains. Little Melkai lay on his belly at his mother's feet with his right hand stretched out toward the dagger while his left clutched tightly to the hem of Seline's dress. His back was shredded; pierced with the deep claw marks of the ferocious beasts.

"Father!" the terrified voice of Daedrin's brother resonated through his mind with a ferocity that caused the young man to crumple and place a hand on either side of his head as he covered his ears and groaned.

"No, no no no no..." he whispered fervently when the vision behind closed lids was assaulted by a brief flicker of Melkai as he reached for a dagger that was struck from his hand by a vicious paw. Daedrin's muscles were taut when he lifted his head and turned to see Kelmîn on his side with throat gashed while his eyes remained locked with those of his wife; one bloodied hand rested atop her own. Choking back more tears Daedrin simply knelt for several minutes there on the ground with head bowed and eyes closed while his body trembled.

At long last he lifted his eyes, reached out and gently scooped up Seline before stumbling to his feet with her already stiff body clenched tightly to his own chest. Slowly he proceeded to carry her to the freshly dug graves where he awkwardly but carefully laid her into one of the holes in the earth and struggled to fold her arms in a symbol of serenity; the knife he left in her hand. With a deep breath he rose, grit his teeth and moved with narrowed eyes back to Melkai. His throat tightened as he bent down, lifted his brother and carried him to the second hole where he proceeded to place the body softly into the ground. For a moment he stood there and looked upon the small face while he fought the quivering that began to creep into his jaw before he turned and moved over to where his father lay.

"I…" he said hoarsely after falling to his knees just inches from the slain form. With much effort he cleared his throat with a cough as a single tear escaped and slid down his cheek. "I hate you," he whispered, and his fists clenched at his side while his face contorted with a mixture of sorrow and rage. "I hate you," he repeated with a voice that was slightly stronger as it rose. "You couldn't help but be cruel, and drive me away… if I had been here, I could have protected mum… kept Melkai safe. That was *your* job and you failed them!" He was practically screaming when he finished, while hot, furious tears ran down both cheeks and he choked back a sob. With teeth grit he slid his arms beneath Kelmîn's stiff form and struggled as he rose to his feet with a grunt and stumbled over to the remaining grave.

After half lying, half dropping his father into the final hole in the earth he moved back to where they had been slain and recovered the dagger and sword. The first he placed gently on the chest of Melkai while the second was tossed carelessly into the grave beside his father. Daedrin walked then slowly over to the shovel, pulled it from the ground and turned to look upon his mother and brother one final time. Taking in a deep breath he swung the tool into one of the now raised mounds of loose dirt and paused briefly to swallow a hard lump of grief as he struggled to maintain his composure and strength before proceeding to cover the bodies of his family.

When the last shovel-full of earth was finally cast Daedrin suddenly flung out his arm and let the tool fly through the air with a furious frustrated expletive before he lifted a hand to rest on his forehead; a dull clunk echoed through the night when the object collided with the side of the farmhouse. He stood there for a while as he took in several deep breaths before he blinked, swallowed and moved over to the edge of the forest where he let his eyes scan the earth for a few moments. His gaze came to rest on some brush near his feet and he stooped low and rose moments later with two large branches clutched tightly in his grasp. These he brought back to the clearing where he broke them over his leg and fashioned with twine from his pack three crude crosses. After carving the names of his family onto them with a small knife he had drawn from his left boot he strolled slowly to each mound and plunged one into the ground at the head of each corresponding grave.

With a heavy gasp he stumbled back several paces, fell to his knees and spoke with a trembling voice as his eyes scanned the markers.

"I… I'm sorry," he choked out while he hung his head. "I should have been here…" his voice trailed off and he took in a deep, grief-filled breath.

"I swear to you, all of you," he finally declared solemnly. "I *will* see your deaths avenged. There will be blood for blood, I swear…"

For several seconds more he simply knelt in silence while his hand turned to a clenched fist that absently thumped the meat of his thigh as he let his arm rise and fall. Finally, with face stained, body worn and clothing filthy, he struggled to his feet and stumbled toward the door of his now ruined home.

He entered the dimly lit dwelling slowly, thinking to himself that this might well be the last time that he did so. *Seems father got his wish after all,* he thought with a pang of agony as memories, now darkened with a sense of horror and foreboding flooded his mind, for everywhere he looked his thoughts were pierced by the tears in the floors and walls while dishes once beautiful were now shattered all around. With a cringe, Daedrin moved quickly over the pieces of a chair before he turned to his right and entered the room that he had once shared with his brother. He swallowed hard as he moved through the room and slowly stepped around the shredded pieces of bedding that were strewn all around.

When he reached the back wall he extended both arms outward to place his hands flat against the wood while his head drooped and he closed his eyes. An image of Melkai flashed through his mind as he became immersed in a vivid memory of his little brother, running through the house in early morning and laughing while Daedrin chased him with a wooden sword before they fought make-believe villains there in the confines of the modest bedroom. The recollection however slowly faded away after a few moments, leaving Daedrin to feel the complete and utter silence of the ruined home.

I am all alone now... the bitter thought drifted through his mind and sunk its claws into the depths of his heart while he took in a deep, labored breath. *Marin...* the name brought fresh tears to his eyes as he pushed away from the wall and wiped his face with a blink. *I must find her,* he thought, *and Skane...* his face twisted with a grimace when he briefly imagined their broken and mangled bodies lying with the rest of those slain within Linull. With a shake of his head, he bent down to his hands and knees to peer under what was left of his bed and breathed with great relief as his eyes took in his bow and quiver; unscathed despite the ruin of the cushions and blankets. His eyes flickered next to the frame of his brother's bed where they took in a small boot knife tucked between the wood and what was left of the mattress. Daedrin blinked and swallowed the lump rising in his throat while he slid closer, extended his arm and removed the blade together with its sheath. He stared at the weapon for several moments while he recalled the exact moment he had gifted this very blade to Melkai before closing his eyes as his fist clenched tightly around the hilt. With a heavy exhale he lifted weary lids and tucked the knife into his right boot before returning his attention to the bow and quiver.

After retrieving and slinging them over his shoulder, he exited the room and proceeded slowly down the hallway with a brief glance at the open door to his left that led to his parent's room; he moved past it without entering. As the hall opened to the wider room beyond he approached the fallen table, bent to one knee and reached out to touch a piece of one of the numerous shattered dishes that layered the floor. He smiled briefly when he imagined Seline gracefully piling on rice and beans before setting a plate in front of him on the table but, his eyes narrowed when he looked up and took in the head of the table where his father had always sat, for the sight brought to his mind those final cruel words that had come from Kelmîn's lips.

Daedrin rose to his feet with a grunt and glared hatefully at the slain form of the Nasci near the open front door before he moved into the kitchen where he found to his dismay and disgust that the beans, rice and bread from the pantry had been pillaged, scattered all over the room and trampled; purposely wasted by creatures of cruel intent. With a scowl he bent down to gather any beans that remained whole when the sound of glass crunching underfoot reached his ears from the other room. Quietly drawing Melkai's knife from his right boot he rose to his feet and moved, ever-so-slowly and carefully to the wall near the open doorway. As he peered around into the room beyond the blur of some dark object suddenly filled his vision and he was struck hard on the forehead. A shock rippled through his whole body while pain that quickly turned to cold flashed briefly, his mind numbed and his world tumbled into darkness…

… The crackling of a fire was the first thing Daedrin noticed as he slowly regained consciousness. With a groan he reached up to feel his forehead and with a bewildered glower he took note of a swollen knot right where his hairline met his brow. With much effort, he examined his surroundings through squint eyes while his head throbbed with a dull ache. He was lying on a bed with a thin mattress, he realized after a few moments; it was off to the side of a small, plainly-furnished room with bare wooden floors that were visible only by the light of a modest flame that crackled and popped from its place on a stone hearth in the corner to his right.

"Well, you might perhaps live to see another day, after all," a soft but gruff voice spoke from over Daedrin's shoulders. "I was beginning to wonder if I had hit you too hard." Daedrin on instinct felt for his sword, only to find that it was not at his side.

"Looking for this, perhaps?" the voice asked while a rather older man came into view. As the stranger moved to seat himself in a chair by the fire he held Daedrin's sword unsheathed in his right hand with the scabbard clutched in his left. He was plainly dressed in a long green cloak, with short and scraggly dark hair above a rough face that was covered in several day old stubble. Daedrin blinked when his eyes took in the disheveled appearance of the man as it flickered in the light of the flames before he scanned the room. His eyes narrowed when he beheld his bow and other possessions lying across the room in the corner, behind and to the left of the stranger.

"Magnificent blade, once I removed the dried blood," the man said as his eyes narrowed. "Though the inscription is certainly strange... stolen, no doubt," he added scornfully.

Daedrin rose to one elbow. "It's not..." he started to say when pain racked his body, the edges of his vision turned white and he nearly fainted. Taking in a slow, steady breath he lay back down and tried again. "That belongs to me," he said angrily, and the man sneered before letting loose a low chuckle.

"Perhaps I've misjudged you, then," he said derisively. "I suppose it is entirely likely that one dressed in such rags as you have adorned yourself with should possess enough wealth to purchase a blade as finely crafted as this." He chuckled but became serious in a moment while he leaned forward. "Where then did you get this blade, if it is indeed rightly yours?"

Daedrin hesitated and closed his eyes for a moment while his weary mind processed what was now unfolding.

Where are you, Creator? He despaired briefly with a feeling of solemn desperation.

"My father gave it to me," he finally said aloud as he opened his eyes. The man frowned and sheathed the weapon before letting it rest across his knees.

"What is your name?" he asked.

The young man hesitated. "Daedrin," he replied finally, and his eyes narrowed with irritation while he rose slowly to sit upright with his back against the wall.

"Well boy," the man said, "perhaps you can grant yourself another day on this earth by explaining your presence in the ruin of that home?"

Daedrin's brow furrowed. "What concern is that of yours?" he demanded angrily while the wheels of his mind began to form a strategy for escape.

The stranger placed both hands, with one atop the other on Daedrin's sword hilt as he replied. "Considering that I am the one who stopped a plundering robber from taking what does not belong to him, I feel I am entitled to whatever answers I seek. You should be more grateful, boy," he added with a sneer. "I'm not in the habit of killing anyone without due justification, and so you still draw breath while a bruise on your head is all you have yet to bear for your wickedness."

Daedrin blinked and allowed his lips to part before he closed them with a pang of grief when the image of the crude markers he had placed at the head of each grave flickered through his mind, bringing with it the crippling notion that he was entirely on his own, no matter the outcome of his encounter with the stranger.

"That home," he said with quiet irritation, "is MY home… or at least it was," he added sorrowfully while he opened heavy eyes that meet the piercing gaze of the old man.

The stranger studied him for a few moments before suddenly tossing the sheathed blade across the room toward Daedrin, who jerked his hand up in surprise and barely caught the sword while immediately battling a fresh wave of nausea for his quick reflexes.

"I beg you excuse my actions," the stranger said as he rose to his feet with a motion to the bruise on Daedrin's head. Some of the harshness in his voice had vanished to give way to a more cheerful, though still gruff tone. The old man exited the room and returned a few moments later with a wooden mug in each hand, the rims of which were spilling over with foam. He offered one to Daedrin, who received it slowly and breathed in the stout aroma of ale as he passed the cup under his nose. He frowned before leaning back with the cup in one hand while the sword rested across his lap.

"I… saw the smoke upon my return from the city," the man declared solemnly after returning to his seat and taking a swig from his mug. "Cordin," he added with a wave of his hand. "The smoke reflected under the moonlight as it rose above the treetops… When I approached the structure that still stood I saw you enter the home in the dead of night with only your sword, yet move back through the main room with a bow and quiver full of arrows. I judged you to be a vagabond, and acted perhaps more brashly than I ought." The stranger's voice trailed off for a moment as his eyes narrowed. "I believe I see the truth now," he added with a gesture to Daedrin's cloak. "The dirt all over your clothes and face, covering your hands and hiding beneath your fingernails… you dug the earth behind the house, didn't you?"

Daedrin averted his gaze at the piercing declaration of this strange man.

"The graves…" he cleared his throat with a gentle harrumph before he was able to continue. "They contain my family." He spoke slowly, and his voice broke as he closed his eyes and struggled for a few moments to regain his composure. "The… Nasci, they slaughtered my mother… my father… even my little brother." He paused and swallowed a hard lump in his throat before looking up with damp red eyes that glinted in the light of the fire. "He was only eight," he choked out in a near whisper.

"I… am sorry," the old man said after a brief pause. "Savage, merciless monsters," he added under his breath with a shake of his head while he looked down at the flames and, for a while neither said anything more.

Finally Daedrin cleared his throat while he collected his thoughts and banished from his mind all but how he should handle this stranger.

"You say you came upon my farm on your return from Cordin," he said as his eyes narrowed and he allowed his fingers to slide slowly over the hilt of his sword. "But," he continued slowly, "I do not know your face…"

The man hesitated while he eyed the young man with what was perhaps an amused expression. "My name is Hadrîn," he said, and Daedrin frowned, for he thought the name to be strange, yet somehow familiar.

"You have never seen my face because I… do not often venture near others," the old man continued. "Nor had I ever laid eyes on your farm before this evening… the smoke drew me in," he added with a grimace. "I might keep to myself as a rule but, I'm not without heart. I feared for a soul perhaps in jeopardy and sought to render aid…" his voice trailed off as he lifted his head to meet Daedrin's narrowed gaze with eyes filled with tears. The young man blinked, taken off guard by the apparent vulnerability of the stranger before him. He swallowed hard and shifted in his seat before taking a sip from his mug and closing his eyes when the golden liquid splashed down his throat.

"Where have you taken me?" he asked finally as he let his gaze rest once more on the old man. Hadrîn coughed and wiped damp eyes on the shoulders of his cloak while he replied.

"You are in my home," he answered. "I live in a small cabin in the pass above your farm," he added with an absent wave of one hand.

Daedrin stared blankly for a few moments.

"Impossible," he declared. "I've traveled all throughout the Basilicus Mountains and found them altogether uninhabited, save for abundant wildlife."

Hadrîn's lips twitched ever so slightly.

"You clearly haven't explored *all* of the mountain range."

The young man glared. "I've hunted from one end to the other; no one lives in the mountains," he said with some irritation while his fingers absently rubbed the grip of his sword and he eyed the man even more warily than before.

"Have you ventured *across* the pass, hmm?" Hadrîn asked with a smirk, and Daedrin scoffed.

"Of course not. The range is far too steep for anyone to cross safely to the other side."

The old man rose to his feet with a light groan and moved over to the wall nearest the fire where he peered out of what Daedrin now realized was a small window.

"That is exactly why I built my cabin here," Hadrîn said with a slight wave of one hand at the darkness beyond the glass. "At the very peak of the mountain, or at least as near as I could reach; the one place least likely to be disturbed. It's cold, to be sure, but not unbearably so."

Daedrin shook his head in disbelief; the pain he found to be slowly subsiding while he took another sip of ale.

"Lies," he scoffed as his eyes narrowed.

Hadrîn glanced back at him. "Would you like to see for yourself?" he asked with a motion to the doorway he had gone through before. "Precious little light at this time of night, but enough to cure your doubt, at least."

Daedrin frowned. "Lead the way," he said finally with a nod to the open doorway. He eyed the old man cautiously when Hadrîn dipped his head and moved past him, through the doorway and into the adjacent room. With a deep breath and a cringe at the slight pain in his temple because of the movement Daedrin slid off the of the mattress to his feet, set his mug on the floor and drew his sword before he followed slowly without taking his eyes off of the stranger.

"You need not fear me," Hadrîn said with a smirk at Daedrin's cautious approach, but the young man glowered as he rubbed the bump on his forehead.

"Time will tell," he said, and his eyes narrowed while the old man sighed as he turned and removed an oil lamp from the wall before lighting it and approaching a door at the back of the room. A rush of frigid air plunged through the building once the handle was turned and the barrier between them and the elements swung open. Hadrîn stepped over the threshold and plunged into darkness pierced only by the faintest of moonlight, accompanied by the light of the flame the stranger carried. Daedrin pulled his cloak tightly around him and followed with a shudder as the cold sent a shiver down his spine while a light breeze touched his face and served to further ease the pain in his temple.

"Over here, boy," Hadrîn said while he moved a few paces away with the light held in one outstretched arm as he peered out into the dark. Daedrin approached slowly, keeping a few paces to the left of the old man as he closed the distance between them with sword raised. His lips parted ever so slightly while his eyes widened in astonishment when he took in the shapes of trees, shrouded in darkness far below.

"Careful," Hadrîn warned. He swung the lamp closer to Daedrin, allowing it to illuminate the edge of a steep cliff just a few paces away. "The mark on your head will be the least of your worries should you venture too close to that precipice." Daedrin's gaze narrowed and he took one step back, then two as he moved away from the stranger.

"I've seen enough," he said with a nod to the open doorway behind them. Hadrîn smirked as he turned on his heels slightly and moved past the young man before pausing briefly at the edge of the entryway to blow out the lamp; he entered the home with Daedrin a few steps behind.

The young man watched with a quiet frown as the stranger refilled his mug from a barrel on the counter.

"You're welcome to more, if your taste is not yet satisfied," Hadrîn offered with a motion to the container before returning to his seat by the fire. Daedrin looked around the room and took in its appearance, lit only by the glow coming through the doorway. Its furnishings were just as plain as the adjacent room, and it had a single small, round wooden table in one corner and a counter along one wall, with two cabinet doors above. In the corner nearest the back door was a small well with what looked to be an iron pot placed underneath. Daedrin shifted with puckered brow as he moved slowly through the room, passed through the doorway and approached the bed where he sheathed his sword slowly before grasping his mug and taking up a cross-legged perch on the bed with the blade across his lap.

"You know," the old man said as his eyes scanned the young man. "I've had more than one opportunity to take your life from you. Had I wished any true harm, you would no longer draw breath." A few moments of silence followed this declaration, interrupted only by the crackling of the fire when Hadrîn placed fresh logs into the flames from a stack near the hearth. Daedrin sipped his ale quietly while he eyed this mysterious man with thoughts racing from one wild idea to the next before he finally broke the silence.

"Why would anyone choose to live at such a dangerous height?" he asked.

Hadrîn was silent for a moment before sneering. "The life I once knew was… taken from me, and so, I exiled myself."

Daedrin's eyes narrowed. "You seemed to know something of the Nasci, when I spoke of them before." He eyed the old man carefully and took note of the clench to Hadrîn's jaw as the stranger's eyes grew dark.

"Too much," Hadrîn declared with a voice that filled with a deep tone; menacing, Daedrin thought it to be.

"What did they take from you?" He asked slowly.

Hadrîn turned his gaze to meet the eyes of the young man with a glare. "You might be content enough with sharing the source of your grief, boy, but that certainly does not mean that I wish to reveal mine to a stranger." His sharp words cut across the room before he averted his gaze to peer once more into the fire as it crackled and popped.

Daedrin frowned. *Perhaps I pushed too soon,* he thought before deciding on a more tactful approach.

"I… apologize." The words were strained as they left his lips, and he coughed to mask the insincerity of his speech. Hadrîn stared into the fire while quietly rubbing his jaw with one hand before he glanced at Daedrin and sighed.

"You… need not be sorry," the old man said finally. "Some wounds… they don't seem to heal." He sighed and took a deep swig from his mug as he looked out the window.

Daedrin tilted his own cup back and drained the last of his ale in one long gulp.

"I… think I shall have that second glass," he said. After rising from his seat he moved to the other room where he quietly turned the valve on the barrel and allowed the liquid to flow freely until the foam spilled ever-so-slightly over the rim. He took one sip before returning to the mattress to watch the flames dance on the hearth while the wheels of his mind turned.

"It seems a lifetime ago," Hadrîn at last broke the silence. The old man chuckled with a half-hearted huff of air. "Though it has been more than that now, I suppose," he added with a quiet frown.

Daedrin's brow furrowed while he studied the old man carefully.

"I… don't follow," he said slowly.

Hadrîn glanced up at him briefly before lowering his gaze once more, looking this time at his mug as he gently rotated the cup and traced the rim with one finger.

"I wasn't always a hermit." The eyes of the old man were hazy as he peered into the golden liquid while it swirled, and Daedrin watched curiously while the old man continued. "I had a life, once. Long ago… so long…" his voice trailed off for a moment and Daedrin merely sat quietly while he observed the stranger.

"You believe that you suffer, lad?" Hadrîn asked as he lifted his eyes to meet the narrowed gaze of the young man. "I've known more sorrow than even you can possibly fathom." The stranger's jaw clenched while he cleared his throat and took a deep swig of ale.

"I…" Daedrin paused as he searched for the words that would perhaps bring the old man to reveal some detail of himself. "Perhaps speaking of what pains you so might offer some release," he said finally.

The old man glanced at him before huffing. "Perhaps," he replied with a frown while he gazed into the fire. "I had a wife," he declared suddenly, "and a daughter." He smiled then, as if lost in some pleasant memory that soon faded, taking with it the curve of his lips and replacing the look with a sour curl beneath angry, fiery eyes. "They were taken from me," he said with a slow nod of his head before he lifted red eyes. "Taken a long time ago," he added mournfully before looking away and clearing his throat. "But, I've already knocked you unconscious, removed you from your home while your own heart was in turmoil... had anyone dared do such deeds to me while I was first in my grief, I would have killed him without question," he added darkly.

Daedrin blinked. "I... haven't decided yet whether you should live or die," he said slowly.

Hadrîn glanced up at him with a sudden chuckle. "You haven't the least bit of tact, have you, lad?" he asked. Daedrin only smirked while the old man shook his head. "Perhaps it is well that I did not strike you down," he added with another chuckle as he drained the last of his mug.

Daedrin felt his eyes narrow while he struggled to contain the sudden urge to remove blade from sheathe. *Enough of this,* he thought.

"What can you tell me of the Nasci?" he asked aloud.

Hadrîn sighed. "Like a dog with a bone," he said with a scowl. Finally he threw up one hand as he leaned back in his chair. "Perhaps some of the knowledge I've gained throughout the years can be useful to you... for the right price," he added with a twitch of his lips while he rubbed his jaw.

Daedrin took in a deep breath and struggled to maintain his calm as anger welled up from deep within.

"Is your life not payment enough?" he asked heatedly, but to his surprise the old man grinned.

"Boy," he said with a slight raise of his hands. "I do not fear you, for there is only one mortal that roams this earth who can bring any permanent harm to me."

Daedrin's eyes narrowed and he leaned forward threateningly.

"Perhaps I should put that faith to the test," he said.

Hadrîn merely shrugged and pulled a small knife from beneath his cloak. Daedrin jerked back with one hand flying to his sword hilt when, to his shock, the old man drew the blade across his own left forearm with a grimace as the skin was gashed deeply. Quickly withdrawing a rag from his cloak Hadrîn placed it beneath the wound to catch the blood when it began to flow.

"Watch," Hadrîn said as he held out his arm so that the light of the fire caught the cut clearly. After a few moments the blood which had at first flowed freely began to slow until after a few moments, it stopped altogether. The torn flesh then began to knit itself back together neatly, leaving the old man's arm completely intact, as if it had never been injured.

"See?" the stranger smirked as he wiped away the remnant of red on his skin. "Hurts, of course, but I can be slain by neither you or even myself."

Daedrin set his mug down on the bed and slowly slid to his feet with sheathed weapon in one hand as he moved over to inspect the old man's arm in astonishment.

"How...?" his voice trailed off as he met Hadrîn's amused gaze.

"Magic made me this way," he declared. "A curse, actually."

Daedrin moved slowly back to his seat on the bed and chugged the last of his ale before he let the mug fall to its side on the mattress.

"Tell me more," he said. His trepidation at the sight of this strange man had been all but forgotten, for his mind reeled as he stared at the bloody rag that Hadrîn had let fall to the floor.

The old man chuckled. "As I said before, that information comes at a price," he reminded him. "I do not know you, lad," he added with a shake of his head. "Nor have I any notion of what you might do with the knowledge I can give you."

Daedrin's brow puckered. "I swore an oath at the graves of my family to avenge their deaths," he said with eyes ablaze as he leaned forward. "Whatever you share with me will serve only the purpose of seeing the Nasci utterly destroyed, no matter the cost."

A fiendish smile slowly spread across Hadrîn's lips. "Fortunately for you, I believe you speak the truth," he said with a slow nod while he shifted in his seat. "Though," he added with a frown, "you would perish long before you saw your goal accomplished, should you attempt it alone, boy."

Daedrin felt his jaw clench. "I handled five of the creatures on my own," he said fiercely.

"Did you? How did you do it?" The old man asked as he abruptly leaned forward.

Daedrin felt his lips twitch, for he was taken aback by the forcefulness of the question.

"My father... he taught me to fight," he said with eyes that narrowed while the old man studied him before nodding slowly.

"Others have tried and failed, but perhaps you have enough skill," he said finally as he broke his stare and leaned back in his seat. "But you are far too ignorant, since you have yet to even mention the real enemy."

Daedrin tilted his head to one side. "What do you mean?" he

asked slowly, and his eyes narrowed when he took in the darkness that filled Hadrîn's eyes.

"Garrôth," the old man's was voice filled with a hateful malice as he uttered the name.

"Nonsense," Daedrin scoffed. "I've only ever heard that name mentioned once in my whole life, and it was met with the fiercest of ridicule by all even as it left the lips of old Barsk."

Hadrîn frowned and rubbed the scruff on his chin. "Barsk... he was a trader?"

"One of the eldest. He was a notorious drunk, and he told a wild tale one visit of a cruel person of great power who was secretly destroying villages and taking people from their beds at night."

"I cannot speak to all of that," the old man said, "but it is a wonder you ever heard the name at all. Garrôth is quite cunning and very, very careful..." His voice trailed off for a moment. "This Barsk... did you ever see him after that visit, when he told his... wild tale?"

Daedrin opened his mouth to speak but stopped with brow furrowed while he thought hard.

"Well, no." He paused, and then shook his head in dismissal. "But he was old; very old. Doubtless he perished as his body finally failed him."

"Somehow I doubt that is what happened to the old man." Hadrîn smirked as he turned his gaze once more to the fire. "To even mention the name is often enough for those who spin wild stories to find themselves beneath Garrôth's blade," he added softly.

Daedrin's lips twitched. "What makes you so certain of the existence of this… Garrôth?" he asked, and Hadrîn turned to meet his eyes with a cold, level stare.

"I knew him, or at least I once did, in another life." He paused with jaw clenching as he continued. "We were friends once, but… that worthless excuse for a life betrayed me. He had the Nasci crafted in secret," he paused when Daedrin's lips parted beneath narrowed eyes. "Oh yes," the old man said with a dip of his head. "The Nasci are by no means a natural part of this world. Garrôth oversaw their creation, and from the depths of his corruption he convinced me that his plans were for the good of all, and I at first believed him but, when the fullness of his plan became clear to me I refused to be a part of his schemes and…" He paused briefly and shook his head before clearing his throat and looking again at Daedrin.

"Garrôth used me to help him destroy his enemies… good men," he added with a frown. "I made sure that he was caught but, he still managed to escape…" Hadrîn's voice trailed off while a single tear slid down one cheek. He quickly brushed it away angrily as he cleared his throat. "In the chaos that ensued his onslaught I took my daughter and fled to a village as far from the castle as we could find but… late one night, nearly a year after Garrôth disappeared he showed up at my door. He told me that he was going to rule Silmaín, and… that he was deeply disappointed by my betrayal." Hadrîn paused and looked into the fire for several moments before lifting his head to peer deeply into Daedrin's eyes; his voice was tight and filled with sorrow when he continued.

"He had his minions – men, loyal to his cause," he added with disgust, "subdue me while he proceeded to drag Hana, my daughter, from her bed and he… he murdered her, right in front me." Daedrin's felt his lips part slightly as Hadrîn's story unfolded.

"He then placed a powerful magical curse on me, the results of which you saw moments ago," he continued with a gesture to his arm. "Such that I cannot die unless Garrôth himself should choose to take my life. Of course he has not done so, but rather allows me to live my life in torment, knowing what I've lost and that, without the release of my spirit through death I shall never be reunited again with those I love."

Daedrin's thoughts were reeling as he looked down at the floor and closed his eyes. Slowly he reached up to touch his forehead when a broken and blurred image of the face of the old man before him flashed through his head, on his knees while tears streamed down his face. Then strange faces began to flicker through his mind's eye, bringing with them a steady, pulsing pain in his temple. He took in a deep breath before letting it out slowly as the flashes faded and the agony subsided. After a few moments more he opened his eyes and blinked when the room flickering in the light of the fire filled his vision once more.

"Too heavy a story for your heart to bear?" Hadrîn asked with an irritated smirk beneath narrowed eyes as Daedrin met his gaze.

The young man frowned. "Nay," he said with a shake of his head. "It's just… that's quite a story you've spun," he added with a chuckle. "How long did it take you to come up with such a wild tale?"

Daedrin knew from the moment the words left lips that he had made a terrible mistake, for a slow, burning fury rolled across the face of Hadrîn as the old man rose from his seat. Daedrin fumbled for his sword-hilt while Hadrîn closed the gap between them in two furious strides. He reached out his arms with lightning speed and closed them around Daedrin's throat before pulling him close.

"You dare insult the memory of my little girl?" he whispered venomously. Daedrin cringed when the hot breath of the old man touched his face while he struggled in vain for a few moments to break free. His breathing began to grow shallow while Hadrîn's hands grew tighter like a vice that cut off his air supply. As his world grew dim he pressed his hands together and slid them up and in between Hadrîn's forearms and pushed outward as hard as his muscles would allow. With a gasp his lungs filled with air when the tension around his throat vanished; he followed through with a hard push that knocked his assailant away. He then rolled quickly to his left and yanked his sword from its sheath as he turned to face the old man, who had fallen hard to his side on the floor. With a head that turned to meet Daedrin's furious gaze with a level stare of his own Hadrîn rose slowly to his feet and chuckled derisively.

"You know that can't hurt me," he said with a light gesture to the naked blade. Daedrin blinked before he sheathed it slowly and raised both hands in front of him.

"I didn't mean to disgrace your daughter," he said slowly. "I..." his voice trailed off as he shook his head. "I'm truly not entirely sure why... why I said those things. Something... came over me." Hadrîn glared for a few moments before he walked slowly back to the chair by the fire and took his seat.

"Such reckless speech will serve to bring you to a sudden end, boy, should you not learn to harness a tight hold over your own tongue," the old man warned as he angrily rubbed his jaw while Daedrin moved to sit once more on the bed in quiet contemplation.

"What did you do," he finally asked softly, "when Garrôth..." his voice trailed off while he eyed the old man warily and rubbed his tender throat.

Hadrîn was quiet for a moment as he leaned to grasp another log from the stack and placed it on the hearth.

"I took Hana's... body, and I fled," he answered quietly. "Hid in Ímrelet with the two dragons who managed to survive the vicious onslaught that quickly followed the murder of my little girl."

Daedrin blinked. "Dragons..." he said slowly. "But they are extinct; all the stories agree on that."

Hadrîn looked up to meet his gaze. "Are they, lad?" he asked as a light twinkle appeared in his eyes. "Sometimes stories are created by design, to hide something that the vanquished wished to be forgotten."

Daedrin shook his head. "Even if that were true, you would have to be well over a hundred to have seen such times."

"Two-hundred and forty now, I believe," Hadrîn replied. "Though I'll admit I'm not entirely certain of that number. The years have a way of all running together when you live such a long life of isolation."

"Impossible." Daedrin shook his head in disbelief, and the old man chuckled while he rose to his feet and moved to the window.

"Is it really so hard to believe, after what you have seen this night?" he asked while he peered into the darkness outside the window with a gesture to his arm.

Daedrin sighed. "I... don't know," he said with a slow shake of his head.

Hadrîn glanced at the young man as he moved back to his seat..

"I only know one thing for certain," Daedrin continued with a sudden fierce gaze as he lifted his eyes. "If Garrôth is indeed real, then he must pay for the atrocities his creatures commit with his blessing, and if the dragons still exist, then I would seek them out. Should the tales of their power and might prove truthful then they could perhaps serve as an instrument of retribution."

The old man's eyes narrowed before he nodded. "Most of the legends concerning the dragons are true," he said. "And nothing would bring me more satisfaction than to see Garrôth finally brought to ruin," he added while a fire kindled beneath heavy lids.

Daedrin felt his lips twitch with the slightest hint of a smile as his imagination was filled with the image a field of Nasci, all brutally slain by his own hand.

Hadrîn sighed. "It is late," he said with a weary yawn. "If you wish, you may sleep tonight on my bed," he added, waving to the mattress where Daedrin sat before rising himself. "I urge caution should you decide to leave. There is only one safe path down the mountain, and you would be hard pressed to find it at this hour." He moved then to the bed with a slight chuckle when Daedrin flinched on his approach.

"Relax," he said as he stooped to one knee, reached under the bed and withdrew a wool blanket. He held it up for a moment before rising to move through the doorway where he disappeared around the corner and left Daedrin suddenly alone to his own thoughts. After a few moments of quiet pondering he slid to his feet, moved across the room and recovered each of his boot knives from the stash in the corner before returning to the mattress with a blade in each hand as he lay down and soon fell fast asleep while still in his boots.

CHAPTER 4

LYSICHITON

Daedrin jerked upright as he woke the next morning with a short scream just barely escaping his lips. His chest heaved with labored breath when he recalled the horrific nightmare in which his unconscious mind had been trapped just moments before. After taking a deep breath he closed his eyes and attempted to calm his racing thoughts until, ever so slowly his mind began to ease, his pulse steadied and he gradually became aware of a smell and sound that he had not sensed in what seemed like an eternity; bacon and eggs sizzling in a pan. With a sharp exhalation of breath that now turned to vapor in the midst of a room left cold in the wake of a roaring fire that had turned to dull embers during the night he swung his legs over the side of the bed and blinked heavy lids above eyes that were weary with exhaustion, for though he had slept through the night his spirit had been allowed no rest.

His stomach growled as he inhaled deeply the incredible aroma, for his last real home-cooked meal seemed naught more now than a distant memory, even though it had only been little more than a day.

He stood up and looked around with momentary confusion while he struggled to remember where he was; his head throbbed slightly and, as he reached up to feel the bump on his forehead, it all came back to him in a rush of disoriented memory. With a sigh and a groan he rolled his neck while he slid the two knives into his boots, strapped his sword-belt around his waist and retrieved his bow before slinging it with its quiver over his shoulder and exited the room.

"Morning," a gruff voice greeted Daedrin as he walked into what he now realized was the kitchen of the Hadrîn's home. The old man was standing over the counter while he ran a small knife, smeared with butter over a piece of bread. He wore the same faded and worn dark green cloak as the night before, but this time there was a sword hanging low on his belt.

"What need have you of a blade?" Daedrin asked as he eyed the stranger warily.

Hadrîn smirked. "This great height is not without its dangers. Wild beasts and predators sometimes make their way this far up the pass." Daedrin frowned, and Hadrîn sighed. "Even though nothing can kill me it still isn't pleasant to sustain injuries," the old man explained with an irritated wave of his hand. "Besides, I have livestock to protect," he added while he returned his attention to the bread. Daedrin nodded slowly and scanned the room with still wary eyes.

"I imagine you won't turn down a hot meal?" Hadrîn asked as he then scooped a portion of bacon and eggs out of a pan that lay on the counter and placed some onto a plate for each of them. Daedrin dipped his head slightly.

"Well," the old man declared. "I raise and harvest my own livestock, which isn't the easiest task with the cold weather, though it does allow for the meats to last considerably longer than usual. I also grow much of my own food in a greenhouse, so all is fresh and quite satisfying, if I do say so myself."

"Sounds like you manage fairly well," Daedrin observed, "despite your seclusion."

Hadrîn smirked sadly. "Well, I've had more than enough time to learn how to survive up here."

After a few moments of uncomfortable silence Hadrîn cleared his throat as he added a slice of buttered toast to each plate before carrying them to the table and motioning for Daedrin to sit. The young man moved slowly to one of the chairs while the stranger retrieved two cups from the cabinet and moved over to fill them from the well before returning to the table and placing one near the plate in front of Daedrin. With a sigh the old man took his own seat and swallowed several large gulps from his own mug while the two watched each other in silence for a few moments until finally, Hadrîn chuckled.

"Eat," he said as he picked up one of two crude pewter forks from the table and took a bite.

Daedrin only sneered and stared absently at the food before him while he recalled the last meal he had eaten, surrounded by his family as they sat together around the table. The words of his father's prayer echoed through his mind and he scoffed quietly. *Protection...* he thought with a gentle grind of his teeth before he picked up his fork. After the first taste his mouth watered and he devoured the rest of his portion in a few moments, wiping his mouth on the sleeve of his cloak and letting his fork clatter to his plate after he had finished.

"How long ago was your last meal?" Hadrîn asked.

"Long enough," Daedrin replied as he sat back in his chair and took a drink from his cup; he closed his eyes when the cool water touched his throat. The old man dipped his head and he returned to his own plate.

"Not the most extravagant meal," he remarked absently, "but also not the worst, I trust?"

Daedrin leaned back in his chair. "It was sufficient," he said.

Hadrîn smirked. "So, might I ask, what were you planning in light of your... current circumstances?" he asked carefully between mouthfuls.

"Well, before I... met you," Daedrin said after a beat of silence with a motion to the bump on his forehead with a frown. "I was planning to return to my village. I..." his voice trailed off and he cleared his throat before continuing. "I had people there, whom I care for deeply." He shook his head and swallowed hard. "I know not whether they are alive or dead..."

Hadrîn sighed, and as he finished his plate he leaned forward to let clasped hands rest on the table. "I can lead you down the mountain," he offered slowly. "If you wish." Daedrin sat in silence for a few moments of quiet reflection before showing his consent with a shrug and a nod. The old man dipped his head, stood and gathered the dishes before moving to the well where he quickly washed and put them away. After retrieving a small towel from the counter he wiped his hands before returning to his seat with a grunt.

"What was it like?" Daedrin asked with a sudden lift of his head as he peered intently at the old man, who blinked at the question.

"What do you mean?" he asked while his brow furrowed.

"Being cursed," Daedrin replied slowly. He eyed Hadrîn carefully as the room fell into silence for a while before the old man spoke softly.

"It... was unpleasant," he said finally as he stared down at his cup on the table with hazy eyes; lost in some far-off place. "I... fell to my knees, next to my daughter..." he shook his head and cleared his throat while he continued in slow, broken sentences. "I... felt pressure, on my right shoulder. It was Garrôth's minions, pulling me back before he... grabbed my face, with his left hand. There was... heat, radiating from his palm... it... filled my head to bursting before he moved away, and I collapsed. His men lifted me again to my knees before, at Garrôth's command, one plunged a blade into my belly," Hadrîn made a stabbing motion toward himself as he spoke. "The pain was... unbearable, but..." the old man shrugged. "I did not perish, as I expected. Instead the wound... knit itself back together, just as you saw last night. Then Garrôth pulled a knife from his own belt, drew it across my cheek."

Hadrîn tilted his head to the side and brushed his fingers over a light scar that began behind and to the top of his jawline before it plunged down to the base of his neck. "I still remember the feel of his hot breath on my face as warm blood tricked down my neck… his words as he whispered them cruelly in my ear…" his voice trailed off, and Daedrin frowned when he beheld the tears that welled up in Hadrîn's eyes before the old man averted his gaze and wiped his face with the back of one hand.

"I am sorry," the young man said finally.

Hadrîn shook his head. "Don't be sorry, lad," he said with a derisive cough. "Be angry," he added as he turned to meet Daedrin's gaze with a cold fire in his eyes until the young man nodded slowly.

"You would lead me back down the mountain?" he asked carefully.

Hadrîn nodded. "I have two horses in the stable," he said, "and it would not take long to pack enough provisions for a few days on the road. Best to leave soon," he added. "The path is long, and not one to trifle with once the sun begins to set."

"Very well," Daedrin consented with a nod as he rose from his seat with a stretch. "Lead the way," he added as the old man followed suit before grabbing his blanket from where he'd left it on the floor, moved to the back door and exited the house. Daedrin strolled to the other room where he folded and rolled the blanket on which he'd laid his head the previous night as he pondered the path that was laid out before him.

Though he had no desire to travel to what remained of his village with this mysterious stranger, he felt at the same time the odd and rather unsettling notion that he already knew the old man well and could trust him. The strange declarations made by the clearly jaded fellow somehow seemed to resound within his troubled heart as truthful, despite a decided lack of evidence, save for the incredible way that Hadrîn's arm had healed itself. With a shake of his head he moved back to the kitchen, approached the well and stooped low to fill his canteen before stepping outside. He found himself blinking under vivid sunlight that reflected off sporadic heaps of snow that lay scattered about amid clusters of trees; a sure sign of the height of the great peak on which he now stood. With a glance at Hadrîn he breathed deeply of the cool mountain air as the old man led him down a narrow dirt path to a small stable roughly a stone's throw from the house where two horses waited, fresh and strong.

"I trust you can handle the rigging?" Hadrîn asked as he retrieved one of two leather saddles from a bench in the corner before moving over to one of the horses, a black stallion, where he proceeded to secure the seat to the back of the noble beast; Daedrin nodded while his eyes took in the magnificence of the beast before him. "His name is Liber," Hadrîn said when he caught the young man staring. "It means 'free', or at least I think that's what it means," he added with a shake of his head.

We could never have afforded a horse so fair, Daedrin thought in wonder as he scanned the strong shoulders and fair coat of the noble creature.

"He's beautiful," he marveled softly, and the admiration was plainly evident in his voice while he approached Liber and reached out with one hand.

"Careful," Hadrîn warned as the horse nickered and Daedrin

withdrew his arm quickly. "He tends to scare easily around strangers," the old man added with a quiet sort of sadness.

"Where did you acquire him?"

Hadrîn smiled lightly. "I guess you could say that I liberated him," he replied. Daedrin tilted his head and Hadrîn frowned.

"Roughly… two years ago, I think, a pair of thrill seeking hunters braved their way up the mountain and chanced upon my humble estate. They had some supplies with them, carried by Liber here. Poor creature was skin and bones, covered in the scars that he still bears, with fresh scabs and bruises as well, barely clinging to life." The stranger paused for a moment as he approached the horse with a raised hand and a smile while he stroked its mane. "I haggled with the two men," he continued, "and purchased him. We've cared for one another ever since."

Daedrin shook his head angrily as he walked around Liber and took in his scarred torso.

"You should've killed them," he said softly, and Hadrîn blinked.

"Well I would be lying if I said that I was not angry enough at the time to entertain the notion, but what kind of man would that make me?"

Daedrin turned to look Hadrîn in the eyes. "A man who corrects injustice," he declared, and the old man chuckled slightly.

"Perhaps," he replied with a shake of his head before he moved to the other horse and brushed its chin softly. "This here is Fidelium," he said, "or 'Faithful'. Though I love Liber and we certainly have a special bond, Fidelium here has been my companion for many years."

Hadrîn turned then to the young man. "Since Liber will likely not take kindly to a stranger riding on his back, Fidelium shall be yours while we ride together."

Daedrin dipped his head slightly in thanks as he approached the beautiful chestnut gelding and stroked its mane while he uttered its name softly. After moving around the steed he grasped the other saddle and slung it onto the back of the horse where he tied it securely it into place before he took the remainder of one of the leather straps and cinched his bedroll to the side of the seat.

"Now," Hadrîn declared as returned from the back of the stable with a leather bag in his hand; his own blanket was rolled and tied to it with twine. "I've packed dried meat with bread and fruit, sufficient enough for the time it will take to travel at least to your village, I should think." After sliding the satchel into a slot on the Liber's saddle, he ran a band around it which he pulled tight before reaching out to grab the saddle horn. With a grunt he pulled himself quickly up, settled into the seat and turned to see Daedrin do the same with Fidelium.

"Lead the way," the young man said with a wave of his hand. Hadrîn nodded and clicked his tongue to urge Liber forward. Daedrin followed while the old man led him out of the stable before moving at a slow trot over to the edge of a precipice.

"It seems impossible to even fathom climbing down," Daedrin said, shaking his head in wonder as he peered out to the valleys and trees far below.

Hadrîn smirked. "When you have climbed the pass as many times as I, it isn't such a difficult task," he boasted as he nudged his horse away from the edge and moved to a narrow road that skirted the side of the mountain range. "Follow me closely, lad," he said over his shoulder.

They moved slowly down the winding path, which Daedrin now realized was nothing more than a game trail, and a very faint one at that. No sound could be heard save the light howling of the wind amidst the falling of the horses hooves' while they carefully followed the path with all its twists and turns down the pass for several hours until finally the ground leveled and they reached the base of the mountain.

"This way," Hadrîn said with a slight nod to his right. They continued quietly for a while with each lost in his own thoughts as they took in the deep greens of the forest slowly fading to brown before Daedrin nudged his horse to a light trot and brought himself alongside Hadrîn.

"What happened to your wife?" he asked quietly. Hadrîn's eyes narrowed at the abrupt personal question while his jaw clenched and he turned to look off into the trees. "You told me of your daughter," Daedrin continued, "but you never mentioned the fate of her mother."

"She fell ill," Hadrîn said finally with a harrumph as he cleared his throat. "A few years before Garrôth…"

Daedrin shook his head. "Say no more. I… should not have asked."

"It… is alright," the old man replied after a beat of silence. "You would think that after all these long years it would be easier to… talk of her. Especially since the king…" he trailed off again, and Daedrin couldn't help but ask, "King?"

Hadrîn sighed. "It's a shame how much history has been lost in such a short time…" he muttered softly, as if to himself before he cleared his throat. "There was a man called Vandin, renowned by all as a gifted healer. He was king of Silmaín before Garrôth slew him. I worked in his estate as a guard, a gatekeeper actually, when I was young, or rather… old by standard reckoning, though not so ancient as I am today." The old man smiled sadly. "My wife, Helena, oh she was beautiful; I've never loved anyone as I loved her…" his voice trailed off as he peered into the brush. "Sickness took hold of her," he said finally, "and I pleaded with Garrôth for the aid of his father. But, the king was away at the time, and so my voice was not heard and… she died." Hadrîn swallowed hard while continued on in silence.

"Why are you here, riding alongside me?" Daedrin asked after a while. "After so long in seclusion, why leave now?"

Hadrîn glanced at him briefly. "I have remained hidden for too long," he said slowly. "Seeing your pain, and your rage… it has served to remind me of what I've lost, and of the one who took them from me. Perhaps it is time to stop hiding and see Garrôth suffer as I have… blood for blood, the guilty must pay," he added with a frown.

"I feel as if I know that phrase," Daedrin mused with a furrow of his brow.

"You could've heard it from a trader, perhaps." Hadrîn shrugged. "It's from the old code of justice as established by Vandin when he first became ruler."

"Our land has need of such a code again, I feel," Daedrin remarked, and Hadrîn nodded.

The young man felt his gaze narrow while he peered into the forest. "Can vengeance sometimes be equated as justice?" he asked finally.

Hadrîn looked over at the young man. "Nay, vengeance I would never call just; but I also would not call it always wrong, either."

"What do you mean?" Daedrin asked.

Hadrîn paused a moment before responding. "Sometimes justice falls short of the mark," he explained. "Ages ago, Garrôth murdered the king with his entire family; his justice could not save them. At that time the dragons deemed it just to abandon the search for Garrôth once he escaped, but he inevitably returned and has wrought death and destruction on the world as a result."

Daedrin nodded slowly as he pondered this notion quietly for a few moments.

"So you deem that sometimes vengeance should be taken for the sake of preserving justice?" he asked.

Hadrîn nodded. "That is what I have come to know."

The young man frowned while they continued for a while in silence broken only by the clattering of the horses' hooves beneath them.

"We are not far from the village, now," Daedrin said suddenly as he surveyed their surroundings, for his eyes began to take in familiar shapes to the trees and land.

Hadrîn glanced at him. "You know these woods well, I take it."

"I've hunted in them since I was a boy," Daedrin replied with a nod as he looked around while memories of hunts with his brother flickered briefly through his mind and brought to his lips a bitter-sweet smile. "I used to take Melkai with me, sometimes," he continued softly. "He was a natural hunter," he added with a smirk that turned slowly to a look of deep sorrow when he swallowed hard.

"Melkai was your brother?" Hadrîn asked quietly.

Daedrin nodded. "Little rascal, he was," he said with a sniffle as a light chuckle escaped. "I miss him..." his voice trailed off to become barely more than a whisper, and he blinked away the tears that had sprung to his eyes. The old man eyed him quietly for a few moments before averting his gaze.

"You will be with him again, lad," he said finally. "Hold on to that," he added with a glance at the young man. Daedrin nodded as he swallowed the lump that rose in his throat and brushed his eyes with the back of his hand.

"Linull is just over that rise," he said, nodding his head forward to a small but familiar hill a stone's throw away and swallowing when he recalled the last time he had seen the mound, for he had stood atop it then with Marin in his arms.

"Are you sure you are ready, lad?" Hadrîn asked softly as he observed the young man carefully. After a few moments Daedrin nodded.

"I... I must know," he stammered and grit his teeth while they moved slowly up the bank until the village came into view. A horrendous odor assaulted their nostrils as a breeze picked up, carrying with it the putrid smell of old blood and decaying flesh. Daedrin coughed and stifled a retch as he placed a hand over his mouth and nose. He glanced at Hadrîn and took note of the old man's scrunched up face while they nudged their horses onward. Daedrin found his that his jaw clenched while his throat tightened when they had closed the distance and the carnage within the village became clearer. As they passed the smithy and moved onto the street the pair wove their horses slowly around the torn and shredded bodies scattered all around while Daedrin peered carefully at each face. Some he recognized with a pang of grief while others were so destroyed and covered with dirt and blood that they were unrecognizable.

"Here," the young man choked with a lifted finger directed to a home on their left once they had passed through the main village square. He dismounted with a cringe when his boots touched the sticky earth. "Bring the pack," he said as he moved through the door, followed closely by Hadrîn. "This... was Tara's home," Daedrin said slowly as he surveyed the main room. "She... was the village healer," he added absently with a glance at the old man.

The table was turned over with one broken leg off and lying to the side amidst broken glass and herbs. Daedrin glowered as he took in the destruction while his eyes scanned for any jar that remained intact. He smirked, for his attention was drawn to a tall shelf off to one side with several containers on the highest perch. Moving over to it he reached up and removed two of the jars before turning and passing them to Hadrîn.

"I assume you've heard of Linellin," he said.

"Is there any who hasn't?" Hadrîn asked while he tucked the jars into his bag. "A wise choice, lad," he added as Daedrin handed him two more containers of the precious crushed leaves.

The old man peered then around the room with a scowl. "Shameful waste," he said softly.

Daedrin nodded before freezing suddenly when his eyes peered over Hadrîn's shoulder and he let one hand creep slowly to the hilt of his sword.

"What is it?" Hadrîn asked softly as he reached for his own blade. A low growl emanated from behind him and the old man closed his eyes briefly before quickly yanking sword from sheath and whirling around. He grunted when the scaly arm of a Nasci collided with his chest, knocking him to the side before the creature pounced at Daedrin, who had just managed to expose his own blade. The young man lunged to the side and hit the floor as the Nasci flew past him and crashed into the wall with a thump and a howl.

Quickly rolling to his feet Daedrin spun to face his foe; he barely managed a frantic swipe that glanced off its scaly hide when the brute pounced once more and pinned him to the ground. For a brief moment all that filled Daedrin's senses was the crushing weight of the creature atop him as rows of lethal fangs were bared and its foul breath filled his nostrils. He struggled to move but found that he was utterly powerless when suddenly blood spurt from the throat of the Nasci and the creature gurgled as it fell to the side. Daedrin gasped when its weight was removed and looked to see Hadrîn standing over him with bloodied sword in hand.

"Are you whole?" he asked as he reached out, grasped Daedrin's arm and pulled him to his feet. The young man nodded while he breathed heavily for a few moments before returning his sword to its sheath.

"I am sorry lad, but I am afraid that we have no more time left to search the dead," Hadrîn said as he wiped his sword with a rag from his tunic.

"No!" Daedrin exclaimed with a shake of his head. "Go if you wish; I'm not leaving until I know for sure!" he added as he took a step forward before being blocked by Hadrîn.

"Listen, boy," the old man ordered as he quickly sheathed his blade, grasped Daedrin by the shoulders and clutched him tightly as he leaned in to look the young man in the eyes. "If you wish to live to fulfill the vow made at the graves of your family then we must leave, now! The Nasci never travel alone; more must be very close. If we stay, we *will* be overwhelmed."

Daedrin jerked away from Hadrîn's grip and turned as he took a few steps while reaching up to clasp his hands behind his head for a moment before grunting in frustration. With a jerk he swung his leg outward with a kick that sent the turned-over flipping to slide across its top on the floor before he angrily moved out of the shop, followed closely by Hadrîn. He swung up into the saddle atop Fidelium while the old man reattached the bag to his own rigging before mounting Liber and, with a kick of their heels they spurred the horses forward and moved quickly around the bodies before exiting the village and plunging once more into the forest. They bore to the west at a brisk trot for several minutes, putting as much distance between themselves and the village as they were able before a shriek and a howl that turned into a chorus of wretched noise echoed through the trees behind them. The pair glanced at one another before spurring their horses to as much of a gallop as the thick brush would allow.

"Follow me," Daedrin yelled over his shoulder as he took the lead and made his way through the trees while his eyes quickly took in familiar surroundings. He directed his steed more to the west with Hadrîn close behind before finally slowing his steed after several minutes of hurried movement.

"We need to keep moving," Hadrîn declared with some irritation.

"Shh," Daedrin commanded while he dipped his head, closed his eyes and strained his ears until a gentle trickling sound reached them from far off. He smiled slightly. "This way," he said as he urged Fidelium forward at a brisk trot toward the noise. After about a half mile the low sound of running water was loud enough for both to hear over the sound of the trotting hooves.

"There," Daedrin said and nudged Fidelium a little to their left when a stream, roughly a stone's throw away came into view. He closed the distance quickly and directed his steed into the shallow creek; the horses' hooves splashed while they moved through the water. Trotting as quickly as the mud beneath would allow they followed the creek south for a few minutes before veering back onto the dirt to their right when the watery trail made a loop before curving to the south-west. Quickly dismounting Daedrin knelt down next to some white budded flowers that were growing sporadically at the edge of the creek.

He smiled as he glanced up at Hadrîn's furrowed brow.

"They are called Lysichiton," the young man said. "I discovered them a few years ago while hunting, and have used them many times to mask my own scent." He proceeded to pluck one of the flowers from its stem before holding it close as his eyes scanned its beautiful appearance. "The key isn't to smell like anything in particular, but to keep from smelling like a man," he added as he removed several more before crushing them with a cringe at the pungent odor released when he did so. Hadrîn watched while Daedrin then proceeded to roll the buds between his hands, causing them to crumble before rubbing them all over his cloak, neck, face and into his hair until every inch of him was covered. He then plucked more flowers, moved to Fidelium and did the same to the horse, speaking gentle words as the horse nickered nervously. Hadrîn smiled and quickly followed suit, and after a few moments more each of them with their steeds were saturated with the foul smelling plant.

"Well," Hadrîn said, "this rotten stench might perhaps do the trick, though we must still be very careful. The Nasci are not a usual predator; masking our scent may not work as well it does on the creatures you've hunted."

Daedrin nodded. "Let's put some distance between us and them, then," he said as he pulled himself back into the saddle, quickly followed by Hadrîn. They moved back into the stream and allowed their steeds a quick drink from the gently flowing water before kicking the horses to a brisk trot. After a few miles they veered left onto the dirt and, in a few minutes more they heard a sudden, shrill cry of the Nasci echo from the distance behind them.

Daedrin smiled grimly at the old man. "Seems to have worked," he said.

"Perhaps," Hadrîn replied with a frown. "We should not waste our advantage. If my guess is correct, we are not far now from Cordin... if we bear to the south and travel through the night we should reach its northern-most gate before the dawn." Daedrin nodded and spurred Fidelium to a more hurried trot. They kept their horses at a quicker pace for several minutes before slowing to a stop for a brief rest.

The few remaining daylight hours were spent in silence, following the pattern of a brisk trot and rest followed by a slow walk and a rest. When at last the sun hid its face behind the horizon they stopped for a break under the concealment of some hanging trees and brambles, not lighting a fire for fear that the Nasci might still be near enough to see the flames. Once the horses had been fed and watered from a small basin that was stored in Hadrîn's gear the old man distributed some bread and cheese from his pack and they ate quietly in the dark.

As he consumed his meager meal Daedrin moved to lean on a nearby tree while he struggled to keep his thoughts free of his family but, their memory combined with the faces of those slain in his village to form images that haunted him in the stillness of the night. The exhaustion he felt from his lack of true rest over the course of the last few days began to creep into his bones until his eyes drooped after a while and he blinked and shook his head with a yawn. He peered out into the dimly lit forest with dew that gleamed slightly under the light of the moon as it settled on grass. After a few moments he felt his lids getting heavy once more, and though he struggled to keep his eyes open they drifted closed…

… Daedrin stumbled through the dark forest as his mind became trapped in the depths of the surreal dream world. His breathing was labored while he ran from… something, though he couldn't quite grasp what it was that held his heart in such terror. He wove around the trees and swatted away leafy vines until he stumbled with a grunt at the base of a hill. Struggling to his feet he clawed through the bramble at its base before crawling up to its peak where his eyes crested the top. He blinked in confusion when the gleaming light of a large bonfire filled his vision, with people dancing around the flames while joyous laughter touched his ears as it echoed across the field between himself and the villagers. Pulling to his feet he stumbled down the hill toward the wonderful sight with a smile when his eyes took in the beautiful form of Marin as she laughed; her arms were outstretched while she danced in a circle with Melkai.

"My love!" she cried when her brilliant blue eyes caught his own as he approached. She released the hands of his brother and ran up to him with a wide grin across her face. He laughed and swooped her up when she collided with him; he spun her around as they embraced. When her feet touched the ground again she smiled up at him and, with raised arms she placed her hands behind his neck and let her fingers become intertwined before she pulled his head down and touched his lips gently with her own.

"Come!" she shouted with a giggle as she turned away. Taking his hand in hers she ran toward the forest and pulled him up the hill that he had stumbled down earlier until they reached its edge where she stopped and he pulled her into a crushing embrace. When he pulled away she smiled with perfect teeth that shone brightly in the moonlight before Daedrin turned, lost his footing and fell face-first down the edge of the rise...

... "Oof!" the air whooshed from Daedrin's lungs when his chest connected hard with the ground and he snapped awake with a blink of momentary confusion while he peered into the dark of the forest. He shook his head and groaned as he pushed himself up to his feet and brushed off the dirt from his cloak. With a pang of grief he closed his eyes, wishing he could return to that wonderful dream before realizing after a few moments that it was actually a memory of one of the best moments he'd had with Marin, for it had been that very night that he had asked her to leave Linull with him and travel the world, and she had agreed with joyous laughter before kissing him hard. He smiled, but his joy quickly faded when his eyes caught two pinpricks of red gleaming in the distance; they disappeared briefly before shining once more. He swallowed hard and backed slowly away when a low growl emanated through the trees and the two lights were joined by four others while the silhouettes of three Nasci became visible under the shining moon.

"Hadrîn!" he yelled as with uncanny swiftness he unslung his bow, fitted an arrow to the string and let it fly at the center of one of the sets of light. He knew that his arrow had struck its mark, for the creature fell with a shrill cry. Upon seeing their companion fall the other Nasci howled and raced toward him. Drawing again he let another projectile follow the first; it struck one of the galloping brutes through its left eye and sent it sprawling head over heels. The remaining creature was too close now to shoot and with barely a moment to spare he let his bow fall and drew his sword, taking brief note that Hadrîn now stood beside him with blade drawn and ready. The Nasci stopped just before it reached them and growled, pawing at the ground as it moved to the right and began to circle the pair.

"Together?" Hadrîn asked with a glance at the young man. Daedrin nodded as they rushed forward and each swung, with Hadrîn from the left and Daedrin from the right, but this Nasci proved more cunning than the others that they had faced. It dodged their attacks easily with a quick step back before pouncing with claws outstretched to the left and the right at each of them. While it flew through the air Daedrin twisted his body but did not dodge the blow completely. He cried out in agony and fell to his knees when the vicious razors sliced through the flesh on his lower back; blood quickly flowed down onto his legs. Hadrîn was unable to dodge the blow at all, for it connected hard with the old man's chest, cutting deeply and sending him backward with a whoosh as the air was forced from his lungs.

With a grunt behind grit teeth Daedrin, while still on his knees turned just in time to barely parry a second blow. His blade cut cleanly between oncoming claws, sending blood spurting while the Nasci howled. Hadrîn rolled now to his feet and clutched his bloodied chest with a momentary grimace before he stumbled toward the brute as it reared back to lunge at Daedrin. He plunged his weapon forward with a grunt when it slipped between the scales of the creature and pierced its thick hide, causing the Nasci to whimper briefly before falling to its side onto the cold earth.

"Blast it, boy," the old man said, dropping his sword with a frown as Daedrin collapsed. The world seemed to be spinning all around the young man while he struggled to maintain consciousness, and he barely noted that Hadrîn had removed his own outer cloak before rolling Daedrin over and pressing hard against the wound. After a few moments more his resolve began to slip as his vision became hazy, and his world was plunged into darkness.

CHAPTER 5

NEW ENEMIES

When Daedrin woke the first thing he sensed was pain; agony that seemed to fill every part of his body, as if the very muscles beneath his skin were lit with a blazing fire. He gasped and opened his eyes only to have dim, blurred surroundings fill his vision while he struggled to speak but found that he could not, for his throat was taut and dry.

"Hush, lad," Hadrîn's voice reached Daedrin's ears as something cool touched his forehead. He felt himself whimper slightly before a cloud settled over him and his mind slipped once more into darkness...

... When at long last his dreamless slumber ended he drearily lifted heavy lids and blinked several times to clear his hazy vision as a dim ray of sunlight caressed his face through an open window, through which the sounds and smells of a busy village touched his ears and filled his nostrils. With brow furrowed he looked around in confusion and found that he was lying down, alone on a mattress in a small room. It was plainly furnished with only the bed beneath him and a small table beside that held a pitcher of water and a pewter cup.

Suddenly feeling just how tight and dry his throat was he quickly reached out and ignored the mug altogether as he raised the container to his lips and took several large gulps; he choked in his haste, and water spilled down the sides of his chin. With a deep, gasping breath he closed his eyes briefly before opening them again and taking a few swallows more of the cool, clear liquid. Wiping the excess from his face with the back of one hand he placed the pitcher back onto the table and swung his legs over the side of the bed. He grimaced when he moved, for he expected severe pain but was surprised to find that there was none at all. Slowly he slid a hand beneath his tunic and felt the skin on his lower back and found that there was no longer any wound, though he could now feel several long, light scars running from side to side, and his flesh tingled slightly with a unique and all too familiar sensation.

Releasing a heavy sigh he looked down to find that he was dressed in a light tunic that was beige in color; his own clothing he could see draped over the bedrail to his right with his weapons bundled close beside while his boots lay on the floor. With a brief roll of his neck he slid to his feet and moved over to his belongings. His tunic and cloak looked to have been freshly washed, though the back portion was now darkened as evidence of his former wounds; the tears in the fabric had been mended and showed only the faintest trace of new stitching.

He rolled his neck and slipped out of the beige tunic and back into his own garments before kneeling and donning his boots. He then rose with a grunt, strapped on his weapons and moved over to the window with eyes that now widened in recognition as they came to rest on a busy street full of life. *Cordin*, he mouthed the name and turned away with a blink at the sharp memories that flooded his mind while he surveyed the familiar architecture of the city he had previously visited once per year with his family.

One eye twitched when he surveyed the room once more and took note of cobwebs hanging low in the corners while his boots left imprints in the dirt that covered the floor beneath them. He turned back to the mattress and carefully placed one hand onto the fabric of the old, faded and stained sheets before turning away with a grimace of disgust at the dust that now covered his fingertips. After wiping his hand on his cloak he turned to the single door that hung on the wall opposite the bed and closed the distance between himself and its handle in two short strides. Quickly he released the latch and stepped over the threshold; the hinges creaked as they shut behind him.

He was in an inn, he realized, though that term was used loosely and with much disgust in his mind while he walked down a short, filthy hallway with ten numbered doors on either side. Taking note of his own room number he moved swiftly down the hall and entered a wide area with a large counter to his left, behind which stood a short, scraggly man. The stranger gave a curt nod when Daedrin entered, a gesture which the young man returned as he approached the bar.

"Greetings," the man said, "and welcome to my inn. How can Mandril be of service to you?" He was rather well-spoken considering the poor appearance of his tunic, which was so faded and torn that its proper color couldn't rightly be guessed.

"You are Mandril, I take it," Daedrin replied.

The innkeeper nodded. "Aye, Mandril is the name, and this is my inn," he declared with a wave of his arm.

Daedrin smirked as he ignored the urge to make his contempt of the place known.

"I… was injured when I was brought here, I believe," he said. "The man who was with me, have you seen him?"

The one called Mandril nodded. "Aye, you were in dire straits, young fellow, and may I add that it is good indeed to see you up and looking quite well," he added with a light bow. "I know not the name of the gentleman who rented out a room and tended to your wounds. Very discreet, he was. As for his whereabouts now, he left with the sunrise, roughly six hours ago, I should think. I've not seen him since."

Daedrin nodded. "Thank you," he said.

Mandril waved his hand in a gesture of nonchalance. "Would you care for a morsel or a drink?" he asked.

Daedrin's stomach suddenly growled fiercely and he nodded before pausing with a frown. "Actually, I… can't pay you," he said regretfully.

Mandril shrugged as he stepped away from the counter and moved through a narrow doorway behind.

"No need to fret about that," his voice echoed from the other room. "The gentleman who brought you in paid in full for a week's stay, meals and drinks included." He returned a few moments later carrying a rough wooden tray laden with meat, cheese, bread and a small chalice filled with a dark red liquid. "Generous man he is, too," Mandril added as he placed the tray in front of Daedrin. "He paid a quarter total more than my services are worth. So please, enjoy!" The innkeeper made a light sweeping gesture toward the food. "You can take it to your room, if you like."

Daedrin dipped his head in thanks and grabbed the tray. "Thank you," he said, and then paused when he started to move away. "You said he paid for a week's stay... how long have I been here?"

Mandril's face scrunched up for a moment. "Well, your friend burst through the door with you in tow three nights ago, I should think."

Daedrin mouthed the words *three nights* while he shook his head.

"Thank you," he said again as he moved away from the counter.

"You're quite welcome, friend," the innkeeper replied. "Just leave the tray on the table when you're finished!" he called out as the young man entered the hallway.

After a few paces Daedrin came to the third door on his left where he turned and pushed it open with his shoulders so as not to disturb the dishes in his hands. Heaving a deep sigh he sat down on the filthy bed with back to the wall and food in his lap while his mind filled to the brim and he munched slowly on the meal before him. His thoughts drifted back to the days when his greatest worry was the winter arriving early and destroying the crops before they could be fully gathered. Now he was alone, save for the companionship of his newfound acquaintance, and his quiet life had been replaced with one simple need; survive.

Perhaps traveling with the old man was a mistake, he thought before reaching back to feel the mended section of his cloak. *Though it seems that he did save me...* his thoughts trailed off and he let his head tilt back to rest against the wall while his eyes closed. *How did it come to this?* he wondered absently as he lifted one hand to rub his forehead. With a grunt of frustration at his racing thoughts he brought his head forward and took a bite of the meat, ham he realized, together with a slice of cheese; the cup he knew from the pleasant aroma to be a sweet red wine. This he gulped down almost greedily as he quickly finished the rest of the food before washing it all down with one final swallow of the dark liquid.

Content with the simple meal he set the tray aside, rolled his neck and took a deep breath while he swung his legs over the side of the bed and stood before moving over to the window. As he stared out into the bustling life of the street outside his heart suddenly longed to be surrounded by those familiar sights and sounds, a notion that was quickly followed by a pang of grief when the image of carnage within his own village flashed briefly through his mind. With a hard swallow he turned on his heels, exited the room and moved quickly through the hallway and back out into the lobby.

"Going out?" Mandril, who was wiping a glass mug with a cloth asked as the young man entered.

Daedrin nodded. "I actually need to contact someone here in the city," he said as he approached the counter. "His name is Salen." To Daedrin's surprise Mandril jumped and the cup in his hand slipped from his grasp before shattering on the floor behind the counter.

"I'm afraid I can't help you," he said with hands that trembled as he bent down to pick up the broken pieces.

"Do… you know who can?" Daedrin asked slowly while he eyed the clearly troubled innkeeper with a frown. Mandril swallowed hard as he rose and moved through the door behind the bar with the shattered glass in hand before returning moments later empty handed; he was wringing his fingers nervously.

"The bar down the street," he declared with a short nod. "Be careful," he added when Daedrin thanked the man before moving toward the entrance. He dipped his head, pulled the handle and stepped outside where he squinted as he was immersed in vivid sunlight that illuminated the numerous townsfolk. Many faces passed by: some gruff-looking but kind, as if they'd endured many a hard season in their life yet did not allow it to darken their hearts while others looked down at their feet as if some great weight rested on their weary shoulders while they navigated the street; all were poorly dressed.

Daedrin ventured forward a few paces, closed his eyes and took in a deep breath as he was immersed in the crowd. He smiled, for his worries momentarily faded away in the wake of the familiar sounds and smells before his joy was interrupted by a thump that caused his eyes to open with a grunt when a burly form ran into him hard; the stranger glared briefly before moving past to whatever destination had so captivated his attention. Daedrin's brow furrowed while he looked around and his mind struggled to recall the street on which he stood, for though he believed it to be one of the many central paths that wound throughout the whole city of Cordin he could not remember having ever laid eyes on it before that moment. All along the sides of the lane were various shops: smithies ringing with the sound of hammers, jewelers shouting their wares while potion vendors promoted their stock to those of simple mind. A little ways down the road to his left he saw a sign that read *"Bull's"* hanging over a seedy looking tavern. Thinking it to be the place spoken of by the innkeeper Daedrin walked the few paces it took to reach the bar and, taking a deep breath he strolled through the door.

Uproarious laughter met his ears the moment he entered and he immediately grimaced with disgust at the condition of the place; ale stained the floor and tables, all of which were surrounded by roughly dressed rabble, while a few rats scrounged for crumbs in the corner. Indeed, the whole establishment seemed host to the worst filth and vermin in the whole city. With a sigh as he ignored all of this Daedrin moved to lean on a counter surrounded by seven high stools and motioned for the bartender; a scrawny, seedy looking fellow in tattered clothes who stepped forward and introduced himself as Nash.

"Whadaya want, eh?" he asked roughly, eying Daedrin's sword as he slowly wiped at the counter with a damp, filthy rag.

Daedrin met his stare evenly. "It… has been some time since I've been in the city," he said, "and I am having trouble getting my bearings. I'm looking for someone, by the name of Salen; perhaps you could deliver a message for me?" A dark look passed over Nash's features.

"Salen, eh? What business 'as an outsider like you with 'im?"

Daedrin scowled. "Can you help me contact him or no?"

Nash eyed Daedrin crossly. "Per'aps," he said, and then added with a nasty grin, "fer the right price, I jus' might be able to see it done."

Daedrin held up his hands. "Alas, I have nothing of any value at present to compensate you," he said. The bartender folded one arm over the other and leaned back as a strange gleam entered his eyes.

"That's a fine blade ye've got there," he observed with a sneer.

Daedrin felt his teeth grind for a moment as he leaned forward. "It's not for sale," he said fiercely. "But I can assure you that should you bring Salen to me, it will be well worth your time," he added while he absently rested his fingers on the hilt of his sword and drove a level stare into the vagabonds' eyes. For a moment he thought that he could almost feel a pang of fear emanate from the mind of the bartender as Nash cleared his throat before diverting his gaze and stepping back.

"Meet me after nightfall, in the alley be'ind the pub," he said as he threw the rag down on the counter and crossed his arms. "Now order a drink, or be off with ye." Daedrin smirked, rose and quickly left the tavern.

The bright cheery sounds of the town outside were quite a contrast to the dark and dreary state of the bar, a fact that Daedrin noted with a touch of relief. A few paces took him back to the inn, over which hung a plain wooden sign with the inscription *"Mandril's"* carved sloppily into the grain. The interior was very plainly furnished Daedrin saw as he took note of the shameful appearance of the lobby for the first time once he had passed through the doors.

Thin, burgundy carpet layered the floor, and a few dead plants stood gloomily in the corners, surrounded by cobwebs; a layer of dust covered the walls and sparse furniture. *That old man certainly picked the worst part of Cordin,* he thought with a shake of his head as he took in the fullness of his surroundings. *Does that make him poor, or perhaps careful...?* he smirked at the thought while he stepped forward and dipped his head at Mandril when he passed the counter on the way back to his room. Swiftly closing the door behind him once he'd reached it he removed his weapons and proceeded to lie down on the bed. After a few minutes of silence interrupted only by his own gloomy thoughts his eyes began to droop and he fell into a light slumber.

Daedrin jerked upright when he woke a few hours later, for he had not meant to fall asleep. With a deep breath he sat up and swung his legs over the side of the bed when he took note of faint moonlight shining through the window. Muttering a quiet curse under his breath he quickly strapped on his weapons, left his room and ignored the frantic warnings of Mandril as he exited the inn. He found himself in a now empty street, dimly lit by a few lanterns that hung from posts outside the doors of some of the shops.

While he walked quickly down the road he let one hand creep to the hilt of his sword as he eyed the shadows all around. His eyes narrowed when he approached the door of the pub, for even though he knew the state of the interior of the establishment its lit windows now seemed almost to beckon as a safe haven from the scoundrels possibly concealed in the darkness; with a frown Daedrin passed by the door and entered the alley behind the tavern. Finding it empty he heaved an exasperated sigh and leaned against the rough wooden wall just to the left of the back door of the establishment.

What am I doing? he wondered with a sneer at the internal monologue that began to unfold in his mind. *Well connected though Salen might be, it would be foolish for him to approach a stranger like this.* He shook his head as he recalled his family's last yearly visit to his cousin just a few months ago, taken earlier than was usual, for Salen had been orphaned when his father had perished suddenly. Kelmîn had offered at that time to take Salen home to live with them but the young man had declined, for he had been given the responsibility of controlling the estate left to him in the absence of his parents.

Daedrin swallowed hard. *How can I tell him...* his thoughts trailed off while his eyes scanned the dark when suddenly a thin, raspy voice touched his ears.

"What have we here?" A voice emanated from the shadows with a veiled, menacing tone. Daedrin jerked away from the building and turned to face the dark as he freed his sword from its sheath; the pale moonlight cast an eerie glow over a cloaked and hooded figure standing in the alley.

"Peace, stranger," Daedrin called out. "I am not looking for any trouble."

"No?" the voice asked. "I hear that you are looking for Salen;

this would seem to suggest that you are indeed looking for trouble." Daedrin smirked as his caution turned to interest.

"You are shorter than the one called Nash whom I came out to meet," he said. "So tell me, what do you know of this arrangement?" The stranger chuckled and suddenly rushed forward before stopping just a few feet short of Daedrin's naked blade. With a flourish the figure pulled back its hood to reveal a devious and crooked grin.

"Salen!" Daedrin cried out in joy and relief when his eyes took in the fair blonde hair and lavish multi-colored cloak of his cousin. Quickly sheathing his blade he leaned forward to give Salen a fervent hand-clasp. "You fool! I could have run you through!"

Salen laughed aloud. "You, cousin?" He said, and his voice was now full and rich as he abandoned the charade. "Why, when last we met you would have been unable to truly harm even your little brother, no matter how much of a nuisance he might've been."

"A lot has changed, cousin," Daedrin said in a downcast voice.

"Well you must tell me why I am hearing of your surprise visit to Cordin from our illustrious, seedy bartender, and not in an advance letter from your father. Where is that old rascal, anyway?"

Daedrin choked back his emotion at the mention of his family. *So he has not heard…*

"All in due time, my friend," he said with a swallow as he clasped his cousins arm once more. "First I beg you come with me to the inn around the corner. I have a… companion, somewhere out in the city, and I must await his return."

"Alright, cousin, lead on, then; we have much to discuss, I

sense." Salen waved his arm in a grand sweeping gesture while he dipped his head, and Daedrin grasped his cousin's shoulder briefly before turning and exiting the alley.

The two walked in quick silence to the inn and shuffled toward Mandril, who dropped the book in his hands with a yelp of surprise as they approached.

"It is alright, Mandril," Daedrin said in bewilderment as he moved to lean on the counter. "This is my cousin, Salen," he added with a wave to the short man at his side.

"Begging your pardon, sir," Mandril said with a bow. "I had not expected you to bring with you such... esteemed company."

"Esteemed company?" Daedrin repeated with a chuckle, to which Salen shrugged and gave a mischievous grin.

"Please," Mandril interjected. "Anything at my inn, anything at all, consider it yours, m'lord."

"*M'lord?*" Daedrin mouthed to his cousin, who only smiled that crooked grin in return. The young man eyed his cousin curiously for a few moments before shrugging his shoulders. "Could you perhaps run two pints of ale to my room, then?" he asked the innkeeper.

"Of course!" Mandril replied with a bow. "I will deliver it to your room momentarily." With that he shuffled around the corner and, in a few moments more the two cousins were sitting down in the privacy of the room with ale in hand. Salen thanked Mandril and placed a small gold piece in the innkeepers trembling fingers before the innkeeper bowed and disappeared. For several minutes the pair sat in silence while they sipped from their mugs; Daedrin looked down at the ground and found it difficult to even speak, for the final images of his family assaulted his mind while Salen quietly observed him.

"So, cousin, would you share with me the cause of your burden?" he asked softly.

Slowly Daedrin lifted red eyes. "Our family..." He choked as cherished memories of wonderful times spent with his brother flickered through his mind for a moment before quickly being stolen by a flash of his violent end.

"No..." Salen whispered in anticipation of what he knew in his heart came next.

"They are gone, Salen," Daedrin's voice broke completely now as grief overwhelmed him suddenly and tears began spilling over his lids and down both cheeks. Salen placed a hand on Daedrin's shoulder while he fought to hold back the wells of his own eyes at this terrible news.

"We were attacked... by the Nasci," Daedrin continued after a few moments, and he struggled to maintain composure as his voice slowly filled with anger. "Those creatures *slaughtered* them," he said sorrowfully before pausing with a hard swallow. "There was nothing that I could do..." he continued in short, broken sentences. "I was in Linull when they came for them... it was attacked as well. I know not whether anyone survived but, the village is gone, destroyed. I fought... did all that I could; killed several of those monsters, but by the time I reached the farm, it was too late. They... they were already gone." Daedrin wiped his eyes as Salen hung his head. "I... I buried them, cousin…" His throat tightened and he looked away. For a few moments he became lost in his own thoughts before the words of Hadrîn came to his mind and he felt his jaw tighten with a cold fury. He reached out to grasp Salen's shoulder and gave it a light shake as his cousin lifted his eyes to meet his gaze. "I need your help," he said solemnly.

Salen's hand clenched Daedrin's wrist "What can I do?"

Daedrin took in a deep, shaky breath. "I need supplies."

Salen nodded as he wiped red eyes. "What are you planning, cousin?" he asked slowly. Daedrin was quiet when he looked away for moment before returning a hate-filled gaze to Salen.

"To make Garrôth suffer," he declared vehemently.

Salen blinked. "Garrôth?" he asked nervously. "Isn't that just a legend?"

Daedrin shook his head. "Hadrîn, the old man I am waiting for has revealed to me some proof of his existence… Garrôth is the one responsible for my family's slaughter," he added as he paused for a moment and looked at his cousin fiercely. "I intend to destroy him," he concluded with a quiet malice.

Salen was quiet for a few moments while he stared at the wall with a frown. "My help you shall have, of course," he said finally.

Daedrin sighed deeply as his lips curled with a mixed look of sorrow, rage and gratitude. "Thank you, cousin."

Salen took in a deep, sharp breath. "I can hardly believe they are really gone," he said softly. "Even little Melkai?" he asked while he lifted red eyes to meet Daedrin's own.

The young man dipped his head. "The Nasci show no mercy…" his voice trailed off and he swallowed hard. "I believe now that I am being hunted by them," he added with a scowl. "That is why I need your help."

After a while Salen nodded his head slowly. "I have some news, then that might perhaps bring some relief." Daedrin tilted his head to one side curiously.

"I received word three nights ago," Salen continued, "that two villagers from Linull had arrived in the city. They were frightened, staying hidden, so I had them brought to my estate where they would be safe." Daedrin stared for a moment in disbelief before leaping from his seat as he cried out with joy and laughter and pulled Salen into a crushing embrace that was interrupted when his cousin was suddenly ripped from his grasp.

"Be still," Hadrîn's voice echoed from behind the now wide-eyed man as the edge of a knife appeared at his throat.

"Hadrîn!" Daedrin exclaimed in anger and confusion while he glared at the old man. "Release him, now!" Hadrîn only eyed the young man warily.

"You are friendly with this… scum?" he asked with clear disdain in every syllable.

Daedrin cursed, for the blade twitched suddenly and caused Salen to flinch while blood trickled from a thin, shallow cut. "He is my cousin, you fool!" he said as his hand crept to the hilt of his sword while the wheels of his mind turned. After a few tense moments of silence Hadrîn withdrew the knife and released Salen with a shove that sent him stumbling into Daedrin, who crashed backwards onto the bed.

"Your cousin here is feared by all in the city; did you know this?" The old man asked.

Daedrin grunted as he pushed Salen off and stood to examine the wound on his cousin's neck before whirling to Hadrîn.

"What are you talking about?!" he asked incredulously while he angrily eyed the old man who now stood leaning against the wall near the door. "What does he mean?" he added with a frown as he turned to see his cousin holding a handkerchief to his neck. "The innkeeper... he seemed terrified of you," he said while his mind wandered back to the glass shattering when Mandril had dropped it at the mention of the name Salen, coupled with the frightened yelp upon seeing them first approach.

His cousin glowered. "Much has changed since my father passed, Daedrin," he said solemnly, and his normal jestful tone was now gone as his eyes darkened. "But I owe you no explanation!" he exclaimed while he lifted a pointed finger at Hadrîn. "My business is no concern of a crazed old man," he added with a curse as he pulled the slightly red rag away from his throat before tucking it back into his cloak with some irritation.

"If you wish to leave this place with breath still in your lungs, you had better start explaining," Hadrîn said darkly.

"Mind your tone," Daedrin warned as he let one hand rest on the hilt of his sword while he cast a glare at the old man. "What's changed, Salen?" he asked; he now eyed his cousin warily when he took in the fullness of Salen's tense features: the bitter look in his eyes with shoulders rigid and jaw set; all seemed entirely foreign to Daedrin as they presented themselves on his usually cheerful friend.

Salen sighed and rubbed his chin. "My father," he chuckled slightly. "Well, it turns out that his wealth was acquired through somewhat... less than reputable methods," he said before throwing one hand into the air. "When I inherited his estate, I received much more than riches: I was given the reputation of my father, as a cunning, ruthless and cruel man. But I am not my father!" he added with an angry wave at Hadrîn before meeting his cousin's narrowed gaze. "You know me, Daedrin; I didn't ask for the life my father left me."

Daedrin frowned. "Why did you not tell me, or Kelmîn?" he asked softly. "We would have gladly helped you."

Salen shook his head. "It... was made clear to me that to involve anyone from the outside would lead to their death," he said with a scowl. "The... men my father was involved with... their corruption runs deep, and their power even deeper. To cross them..." his voice trailed off as he turned to look out the window.

Hadrîn sighed and cast his gaze to Daedrin. "You vouch for this man?" he asked with eyes that narrowed when the young man slowly nodded.

"Salen... has always been a faithful friend to me, and his word he has never broken," he said. "He has vowed to give whatever supplies he can spare," Daedrin added, turning to face the old man, who nodded when he met the young man's gaze.

"Very well. I trust you can use your influence to ensure that our arrival and departure from Cordin remains a mystery to any prying eyes?"

Salen nodded as he turned to face Hadrîn. "Daedrin has told me of… Garrôth," he paused with a frown. "The idea of such a legend truly existing is not one I like to fathom, but my cousin seems convinced."

Hadrîn sighed as he turned to glare at Daedrin. "You need to keep a stronger hold on your tongue, boy," he declared angrily. "If word reaches Garrôth's ear that I am roaming the wide world again he will see to it that we come to a swift and unpleasant end. The fewer who know of our plans, the greater our chance for survival."

"If there is anyone I trust with such knowledge, it is Salen," Daedrin argued. "We need help," he added. "Doubtless the Nasci will not rest until they have found us out, but we can't hope to evade them without aid."

Hadrîn sighed as he slowly nodded. "Very well, but if you cross us," he added with an angry step forward, at which Salen lifted both hands up to his chest with palms outward.

"I assure you, I have no intention of seeing Daedrin come to any harm," he said. "Nor anyone whom he should choose to travel with," he added as he eyed the old man scornfully. "With that in mind," he continued slowly, "the safest place for you both is at my estate. The guards are entirely loyal to me, and no citizen would dare risk my wrath by approaching the dwelling without my blessing; safe from prying eyes," he smirked and glanced at Hadrîn. "Besides, there you can convene with Skane and Tara," he added slowly with a glance at his cousin.

"They are the ones who survived?" Daedrin asked quietly.

Salen nodded. "They have endured much," he said softly. "But they are whole. Seeing you would doubtless bring great joy to their heavy hearts, as it will to yours, I imagine."

Hadrîn's eyes narrowed when he met Daedrin's gaze. "Some made it safely away from Linull?" he asked, and Daedrin nodded, though his eyes glossed over as the face of Marin filled his mind's eye briefly.

"I... am glad for survivors," he said softly while he looked away. "But I had hoped that perhaps Marin..." his voice trailed off and he closed his eyes.

"I am sorry, cousin," Salen said with a hard swallow as he reached out to place a hand on Daedrin's shoulder. "But at least some still live," he added with a smile that was returned weakly by the young man.

Hadrîn watched the encounter quietly for a moment before coughing lightly.

"Provided those who still live can be trusted it would be well to go to them; the more able-bodied hands we have, the better. We have two horses housed in the stable behind the inn," he added with a glance at Salen, who gave a short nod.

"There's more than enough room in my own stables; I shall have the innkeeper fetch them for you," he offered, "along with your provisions," he added with a nod to the pack at Hadrîn's feet by the door.

Daedrin shook his head. "That isn't necessary —"

"It's no trouble at all," Salen interrupted his cousin with a raised hand.

Daedrin shrugged and nodded. "Very well. Thank you."

Salen nodded and gave Daedrin's shoulder a solid pat.

"All will be well, cousin," he promised softly, and Daedrin smiled weakly before Salen cleared his throat and averted his gaze. "Well, follow me, then. The sooner we get you both safely to my estate, the better," he added as he moved to the door and exited the room. Daedrin and Hadrîn exchanged a brief glance before following close behind.

"Going out again so late, sirs?" Mandril asked while he eyed Salen nervously when they entered the lobby.

"Indeed," Salen replied, "and if you would be so kind as to gather the two horses of my companions here and have them delivered to my estate, I would be most obliged," he added as he retrieved three small coins that glittered gold in the light of the lamps when he handed them to the innkeeper.

Mandril bowed low. "It will be done this very hour, m'lord," he said before shuffling away from the counter and through the door to the hallway.

When the rest approached the front entrance to the inn Hadrîn made a sweeping gesture with his arm as he opened the door and allowed the other two to shuffle past him. After they all had exited the inn and began to walk down the path Hadrîn gently tugged

Daedrin's arm and gestured for him to slow his walk; Salen eyed them curiously but made no objection when they fell back a few paces and conversed quietly.

"I feel I must ask," Hadrîn said, "cousin or no, are you completely certain that Salen can be trusted?"

Daedrin frowned while he looked around in quiet thought. "I've known Salen since I was a small boy," he said finally. "I would trust very few in this world, but with him I would entrust my own life." Hadrîn remained quiet for a few moments while they walked.

"I pray that your faith is not misplaced, boy," he said at length.

Daedrin glared at the old man. "Of course it isn't misplaced," he declared angrily as he quickened his pace until he came to walk alongside his cousin.

Hadrîn followed the pair in silence while they talked and laughed, and after a roughly fifteen minute walk they arrived at a rather splendid looking manor with a large set of ornate wooden doors atop a wide set of polished stone stairs. Two men, dressed in plain light armor with swords hanging low on their belts stood on either side of the entrance.

"Welcome to my estate!" Salen exclaimed with a mischievous grin. "You will not find a more secure place in all of Cordin," he added as they moved up the steps. When they drew nearer the two guards pulled open the heavy, creaky double doors to reveal a lavishly decorated interior with several servants bustling to and fro. Bright lights were glowing from extravagant chandeliers, which shed their light on the deep red satin that carpeted the floor. A winding staircase of polished oak led up to a second story, and high doorways that led to even more richly decorated rooms were on all sides. Daedrin and Hadrîn followed as Salen led them up the staircase and down a long hallway to a tall door at the end of the hall, which he opened before gesturing for them to enter.

Daedrin was filled with joy for a moment as he and Hadrîn stepped inside, but his joy quickly turned cold when he took in the fullness of what was before him, for though there were indeed two people in the room they lay bound and gagged on their bellies in the corner with backs to the door. Daedrin whirled around angrily when the door suddenly slammed shut and the sound of a bolt clinking loudly into place could be heard from the other side; it rang out for a moment before the room was plunged into an ominous silence.

CHAPTER 6

OLD FRIENDS

Salen stood still for a few moments with a quiet frown across his face as a clamor of protest erupted from within the now sealed room. Reaching forward he placed one hand on the door and closed heavy eyes while he wondered if he was indeed making the right decision. Daedrin was family, his only living relative in fact, but what else was he to do? Garrôth was slowly casting off the shroud of mystery surrounding his existence as he rose rapidly to dominant power. Salen wasn't looking out only for himself but for all of the inhabitants of Cordin, for without continuing the deal his family had made with Garrôth the city surely would have been laid waste long ago. His eyes narrowed when he recalled the dark day when the most powerful of the Nasci had first approached him…

… *"Stand still, stranger," a deep, monstrous voice spoke from the shadows, and Salen froze mid-stride along the dark alley behind Bulls Tavern as his hand crept to the dagger hidden under his cloak.*

"Stay your hand, fool, or I shall take it from you," the voice snarled, and sweat began to creep down Salen's neck.

"What harm have I done you, stranger, to cause such enmity between us?"

he asked.

"You have committed no treachery… yet."

Salen scowled. "Come out of the shadows and face me!" he challenged. "Or are you a coward that you should skulk about in the dark?"

A deep, low rumble emanated from the shadows; a growl, Salen realized. Slowly a creature slunk into the light just a few yards away from where he stood, the sight of which caused the hair to rise on the back of Salen's neck as tingles ran down his spine, for before him stood one of the Nasci, a creature that before that moment had to Salen only been legend.

"Do you fear me, Salen?" The creature asked as it now called him by name while its red eyes glowed eerily in the moonlight.

Salen swallowed hard. "Nay, foul creature," he answered. "You are nothing more than a beast; powerful and deadly no doubt, but a beast nonetheless."

The creature growled again, louder this time as it took a step closer.

"You keep far too loose a hold on your tongue, human. Perhaps you would like me to remove it for you?" Salen cringed at the ferocity of the words and slowly rubbed his jaw before swallowing hard and bowing slightly.

"My apologies," he said. "Pray tell, what business have you with me?"

The Nasci snarled. "My master knows that since the passing of your father, you now control the wealth he once possessed, and with it a seat of great power and influence in this… place." The creature looked about with a cringe of clear disgust. "He also knows that you use this power in an… unwise manner. Rather than see you punished for your ignorance, he in his benevolence wishes to extend to you a chance for mercy. This very night an army of my companions is poised outside the city walls, ready to lay waste to all the wretched inhabitants residing here. If you do not do as my master commands…" the voice of the creature trailed off as a hideous, cruel grin spread across its face. "I shall give the order to have Cordin utterly destroyed."

Salen's eyes widened in shock. "Tell me then, what must I do to prevent this tragedy?"

The face of the Nasci twisted in an odd fashion, not unlike a hideous smile. "Cease your efforts to find those who have gone missing, and make the same pledge your father made to my master; to commit your resources and servitude to Garrôth, rightful leader and conqueror of this realm."

Salen blinked as the gravity of the situation washed over him. Never could he have imagined so terrible a scenario being laid out. Yet how could he refuse? He had no way of knowing if the beast was telling the truth or merely bluffing, but it did not matter either way; he could not risk the lives of everyone in the entire city, no matter the cost.

"My power I give to Garrôth, to do as he will," he declared with a light bow. "Please, only spare my city; no good can come of its destruction."

The Nasci snarled with satisfaction while a deep, throaty chuckle emanated from its shriveled maw.

"I shall deliver this news to my master. Fear not, for he extends mercy where it has been earned; your city shall be spared." The creature then leapt forward suddenly with a swift stroke at the back of Salen's legs that caused him to fall to his knees as the creature moved in so close that Salen could feel its hot breath on his face.

"Mark my words, for they come from Shrem, captain of the Nasci and right hand of my master. Be wary, pitiful wretch, for your every move will be closely watched. One small step outside the bounds of your new contract and I shall not hesitate to see this city burned to the ground before escorting you personally to the *torture chambers of my master." With a snort the brute slunk back and disappeared into the shadows...*

... Salen shuddered and blinked as his conscious mind left the memory and he backed away from the door. Slowly he moved through the hallway and down the stairs before exiting his home by way of the front door. His guards bowed when he passed, a gesture which he absently returned with a slight nod as he walked down the lane in front of his estate.

His life had been filled with more moments of terror than anything else since that night, for Shrem visited Salen once every fortnight. The creature brought with him on occasion a name of one of the inhabitants of the city whom Salen was to have delivered to Garrôth in secret, though to what end he could only guess. Still, the most horrifying command of all had come only four nights ago when Shrem made it clear to him that any who made their way to Cordin from the village of Linull were to be captured and delivered to his master.

Salen had hardly slept since, for he agonized over the command each night, for he deeply loved his family and knew many who called Linull their home, though his heart now ached with the knowledge of the slaughter of that fair village. *It isn't fair to the boy,* Salen thought, *but what can I do differently? If I do not deliver him with his companions to Garrôth as commanded, then Shrem will destroy Cordin and slaughter many more innocents, and I will be responsible. As it always has the good of the many calls for the sacrifice of the few, does it not?*

"Blast!" Salen grunted in frustration as he pounded his fist against the wall of a nearby building. *Can I really justify turning my own blood over to the hand of such a villain?* He shook his head and sighed while he leaned back against the wall and rubbed his forehead in irritation. He had already turned over several perhaps innocent men to Garrôth, a fact that served to explain and subsequently end his investigation into the mysterious and occasional disappearance of those within Cordin but, to sacrifice his own family was an entirely different matter. In any case, he knew that whatever the cost either way he had to make a terrible decision and, as Salen weighed all the options with the consequences of each, his mind was finally made up. With a deep sigh he jerked himself upright and squared his shoulders while he strolled back toward his house...

... Meanwhile, after ceasing their efforts to force open the door Daedrin and Hadrîn quickly moved to set loose the bonds that held the survivors of Linull. Tara rose to give Daedrin a quick hug with a sigh of relief at his familiar face while Skane reached out an arm in expectation of a fervent hand-clasp with that was not returned. For a moment his arm hung in the air awkwardly before he let it fall with a hard swallow at the look of cold fury etched into the young man's features while he eyed Skane until, with a sudden motion Daedrin swung his right arm; his clenched fist connected squarely on the jaw of the burly blacksmith. The blow sent Skane hurling backwards while Daedrin lunged forward, tackled him to the ground and swung wildly as a pained, angry cry escaped his lips. His friend made no attempt to fight back; instead he only raised his arms in defense as blow after blow was landed.

Clunk! Daedrin was suddenly sent sprawling away from Skane when a sharp pain shocked his senses. He lay sideways on the floor and breathed heavily for a few moments before reaching up to feel the side of his head as the ache slowly subsided. His fingertips came away red when he removed his hand and he looked up to see Tara kneeling beside Skane with a wooden staff lying on the floor beside her; freshly spattered blood covered its tip. She glared at him for a moment with a mixed look of shock, anger and confusion before returning her attention fully to the injured blacksmith.

With teeth grinding beneath hate filled eyes Daedrin rose to his feet and took a step toward them, a gesture which Tara responded to with a quick grasp of her staff as she rose to her feet and brandished it defensively.

"Step back," she warned. Daedrin ignored her completely while he stared hard at the now battered face of the man who had ever been his closest friend.

"I *buried* them," Daedrin choked as a single tear escaped and slid down one cheek and his voice rose while emotion flooded each trembling word. "You *swore* that you would warn them yourself, but I *buried* them!" Slowly Tara lowered her staff and swallowed hard as she surveyed the tormented features of the man before her.

"Buried whom?" she asked softly. He did not answer but instead turned away as he moved to one corner and slumped down with his back against the wall. Hadrîn moved over to stand quietly next to Daedrin while Tara knelt once more beside Skane and reached out a hand that was swatted away while the man pushed himself backward, sliding along the floor until his back came to rest against the wall. He lay there for several moments heaving deep, wrenching sobs; a strange and heartbreaking sight for Tara, who was unaccustomed to seeing such a strong man cry. She remained on her knees in awkward uncertainty as the only sound to break the silence were the muffled cries of the broken man.

Finally Daedrin spoke from his perch in the corner.

"Why has Salen done this?" he asked with a voice that was strained through a tense throat. Tara answered after a few moments.

"I don't know," she replied; her own raspy voice was hoarse before she cleared her throat and rose to her feet. "When we escaped Linull we fled to Cordin, arriving... well, I'm not sure when exactly, as there has been no sense of time in this room. I'm starving, at least," she added with a grimace. "We took up lodging at an inn upon our arrival, and Salen somehow heard of our plight and reached out to us, welcoming us into his home with open arms at first, and we were grateful. Not two minutes through the door of his mansion though he turned on us. He took us captive and removed our weapons, or at least Skane's dagger." She smirked while she lifted her cloak of a faded grayish green and gestured to her boot. "Thankfully the incompetent fool neglected to find my own. We've been locked in here since then."

Daedrin shook his head. "You've been here for three nights then, according to Salen," he told her before he let loose a frustrated sigh. "This doesn't make any sense," he added while his brow furrowed and he rubbed his forehead with one hand.

"His freedom has been forfeit to Garrôth," Hadrîn interjected heavily, locking eyes one by one with all in the room as complete silence followed this declaration.

"Impossible," Daedrin argued. "I know my cousin well. He would forfeit his own life before betraying those he loves."

"Perhaps, but Garrôth has ways of manipulation far more treacherous than anything you can imagine."

Tara blinked. "Garrôth?" she asked with a glance toward Skane as his sobs subsided at the mention of the name; there was a beat of silence while Hadrîn exchanged a wary glance with Daedrin.

"He is the one responsible for what happened to our village," the young man said with a sigh as his jaw clenched.

"I've never heard the name before," Tara remarked with a shake of her head. "Though it seems I'm the only one who hasn't," she added as she cast her gaze to the now attentive stare of the blacksmith.

Daedrin sighed. "We," he nodded with a glare at Skane, "heard the name a few years ago, if memory serves me. Barsk spoke it during a night of drink at the tavern."

Tara huffed and squared her shoulders. "Since when can the word of an old, drunken merchant be trusted?"

"Rarely can it ever," Hadrîn interjected. "But, when one dares utter the name Garrôth you can be certain that he knows exactly of whom he is speaking."

"And who might that be?"

"One who does not like his name to be brought into the light," the old man replied solemnly. "Doubtless it is for this reason we have all been taken."

Tara eyed the stranger with narrowed eyes before turning to Daedrin. "Who is this old man who speaks such nonsense," she asked incredulously, and the young man felt his jaw twitch for a moment before he responded.

"His name is Hadrîn," he replied slowly. "I… met him in the wild, after fleeing the Nasci. He has done nothing since our meeting to betray my trust. In fact, he saved my life not long before we came here."

Tara frowned. "What reason would this Garrôth have for the needless slaughter of so innocent a village?" she asked heavily, and Daedrin shook his head.

"I wish I knew," he replied softly.

"Isn't it obvious?" Hadrîn asked with an irritated edge to his voice. "Linellin; Garrôth must be nearing the end of his schemes, whatever they might be, and the use of that incredible herb would be instrumental in his seizing the realm."

Daedrin swallowed hard and glowered. "You believe that we all lost our homes, our families… over a plant?"

Hadrîn dipped his head. "What other explanation could there be? I've never heard of an entire village being laid waste before now. Such a bold act must have immense rewards for him to risk such a venture."

"It doesn't really matter," Tara interrupted as she crossed her arms and began to pace angrily. "Garrôth or no, it is Salen who is our

125

enemy at present."

Daedrin nodded. "On that we can agree, for now," he said as he accepted the now outstretched arm of Hadrîn and rose to his feet. "Whatever his reasons it is clear that Salen has betrayed us all." He sighed and rubbed his temple as he craned his neck to one side slowly and became immersed in thought. "I had hoped to receive his aid," he said at last. "I do not like the idea of having one with such wealth and power as our enemy," he added with a shake of his head. "Even if we make it out of this mansion we would be hard-pressed to get outside the walls of the city unnoticed."

"We must," Hadrîn interjected. "If we cannot then by this time tomorrow we will all be locked away in the dungeons beneath the ruin of the old castle, where we will be tortured endlessly until Garrôth has extracted all useful information and sees our shoulders relieved of our heads." The old man frowned at the bewildered and disturbed faces of Daedrin's companions. "Our only chance is to get away from this place and make our way up the Basilicus Mountains."

Tara huffed. "Why would we not journey to one of the outlying cities, where we can start over?"

"After all the trouble he has gone through to see us captured, Garrôth would not allow us to escape so easily," the old man said with a shake of his head.

"You seem to know a lot about this mythical person," Tara declared as her eyes narrowed. "If he truly exists I could perhaps see why he would be so interested in an old man who knows his secrets, but why would he care so much about killing us?"

"Why does that matter?" Hadrîn asked while his lips curled in irritation. "Perhaps the reason is as simple as his pride becoming wounded by the three of you escaping his clutches, but at the very least we can be certain that you are being hunted by the Nasci."

"He's right," Daedrin interjected. "Hadrîn and I, we went to Linull after..." his voice trailed off and he cleared his throat before taking in a deep breath. "I... wished to see if Marin, and Skane..." he coughed and tossed an angry glance at the red eyes of the blacksmith before shaking his head. "The Nasci were watching the village, and we were ambushed by one before being pursued by countless others. We are very fortunate to have escaped," he added with a sidelong glance at Hadrîn.

"You speak as if these mindless creatures somehow know that we still live," Tara argued with a toss of her hand.

Hadrîn shook his head. "They are not without intelligence," he explained. "They can reason and speak, just as you and I, though their will is completely bent to that of Garrôth."

Tara sighed as she closed her eyes for a moment before turning to face the old man. "Even if all of this were true, why would it matter? Why would they be so concerned with our escape?"

Hadrîn opened his mouth to speak but paused with puckered brow instead. "I do not know," he finally said slowly. "And that does indeed trouble me some. The fact that we made it to Cordin where it should be safe but are instead captured by Salen, someone who should be loyal to Daedrin... there is something bigger here, a dark scheme, I fear, which my eyes cannot yet see."

Tara sighed and moved a few paces away to one corner of the room with hands on her hips as she scowled and gave Daedrin a dark look beneath narrowed brows before turning her gaze to the old man.

"Why the mountains?" she asked.

"There is a valley nestled at their peak," Hadrîn answered after a brief pause, "where a city lies in secret. The dragons call it Ímrelet and it is their safe haven, for though its location is known to Garrôth he has no way to seek it out, since the only method of entry is through the air, carried by dragon…" his voice trailed off while he rubbed his chin. "The council sends out a weekly patrol in the late watches of the night, or at least they once did… if we can travel high up the pass we could light a fire, large enough to perhaps attract the attention of any dragon passing overhead. It shouldn't take much explaining for them to agree to bring us within the safety of their walls."

Tara shook her head. "Dragons," she muttered the name with a blink. "First a person who's name I've never heard, and now I am to believe that extinct creatures of legend will rescue us?"

"Until just a few days ago the Nasci were legends to your mind, were they not?" Hadrîn asked with a smirk. "Your life has been completely changed," he added bluntly. "You must now adapt, or perish with your ignorance intact."

Tara blinked at the bold words before whirling to face Daedrin. "This is madness," she exclaimed. "Are we really to follow the word of this stranger?" she asked as she drilled a stare into the narrowed gaze of the young man.

The young man heaved an exasperated sigh and turned his face away while the wheels of his mind turned. "I see no other option," he said finally with a glance at Hadrîn before returning his attention to Tara. "We aren't safe in Cordin, and I feel we would only endanger any of the outlying villages should we venture there. We are being hunted," he added with a frown. "At the very least the mountain pass would offer our best chance to shake off any pursuers."

After a beat of silence Tara sighed. "Very well," she said. "I trust you, Daedrin," she added as she locked eyes with the young man. "But we still have to escape this place, and as resourceful as you've made Salen out to be I don't like our chances."

"I only saw two guards when we first entered," Daedrin replied, but Hadrîn quickly shook his head.

"Do you really believe that one with the wealth and influence that Salen controls would be so foolish as to keep safe his mansion with only two guards?" he asked crossly. "The servants are his real protection."

Daedrin felt himself chuckle slightly.

"The servants?" he asked incredulously. "If I can handle several Nasci then servants should be the least of our worries."

"Perhaps leaving with you was a mistake," the old man said quietly before sighing and lifting his head to meet the fiery gaze of the young man at this declaration. "They were all secretly armed for one thing, and several made eye contact with us when we first entered. Unusual for servants, don't you think? And did you not see their clothes? Too lavish for servitude, cut in such a manner as to allow for unrestricted and swift movement."

Daedrin's brow furrowed as he shook his head. "Well I will *not* go quietly," he declared vehemently. "If I am to die before seeing Garrôth destroyed, it will be right here, slaying as many traitors as I can before I draw my final breath!" After releasing sword from sheath he pointed with his free hand. "When that door opens, we don't hesitate. No matter who comes through; we strike." He locked eyes with Hadrîn who nodded slowly.

"Are you certain?" he asked softly. "If your cousin should walk through that door, will you truly be able to swing your blade?"

Daedrin met his eyes with a cold, level stare. "Nothing will keep me from fulfilling my oath," he declared icily. "Salen has chosen his fate." He turned in time to see Skane shuffle slowly to his feet while rubbing his swollen face as he looked at Daedrin, who stared back with dead eyes.

"I'm with you, lad," the blacksmith said as he took in a deep, shaky breath. "If you'll have me," he added quietly with downcast eyes.

After a brief pause in which Daedrin only glared at the blacksmith Tara stepped forward.

"Whatever is between the two of you, it doesn't matter right now," she said. "We need to be united if we hope to escape this place."

"She's right, lad," Hadrîn interjected. "Leave the settling of personal quarrels to the security of the wilderness."

After several moments of silence Daedrin only turned to put his back against the wall by the door and slid down to the floor before placing his sword across his knees and closing his eyes. The others chattered on but the sound of their voices faded into the distance as the wheels of his weary mind struggled to turn. Brief flashes filled the vision behind his closed lids of strange people and places and, for a moment a strange valley took center focus; it glowed with a faint green light. His head turned to one side and he grimaced when the image suddenly blurred before disappearing altogether in a rush like leaves carried by the wind, for it was penetrated by the sound of a sudden thunderous clang erupting from the other side of the doors.

Daedrin's eyes snapped open as he jumped to his feet and stood flat against the wall with sword held close to his chest, a position which Hadrîn copied on the opposite side while Skane shifted on his feet, ready to lunge forward; Tara's grip tightened around her staff. After several moments however, nothing happened; the doors remained closed, and no sound was heard save the breathing of the group as they exchanged wary looks with one another.

Slowly Skane moved forward and cautiously reached out to grasp the handle of the door closest to Hadrîn and gave it a gentle tug. The latch released, allowing it to creak open slightly while the knuckles of Daedrin and Hadrîn cracked lightly as each tightened the grip around his sword hilt. After returning the old man's wary look with a nod Skane pulled the door open completely to reveal the hallway beyond as completely empty. He moved forward and peered in both directions, but he did not see any immediate threat; even the servants of the manor were nowhere in sight. He stepped back while Daedrin moved around him, motioning for the others to follow as he crept cautiously through the open doorway with sword outstretched. Hadrîn let all the others pass before taking up the rear of the procession with eyes that vigilantly searched for any sign of danger.

They made their way single file through the long hall to the top of the stairs and then down before pausing at the base of the front doors of the estate where Daedrin waved the group in closer and spoke just above a whisper.

"This doesn't feel right," he mused with a shake of his head. "Either we have a secret ally, or a trap is now being laid."

Hadrîn frowned. "If we have been freed by an ally then we need to move quickly; if a trap, well… nothing for it but to hope we can outwit whomever is pitted against us. In any case we should first make our way to the stable, in case Mandril has already brought our horses."

Daedrin nodded in agreement and sheathed his weapon as he reached for the handle of the nearest door.

"Best not to draw attention when we enter the public street, I think," he said.

Hadrîn nodded and sheathed his own blade while Daedrin pushed open the massive double doors and stepped out onto the stairs outside; the guards were nowhere to be seen. The rest quickly followed, with Skane pausing briefly to shut the door behind them. A few steps took them out onto the street where the shadows of the moonless night were dispelled only by the light of the street-lamps.

The group casually strolled behind Daedrin while he led them around the mansion until a rather large stable came into view.

The architecture was very ornate, with dark-stained wood that displayed the intricate carvings that roamed the pillars and braces; two oil lamps burned dimly above a hallway with rows of stalls on either side. Daedrin grasped one of the lanterns and removed it from its stand before he cautiously entered the dwelling, followed closely by Hadrîn who held the other lantern.

"Search that side," Daedrin ordered with a point to his left as he moved to the right row of stalls and peered into each while the group moved quickly through the stable. A few of them they found empty, though most contained beautiful horses of various shades; their own steeds however were nowhere in sight.

"They must still be at the stable behind the inn," Daedrin observed when they had all reached the back wall of the structure.

"We should take a different route back," Hadrîn said grimly. "The less we are seen, the better, I feel."

Daedrin nodded his assent. "I know the city well; there are a few different avenues we can take, one of which will bring us to an alley beside the stable."

"Lead on, then," Hadrîn said with a wave of his arm as Daedrin moved past the group and carefully peered around the entrance once he had reached it. Seeing no sign of danger he continued moving to his left down the main road in a direction that at first led them further away from the inn. After a couple of minutes however he turned again to the left, leaving behind the torch light of the main avenue while he entered a narrow lane that cut between two buildings before connecting to another small path roughly a hundred paces down. Faint shadows beneath shrouded silhouettes were all that could be seen under the dim rays of the moon as they moved quickly down the alley before pausing after taking another left at the crossing; here Daedrin motioned for the others to gather in close.

"We must be careful down these next few lanes," he warned just above a whisper. "Cordin isn't always safe to travelers at night once they have ventured away from the main road."

They all nodded and made such motions toward their weapons as to indicate readiness to any vagabond who should chance a glimpse at them from the shadows.

Continuing in the same order as before the group moved in silence through the dark with all peering closely at their surroundings. Every shadow now seemed almost menacing, as if danger lurked behind every corner and trash heap but, after several minutes of this the faint light of street lamps could once again be seen just a few hundred paces ahead of them.

Daedrin held up his hand and stopped.

"We're here," he said quietly as he pointed up at a thatch roof that just barely covered a ragged and foul smelling stable. Horses nickered when Daedrin and Hadrîn entered with a smirk and cough of disgust at the unkempt state of the place; Tara and Skane remained outside to stand guard. Inside the structure they found Liber, along with Fidelium and one other; an old, scraggly brown mare. Hadrîn nudged Daedrin's arm gently.

"We should take that one, as well," he said with a motion to the mare.

Daedrin frowned. "I don't much like the idea of becoming a thief."

"When my life is at stake I do not care about such trivial crimes," the old man declared pointedly. "I certainly have no intention of returning to Garrôth's torture chambers, and if taking this mare will help our escape, then a thief I will gladly become."

Daedrin sighed and nodded after a moment as he moved over to the horse.

"It looks as if we would be doing this poor girl a favor, anyway," he reasoned while he gently brushed the disheveled mane and took in its battered and scarred appearance.

Hadrîn huffed in agreement. "I can finish here," he said. "You should gather our provisions from our room whilst I finish," he added, and Daedrin nodded as he moved to a door at the side of the stable, through which was the same hallway that led to the room that Hadrîn had rented.

After moving quickly down the passage he quietly opened the eighth door to his right and was surprised to find an extra pack full of provisions with the bag of food and water that he and Hadrîn had brought with them to Cordin, along with two blankets bundled tightly with twine. Pausing for only a moment before muttering a silent thanks to the innkeeper he grabbed it all and hurried back to the stable where he found the others in their saddles, ready to depart. After handing one bag of stores to Tara who sat astride the mare he passed the blankets to Skane who was seated behind Hadrîn. The young man then tied the remaining pouch to his own horse and pulled himself up into the saddle.

"We should leave by way of the north gate, if the mountains are to be our destination" he said with a glance at Hadrîn, who nodded.

"Should anything foul arise causing us to be separated," Daedrin added, "bear northeast after exiting the city by that gate. There is a cluster of trees with two that have grown together over the years a few miles inside the forest where we can regroup."

They all nodded, and with a sigh Daedrin nudged Fidelium forward and exited the stable with the others close behind.

CHAPTER 7

A TRAGIC PAST

The moon shone bright, for the clouds which had previously concealed its light had parted to allow its gentle rays to touch the land. As they made their way back onto the main village street the dull click-clack sound made by the horses' hooves when they struck the cobblestone road now seemed horrifically loud amidst the silence of the night. They moved at as brisk a trot as they dared without drawing unnecessary attention and yet despite such caution Daedrin's gaze was drawn sharply to their right by a sudden yell.

"Ay, horse thief!" a short, thin, reedy sort of man yelled while he ran toward them with a drawn dagger in his left hand. The company immediately brandished their weapons, causing the man to slow to a stop several paces away.

"Easy, stranger," Daedrin warned with his sword bared menacingly. The man cursed and spat as if ignoring the naked blades before him.

"That's *my* horse that lady of yours is sittin' on," he said with a pointed finger at the mare beneath Tara. "My brand…" the stranger trailed off while his head tilted to one side and he leaned in slightly to peer closely at the haunch of Liber before he blinked and lifted one bony finger. "What... what's my mark doing on *your* horse?" he asked, looking with bloodshot eyes at Hadrîn's seemingly bewildered face when the man repeated his question, louder this time as his voice rose to a slight screech.

Lamps had begun to glow through the windows of nearby homes as a clear indication that the village was quickly waking to inspect the ruckus taking place outside their doors. The horses brayed nervously when the stranger suddenly marched a few paces toward Hadrîn before stopping and raising his dagger.

"That's my cousin's horse you're sittin' on! My cousin's horse!" he cried while rubbing his temples with the heels of both hands as he began to pace and mutter under his breath. "Not seen him in years... years he's been gone, gone."

Daedrin, taking full advantage of the stranger's distraction suddenly nudged his horse forward, thrust his sword outward and plunged it cleanly through the left shoulder of the man, whose ravings turned quickly to cries of agony when the sword pierced his flesh and caused his dagger fell to the ground with a clatter. With a sharp follow through Daedrin brought the hilt of the blade down hard on the screaming man's temple, a move which sent him crumpling to the ground, unconscious.

"Come on!" he yelled over his shoulder, leaving no time for his companions to question what had just transpired as he spurred his horse to a gallop that they were all quick to follow. Cries of shock and outrage behind could just barely be heard over the pounding of the horses' hooves while they charged down the lane and around the corner where they were away from any eyes that may have been searching from the side of the fallen stranger.

With a quick turn to the right Daedrin led them off of the main road to a narrower side street until after a few moments they could just make out the outline of a large wall off in the distance where an enormous gate rested. It was closed and locked tight, and two sentries fitted in armor with swords at their sides and small horns round their necks could be seen standing guard on either side. Daedrin held up his hand and slowed his horse before coming to a stop a few hundred paces from their exit.

"I had forgotten that these gates typically do not open for anyone after nightfall," he admitted as he absently wiped clean his blade before he returned the weapon to its sheath.

Hadrîn frowned. "We can certainly handle two guards," he replied, "but doubtless these are good men and soldiers to whom I do not wish to deal any harm."

Daedrin shook his head. "Our escape must not be questioned until we are many leagues from this place. I see no other choice."

"Like ye 'ad no choice but to run that man through and leave 'im bleedin' in the street?" Skane interjected angrily.

Daedrin met his stare evenly and resisted the sudden urge to unleash his blade on the blacksmith.

"There was no time for anything else," he said angrily while ignoring the scowl across Skane's battered face. "That stranger was clearly crazed, and dangerous. A few moments more and we would have been dealing with more questions than we cared to answer."

"And if we don't move soon we will have most of this section of the city out on alert looking for anyone with a horse bearing that mark," Hadrîn added as he pointed to the brand on the mare. "The people of Cordin do not take kindly to a horse thief, nor certainly the assault of its owner."

"You stole these horses?" Tara interjected incredulously.

"Keep your voice down!" Daedrin responded sharply. "We took the mare," he added softly with a wary glance at Hadrîn. "But why did he believe that your steed bears his own mark?" he asked, and the old man smirked with eyes that darted between Liber's haunch and the steed beneath Tara as she huffed and crossed her arms while she leaned back in the saddle and fiddled with her staff.

"Likely because it does," Hadrîn replied dryly. "Though I highly doubt it was his mark," he added with a scowl. "Didn't you smell the liquor on his breath? Likely it is the brand of whomever raised the steeds before they were sold, and his drunken mind believed my horse to be his own..." his voice trailed off then while he looked past the young man to the guards. "But we have a more pressing problem, I fear," he said softly with a nod to the sentries. "See that emblem?"

"I don't recognize it," Daedrin said with a light shake of his head as he strained to examine what appeared to be the form of some strange creature emblazoned on the breastplate of each soldier.

"I believe that I have," Hadrîn whispered, and the young man turned to see a dark look on the face of his companion.

"What is it?" he asked while his hand crept instinctively toward the hilt of his sword.

"That," Hadrîn replied, "if it is indeed what I believe it to be, is a form that I have not seen in quite a long time, from before the kingdom fell."

Skane and Tara exchanged a puzzled glance with each other while Hadrîn rubbed his jaw absently and continued.

"It looks like one of the royal guard... powerful creatures they were, called themselves Grenleth; ancient ancestor of the dragons, I believe. They served only one purpose, and that was to protect the King and his family but, they vanished into the wilderness after their masters were slain. I have never seen their form in the shape of such a symbol... and their existence is now a memory known only to myself and Garrôth, I should think. The dragons know it as well, of course, but even if they had expanded their resistance enough to have men in uniform they would not use the image of such dishonored creatures."

He paused briefly and frowned. "I fear that its appearance on the armor of man shows that Garrôth has taken the image of the Grenleth and twisted it into an emblem to serve his own malicious purposes..."

Tara shook her head and muttered under her breath as Hadrîn trailed off while Skane only stared with a single raised brow with his mouth parted slightly at the numerous declarations that had come from the old man's lips. Daedrin however found that his blood seemed to turn hot in his veins as the full implications of Hadrîn's statements became clear.

"These men are... *traitors?*" he asked in a quiet, icy tone while he stared hard at the two guards.

"Perhaps," Hadrîn replied. "Garrôth has always employed men to his service but, his seeds of death have taken root far deeper than I could have imagined if his followers now stand openly in uniform."

Daedrin's knuckles turned white while his vision became filled with a hazy anger as his fist clenched and with a sudden uncanny swiftness he slung his bow off his shoulder, placed an arrow on the string and let it fly. It hit its target with deadly precision; straight through the left eye of the guard to the right of the gate. Before the second had a chance to cry out or even truly register what had happened to his companion another projectile was in the air; it blasted straight through his throat and pinned him to the wooden wall behind where he tugged at it frantically for a few seconds before slumping down, motionless. Gasps of horror and shock erupted from Skane and Tara but they were left with no time to object, for Daedrin had already kicked his horse to a brisk trot while the first guard he had slain fell to the ground with a dull thump of armor.

After exchanging uneasy glances the others spurred their own steeds forward at a pace that quickly brought them beside Daedrin, who had already dismounted in front of the gates. He quickly retrieved his arrows with a step to the side when the left-most guard fell from his place on the wall before he wiped and placed the feathered shafts back into his quiver. He ignored the wide-eyed stare from Skane as the blacksmith let his gaze pass over the slain forms of the two men before he reached out with his burly arms and drew open the city gates.

In a few moments more the entrance had been closed and all were quickly galloping down a dirt path as fast as the horses could carry them. Soon they plunged beneath a canopy of trees until, as they rounded a corner Daedrin led them off the path and pressed deeper into the dark forest. After several minutes of maneuvering through thick brush and timber he slowed his horse near a cluster of trees, two of which were growing together.

When Hadrîn reigned in Liber he nearly leaped out of the saddle, rushed suddenly to Daedrin and yanked him out off of Fidelium by one arm. As the young man hit the ground with a thud that knocked the wind from his lungs Hadrîn quickly straddled him with sword bared menacingly under the pale moonlight that drifted through the treetops.

Tara dismounted quickly and moved toward them with a twirl of her staff when, with a twist and a kick Daedrin shifted his weight, flung Hadrîn to the side and drew his own blade while he rolled to his feet.

"Have you gone mad, old man?" he raged. "If ever you dare to draw your blade on me again I will not hesitate to kill you where you stand!"

Hadrîn rose slowly to his feet and for a few moments they both breathed heavily while they faced one another in silence with weapons brandished. Tara, with Skane now on his feet behind moved to stand between them with her staff raised defensively.

"Enough!" she exclaimed with a glare at each of them. At first it seemed as if neither Daedrin nor Hadrîn had even heard her but, after a few moments the old man heaved a deep sigh and sheathed his sword, though the fire in his eyes continued to blaze.

"As if the threat of Garrôth and the Nasci are not enough, we will be lucky indeed not to have the entire city guard on our trail after that stunt you pulled!" he declared angrily. "You just *killed* two men back there," he raised an arm and pointed back the way they had come. "City guards no less," he added vehemently.

"Men?" Daedrin responded coldly while he slowly lowered his blade. "I saw not men who fell when my arrows pierced them," his voice became venomous and grew louder as he continued. "I saw villains; naught more than traitors to all that is good. Any who would serve Garrôth is just as responsible for the deaths of my family, of *Marin*, as the Nasci themselves, and even the release of death is far too easy a punishment for them!"

He was nearly screaming with chest heaving when he had finished and sheathed his sword roughly.

"If you do not care for the way I defeat our enemies then you need not continue the journey," he raged on. "If I must seek retribution by myself, then so be it!" With this he averted his gaze, moved around Tara and brushed past Hadrîn before remounting Fidelium; his chest rose and fell with labored breath while he looked off into the night.

Hadrîn sighed finally with a shake of his head as he moved to mount his own horse; he was followed quickly by Skane and Tara.

"For the moment we must bear to the northeast," he mused while he rubbed his jaw and peered into the forest. "There is an old outpost several miles to the northwest that was abandoned long ago. We will cross a stream to the east that should suffice to throw any pursuers off our trail before we approach the outpost, which should provide sufficient cover with shelter for the night." He glanced at Daedrin, who waved his hand absently. Hadrîn nodded, nudged his horse forward and began making his way through the forest while the rest followed with Daedrin at the rear this time; his right hand clutched the hilt of his sword as poisonous thoughts worked through his mind. They trudged on at a brisk pace in silence for nearly an hour before Hadrîn stopped to allow the horses' a brief rest. After a few minutes they continued in the same order, except this time Tara kept her horse close beside Liber while she conversed quietly with Skane.

"How are you feeling?" she asked softly with a short glance over her shoulder at Daedrin. The burly blacksmith stared blankly into the night for several moments before he responded.

"Ye don't mean my face, do ye love?" he asked.

"Not entirely, no," she eyed his battered features as the man blinked but said nothing. "I imagine that you can forgive the beating he gave you but…" her voice trailed off and she frowned. "I saw the look in your eyes, back at the gate, after…" she paused and watched the blacksmith carefully.

"He *murdered* those men…" Skane said softly.

Tara felt her eyes narrow. "One might think of it as an

execution."

"Is that what ye would call it?" Skane asked as he now eyed her with a glare.

After a moment the healer sighed. "I'm not in the place to judge his actions," she said softly while she stared into the dark of the forest as her mind became immersed in memory. "He saved my life," she added while she returned her attention to the blacksmith.

Skane shook his head. "Saving ye doesn't redeem him of what he's done this night," he argued, and a solemn silence followed his statement. "It's their eyes," he spoke again just above a whisper as he stared into the forest once more. "I can't get that 'orrified look of pain and terror out of my mind..." His voice trailed off before he cleared his throat and turned again to Tara. "Did ye stop to look?" he asked heatedly, "or did ye give no heed at all to the lives he slaughtered back at the gate?"

"They haunt me as well," the young woman replied softly.

"You know Daedrin well, I gather," Hadrîn interrupted suddenly with a backward glance at Skane, who nodded.

"Aye, I've known him for 'alf his life."

Hadrîn dipped his head slightly. "You knew his family, as well?" he asked, and Skane nodded again.

"Of course you must know that they are the ones he buried," Hadrîn added after a brief pause; Skane swallowed hard as the anger on his face suddenly dissipated while Tara dipped her head and closed her eyes.

"I... I saw... I went to warn them but... I was too late..."

Skane's voice trailed off as he took in a deep, shaky breath.

"He dug their graves himself," Hadrîn continued softly, "burying them behind the ruin of his home. Because of your failure he has lost those he loved," he added with a sneer while Skane hung his head. "His actions might be reckless but they do not make him a monster as you suggest, for such agony can cause a man to do without question even the most heinous of deeds." Neither Tara nor Skane said anything more as they continued on in silence with each lost in their own thoughts.

Meanwhile Daedrin couldn't keep his own mind from wandering in quiet agony while he stared into the darkness surrounding him, taking note only for a moment the heated look on Skane's face while he spoke with Tara. He closed his eyes as cherished memories of Marin washed over him, bringing with them a bittersweet sense of longing when a vision appeared in his mind of her smile as her beautiful form moved toward him in her simple dress while her hair flowed in the wind. His heart seemed to skip a beat when the memory flashed and was replaced for a moment by a fleeting image of her lips suddenly dripping with blood beneath grey, dead eyes. He shuddered with a gasp, opened his eyes and blinked when his vision was suddenly interrupted by Tara when she slowed her horse to come alongside him.

"How are you?" she asked; her raspy voice resonated with a gentle concern. Daedrin merely averted his gaze and said nothing. The healer frowned and, after a moment of quiet indecision she placed a slender hand on his shoulder.

"Daedrin…" her voice trailed off while she collected her thoughts. "The old man told me of your family," she continued after a while. "I… I'm sorry." She swallowed hard as she eyed the now clenched jaw of the man before her.

"We were going to travel, Skane and I," Daedrin said softly; he seemed not to have heard Tara at all. She kept silent and watched him while he continued. "Marin was going to leave with us, with… me." Daedrin smiled weakly as he became lost in memory, but his joy quickly faded. "I spoke to my father about it many times but, he was always quick to dismiss it as fantasy. It was the last thing he and I spoke of, before…" his voice trailed off and Tara felt tears now spring to her eyes when she took note of the strain that entered Daedrin's voice before he cleared his throat. "He told me that if I left the farm to travel with Skane and the 'village harlot' then I would no longer be his son." He snorted softly and shook his head. "Those were the last words I ever heard come from his lips."

He became silent and Tara said nothing at first, for there seemed to be naught good to say but, after several minutes of quiet prayer she spoke softly.

"I know that your father loved you, Daedrin, despite your differences. Kelmîn just… wasn't the best at expressing those feelings."

Daedrin nodded and turned his face away as a tear spilled down one cheek. After wiping it away angrily he cleared his throat and smiled weakly.

"I am glad that you made it to safety, Tara," he said, and she smiled before her lips curled slightly.

"Can I ask something of you?" she said, and after a beat of silence Daedrin dipped his head. "You and Skane have always been close," she continued, "and I feel as if I know what has happened to cause such enmity between you and he but...?" her voice trailed off, and the clenching of Daedrin's jaw did not go unnoticed when he replied.

"If he still had honor then perhaps he would have shared with you the reason," he said sharply; with an angry sigh his teeth ground together before he continued. "You of course know that I was injured the night the Nasci attacked. Nevertheless I wanted to go home and warn my family but, Skane swore to me that he would go to them himself, and yet... I found them dead. I feared then that he himself must have been slain somewhere in the wilderness and yet... after burying my own kin I discover him in Cordin, alive and well."

Silence ensued his heated monologue interrupted only by the chirping of crickets from the darkness of the surrounding forest.

"Perhaps he deserved the beating you gave him," Tara interjected finally as she peered into the brush. "But I know at least that Skane left to warn your family and bring them back with him to the village, but he was too late. They... were already slain."

Daedrin turned to look at her. "He told you this?"

She nodded. "Just moments ago. I... know that you are suffering," she added softly as she placed a hand gently on his shoulder, "perhaps a great deal more than the rest of us. However you do not suffer alone; we all have lost much that we held dear..."

she cast a heavy look at his weary face before removing her hand and turning away to ride beside him in silence.

Daedrin peered into the dark with a frown at his own thoughts as they trudged on for a few miles that were filled only with the chirping of crickets accompanied by the gentle clip-clop of the horses' hooves until eventually the trickling sound of flowing water reached his ears. He glanced forward to see a modest stream in the distance; the clear liquid glimmered under the rays of the moon as it bounced over smooth dirt and pebbles. He and Tara followed closely when Hadrîn directed Liber into the water upon his approach before changing direction and following it to the west while it wound through the trees. They splashed through the spring for several miles before the old man left the water behind and directed them straight to the north as they continued to make their way through the forest. After a few more minutes of silence Daedrin finally turned to Tara and had just opened his mouth to speak when he was interrupted by Hadrîn as the old man called out, "Whoa!" and the company halted.

"We're here," he declared once Daedrin and Tara had nudged their horses closer.

They had come to a small clearing made up of a hill that reached almost to the height of the surrounding trees. The outpost that Hadrîn had spoken of before could be seen atop the raised mound, though it was nothing more than a ruin now. Weathered grey stones could be seen laying all around them as the old man led them up an overgrown path that was covered in green moss, and as they reached top of the rise they passed through a broken wall to their left that rounded roughly a quarter of the hills mass. The rest of the structure appeared to have either decayed completely or had fallen over the edge to the earth below.

Even Daedrin's inexperienced eyes could see that the outpost had been very strategically placed, as there was no easy method of entry save for the way they had come, and the edges all around plunged steeply to the bottom. The view all around, though overgrown by the surrounding forest gave an excellent view of the countryside in all directions but, well-placed as it was, the hilltop was small, for the company with their horses fit into the center of the decayed structure with no more than a few paces around them.

They all dismounted slowly with a stretch of stiff joints from the hours on horseback before moving to tie their steeds to crooks in the nearby stones. When this was done Hadrîn motioned for everyone to come closer; he spoke softly once all were near.

"We should keep watch until the light of day," he said as he exchanged a careful glance with each of them. "It troubles me that we neither saw nor heard any sign of pursuers, and," he added with narrowed eyes, "it is strange indeed that the city guard would not pursue those who slayed some of their own…"

"You think we are being followed," Tara observed with a wary look into the trees below, for the very shadows of the towering timber now seemed suddenly menacing.

Hadrîn nodded. "If Salen is working for Garrôth as I believe he is then doubtless his master has been informed of my presence. This could perhaps have changed his plans for each of you…" he paused as he rubbed his chin. "I suspect that we are being watched closely by those who would report back to Garrôth the details of my involvement with those whom he clearly wishes dead."

Tara huffed as she moved in close to meet Hadrîn's eyes with a sudden, level stare.

"You still cling to that name," she said, "speaking of Garrôth and dragons as if they are as real as you and me, with such confidence that I almost think you truly believe what you are saying."

"Because it is the truth, madam," Hadrîn said dryly. "Ride with us long enough and you shall receive all the proof that you desire."

Tara sighed and lifted her hand in an irritated gesture before she moved away to the edge of the hill and stared out into the dark below.

Daedrin frowned as he watched her while she moved away before he returned his attention to the old man.

"Why would Garrôth care that you are involved?" he asked.

Hadrîn smirked while his eyes narrowed. "There was a time not so long ago when I was held captive in his dungeons," he said softly. "He... believed after a time that he had broken my mind, though he was not as successful as he had thought. When I at last had an advantage I seized the brief opportunity and fled, hiding myself away at the top of the mountain where I built my cabin. It... is unfortunate that he should so soon learn of my presence out in the wide world once more... I would have liked to remain hidden from his scheming eyes."

With a frustrated sigh he fell silent as he moved over to his saddlebags, followed by Daedrin while Skane remained at the edge of the hill and peered into the night. The pair quickly set up camp in the most defensible manner possible, with the heads of their bedrolls at the foot of the remaining stone wall. When this was done Daedrin rummaged through the new pack from the inn and withdrew bread and cheese with dried meat; he ate a few bites before grasping a clean cloth and bundling up a large morsel which he brought to Tara where she stood near the edge of the fallen structure. She glanced sideways at him as he approached and extended the bundle to her with one hand.

"Eat," he said, and she took the cloth from him without hesitation and drank from her canteen between mouthfuls. For a while they only stood in silence while she ate; Skane and Hadrîn conversed quietly behind them after lying down on their bedrolls.

"I…" Daedrin started to speak but paused. Tara glanced at him as she finished the last of her food and washed it down with a final swig of water while she waited for him to continue. Finally, Daedrin frowned and let one hand rub the hilt of his sword absently.

"When I… saw my family, slain as they were I… something inside of me perished, I think." He spoke in slow, broken sentences as he struggled to piece his thoughts together. "I haven't… I haven't felt goodness or, anything other than anger since that moment." His face scrunched up while his jaw clenched and he fell silent while he looked out into the dark with his mind wandering until after a while Tara cleared her throat.

"Did I ever tell you about my father?" she asked.

Daedrin shook his head. "I thought you never knew him." He watched carefully as the young woman's eyes narrowed.

"I knew him," she said slowly, "but… the thought of him brings nothing but pain, even after all these years." She sighed before continuing.

"He was a terrible man, my father, yet I adored him as a girl. He would be gone for weeks at a time, leaving myself with my mother and older brother alone at our home in the forest. When he returned he always brought with him the stench of drink, and an unbridled anger at how horrid his life had turned out. But, he was kind to me; spoiled me, even," she huffed and shook her head as she smiled ever so slightly. "He always gave to me some new trinket from whatever far away town he had visited. But my mother, my brother…" her lips curled downward. "Well to them he was not so kind. They only ever felt the brunt of his anger, always receiving fresh bruises before he would go away again."

She sighed while she stared into the night. "I was always there to patch them up," she continued, "stitch up the cuts while we fearfully awaited his next visit. This was the pattern for our lives, one that led me to harbor a growing resentment with a feeling of dread at the thought of my father's return…" She glanced at Daedrin briefly as with narrowed eyes he watched her while she returned her gaze to the forest. "One afternoon, just days after my sixteenth birthday my father came up the lane to the house, but he was not alone this time. Two men were with him, a rough sort, armed with short daggers in hand. My father… he was bruised and bloodied, pushed forward by the two strangers with hands tied behind his back. These men yelled for my mother and threw my father down at the feet of her and my brother when they came out of the house. They kicked him and spat curses, and when my mother ran to my father one of the strangers struck her, sent her sprawling to the ground. When my brother drew his sword, the men moved quickly, disarming him and... slitting his throat."

She paused for a moment as her eyes closed; Daedrin blinked and swallowed hard while he listened carefully to her story. "It all happened so quickly," she continued softly. "My brother fell to the ground... clutching his throat as his blood quickly soaked the ground. My father tried to rise, but they kicked him, over and over again. My mother was hysterical, just kneeling there on the ground, sobbing. I watched it all from the woods just a stone's throw from the house, unable to speak, petrified with fear. After what seemed like an eternity, the kicking stopped and the two men moved then to my mother and... they..." She trailed off as a single tear escaped her closed lids and slid down her cheeks before she slowly opened her eyes and took in a deep, shaky breath. "They slit her throat, and laughed manically as she writhed on the ground."

Tara's lip quivered slightly as she continued. "I started to move then," she said, "the shock I think wore off, replaced with a cold purpose. I strode toward the strange men... they made obscene calls as I approached. So I stopped a few paces away... undid the top button of my blouse and reached behind to tug at the laces and as they took the bait and moved close to me, I withdrew a short dagger

I always carry behind my dress, and made one quick motion," she jerked her hand forward with fist clenched before letting it fall with a frown. "I plunged it into the stomach of the nearest of them, slicing him open and leaving him on the ground holding his own insides. While the other was still petrified with shock I lunged, stuck my knife into his chest and knocked him to the ground as he cried out. I stabbed him, again, and again, and again…"

Her voice trailed off again and she blinked when two tears escaped her lids and followed the first; they slowly slid down her fair face before she took in a shaky breath. "Eventually," she said as she exhaled, "when his chest was nothing more than pudding I stopped and moved over to stand before my father. He stared at me with wide, red eyes but said nothing, and after a few moments I moved behind him and cut him loose. He fell forward, caught himself with his hands in the dirt and sobbed, saying he was sorry and that it was his fault, he was so sorry…" Tara fell silent while Daedrin looked down at her in complete shock before he blinked red eyes and swallowed painfully.

"Tara I… I am truly sorry. I cannot imagine…" he shook his head. "What happened to your father?" he asked quietly, and after a few moments Tara turned to look him right in the eyes.

"I slit his throat," she declared, and Daedrin blinked. "While he knelt there sobbing, I reached out my dagger and I drew it across his neck and watched as he bled out on the ground beside the rest of my family." Tara shook her head. "I was completely lost for a long time after that," she mused while she stared into the night. "Estranged myself from the rest of the world, traveled everywhere and slayed any vagabond I came across whom I deemed worthy of death, until I eventually came to Linull. The people there... well, they were very different from anyone I had ever met. So kind and compassionate, so forgiving, despite the harshness of the world around them. So I stayed for a while, got to know a few people, asked questions."

Tara smiled now as she wiped her face. "Of course, you and I both know exactly why everyone in the village was so different."

Daedrin nodded and returned her look with a smirk of his own. "Indeed," he replied, "though it seems not to matter now."

Tara frowned while her head tilted to one side and she glanced at his face briefly. "Why not?"

Daedrin shrugged. "Their faith ultimately got them nowhere," he replied, "for in the end, all but we three," he motioned to Tara, himself and Skane, "are alive to remember."

Tara shook her head. "Daedrin, I've... you're the first person to whom I've ever revealed my past," she said softly before turning to gaze into his eyes. "I... wanted you to know the darkness from which I walked before Linull. The people there saved me from that darkness," she added, and the passion was clearly evident in her voice.

Daedrin felt his eyes narrow while he looked into the deep green wells of her own before he averted his gaze and scoffed. "That's exactly my point," he argued. "The *people* saved you. Their goodness saved you. Their faith, however did nothing to save them from the fate the Nasci unleashed. Just like the prayer from my father for protection each day did nothing for my family," he added vehemently as his jaw clenched.

Tara frowned while she eyed the young man carefully. "I... cannot believe that," she said softly with a gentle shake of her head. "I may not understand why this has happened to us, to them, or why our prayers seem to go unanswered, but I know that their faith in the Creator is what made them who they were, and it's what has made me who I am today; one who brings healing, instead of death."

"They spent their entire lives... *I* spent my entire life believing in someone whose benevolence I can only question," Daedrin remarked as his fist clenched in anger and his voice trembled slightly. "A Creator with the power that we all believed in should have intervened..."

Tara sighed deeply. "You may be right," she said. "But if I stop believing now, I fear I will lose myself again," she added with a voice that was barely above a whisper before she cleared throat. "I choose now to believe that there is a purpose behind what happened to my friends." She then gently grabbed his arm. "Even what happened to your family," she added softly; Daedrin jerked away and averted his gaze.

"Daedrin, I have seen in you this night the same broken vessel that I once was... the same reckless hate. I have done many terrible things in my life, such that I sometimes wonder if I am even worthy of redemption." She paused and placed a hand on his shoulder. "I pray that you find your purpose soon, before you descend as deep into the darkness as I once did." With this she took a step back and moved away, leaving Daedrin alone to his own quiet reflection as he peered into the dark…

CHAPTER 8

FORGIVENESS

Beady red eyes glimmered ever so slightly in the pale moonlight of the forest just south of where Daedrin and the company had made their camp. The Nasci behind the eyes who was called Crevan growled softly with eager anticipation of the battle to come. All he needed was a sign, a clear indication of what the old man was up to and he would report back to his master and then... he would wait no longer. Then he would strike with the full force of those under his command. The creature adjusted its weight and a small twig popped under his paw; it was barely more than a whisper, nevertheless Crevan froze and held his breath while he watched carefully for any sign that the human standing at the edge of the hill had heard the sound. After several minutes Crevan saw no indication of alarm and let himself breathe a little easier, though he remained tense, for a mistake now would most certainly go unforgiven by his master.

He shuddered as he recalled the last time one of his kind who had displeased Garrôth; the wretched shrieks of the creature had echoed through the dark caverns before suddenly being silenced.

"Captain," a raspy voice caused Crevan's stubby tail to twitch in

160

irritation as it whispered in his ear.

"What is it, Lern?" he responded sharply without taking his eyes off of the human atop the mound.

"The company grows restless," the one called Lern replied. "Little patience have they for this skulking about in the dark of the forest."

Crevan growled with a deep, almost imperceptible rumble.

"The time for spilling blood will come," he turned his head ever so slightly so as to look upon his comrade. "Patience, Lern," he added with a gleam in his eye as he looked back to the hill. "Soon these wretched, two-legged beasts will give us to what our master desires, and then their lives will be ours."

Daedrin was deep in his own thoughts when he heard a sound so low that it could have been nothing more than wind rustling the leaves in the trees but, it was one he knew well from all his time hunting; some creature was moving through the bramble under the cover of darkness. For a moment he thought that he caught a glimpse of two glints of red when they flickered briefly from the darkness. He did not however let his face betray any sign of alarm as he instead calmly remained still for several minutes before he casually moved away from the edge of the hill with a stretch and a yawn. Tara and the others he saw were already bundled up in their bed rolls; sound asleep. After moving over to where Hadrîn lay he bent to one knee and gently shook him awake before whispering in his ear.

"We are indeed being watched," he said. "Not by men but by

Nasci I think, though I do not know the number of our enemies."
Hadrîn sat up slowly and stretched ever so slightly as he rubbed his
face with his hands.

"I had hoped that my fear was nothing more than the paranoia
of an old man," he said with an exasperated sigh. "We must deal with
this before we venture too high up the mountain. It would not do
well for Garrôth to learn that I am seeking the dragons again after..."
he trailed off and brushed his chin as if deep in thought. "We can
lead them along narrow paths as we climb... perhaps lose them as we
progress higher into the mountains but, that is highly unlikely," he
added with a shake of his head. "The Nasci will not abandon a direct
order so easily... doubtless we will be forced to face them, but at
least the climb will allow us to choose our battle ground. In the
meantime it might be wise to utilize an ancient practice; perhaps warn
our allies of the enemy that follows."

Daedrin let his head tilt to the side. "How?" he asked, and for a
moment Hadrîn stared off into the night while he rubbed his chin
with one hand.

"The dragons," he began slowly, "while not harnessing magic
themselves still possess some extraordinary abilities. Perhaps the
most powerful of these is something that they call extrasensory
perception. At its base it grants any dragon the ability to sense or
even manipulate the base feelings or rudimentary essence of thought
in nearby sentient beings. They used it as a guide in older days for
governing the people of the land, lending aid or counsel when
needed." With a grunt Hadrîn lowered himself to one elbow and

tilted to face Daedrin as the young man shifted to crouch on the heels of his feet.

"When the royal family was given the authority to govern Silmaín," Hadrîn continued, "the eldest of the dragons shared this ability with King Vandin, along with his direct descendants. When this was done, the power was unexpectedly enhanced by the magic of the King, developing the capacity to actually communicate, as well as feel." Hadrîn paused and scratched the scruff on his chin. "This practice has of course been all but lost in the ages since the fall of the kingdom but, if they still harness this power to monitor Silmaín as they once did when on patrol then there is perhaps a chance that we could reach out to them. If our thoughts are felt as they lay eyes on the signal fire we could alert them to our pursuers, if we've not yet shaken them."

Daedrin smirked. "I think I'd rather trust in my own instincts," he said, and Hadrîn chuckled lightly.

"Instinct can only carry you so far in this realm, lad." He rose to his feet with a grunt. "For now, get some rest," he added as he eyed the drooping lids of the troubled young man. "I will take your place as sentry."

With a short nod Daedrin moved to the remaining small, empty pallet and laid down his head. Weary though he was he hesitated to let sleep take hold for fear that his nightmares of late would haunt his dreams once more but, after a while the peaceful sound of crickets and other insects chirping in the night brought some semblance of calm to his mind and he sunk into a deep slumber...

… As the suns first rays began to peek over the horizon Daedrin slowly lifted heavy lids. With a stretch and a yawn he sat up and looked around with bleary eyes that quickly narrowed in confusion, for his companions were nowhere in sight. After jumping to his feet in alarm he blinked and looked frantically around as he moved from one end of the hill to the other but, he saw no sign that they had ever even been to fallen structure, save for his own bedroll. With a brief pause to take a breath he knelt to search the ground more closely and his eyes took in one sign; a small scuff at the edge of the hill, quickly followed by several more. These he tracked down to the base of the mound, and as he continued around to the far side he saw droplets of blood splattered around in the dirt. His pulse began to quicken as he moved slowly around a large, blood-soaked portion of wall that looked to have collapsed before sliding to rest at the base of the hill. As he crept past the stone he choked, for there lay his companions; mangled, bloodied and broken. With a despairing cry, he ran forward and fell to his knees beside Tara…

… "Agh!" Daedrin cried aloud as he woke from his slumber, rose rapidly to his feet and spun from side to side with one of his knives suddenly in hand while he breathed heavily.

The sun was just beginning to peek over the tops of the trees to cast its first dim rays on the land, and he beheld in its light Hadrîn, sleeping soundly beside him while Skane now stood at the edge of the hill keeping vigilant watch; Tara watched him with furrowed brow from her perch on the balls of her feet near the horses while she munched on a piece of bread.

"Sleep well?"

Daedrin jumped at the sound of Hadrîn's voice and looked down to see the old man now sitting up with bleary but narrowed eyes; the young man only frowned as he moved away to the edge of the hill opposite Skane. After closing his eyes he took in careful, deep breaths, and after a while his pulse began to slow until it eventually began to settle to a steadier rhythm. With a final deep sigh he turned, ignoring Tara's concerned gaze when he moved past her to Liber where he quietly withdrew his canteen and took a long swig as he leaned against the horse with one arm. With a shake of his head he tucked the water skin back into the pouch on his belt and withdrew a morsel from his pack with a scowl at how little was left before he consumed a portion and moved back to his pallet; this he found that Hadrîn had already rolled up and placed next to his own along with the ones for Skane and Tara.

"We must be careful if we wish our vittles to last as long as needed," Daedrin remarked absently as he approached and picked up two of the bedrolls.

Hadrîn paused while his eyes narrowed before he grabbed the remaining pallets. "You have your bow," he observed as he eyed the quiver on the young mans' back.

"Hunting becomes much more difficult this time of year," Daedrin replied with an irritated twitch of his lips. "The wildlife slink away into their corners to keep warm for the winter."

Hadrîn smirked. "Then we shall have to make it safely to Ímrelet before it comes to that."

Daedrin huffed and shook his head as they moved quietly over to the horses where, with a brief reassuring smile he passed Tara before attaching the two pallets in his hands to the saddle atop Fidelium.

"Tara," he called out with a wave after she had looked his way. "We are being pursued," he told her softly once she had approached; she was closely followed by the old man. "By the Nasci, I believe," Daedrin added, "though I don't know how many."

The healer nodded with a quiet frown as she motioned to the blacksmith. "Skane," she called out and beckoned for him to approach.

Daedrin felt his jaw clench as the man drew nearer. "Last night I conversed with Hadrîn," he said, ignoring the blacksmith when he drew near. "It is unlikely that we will be able to easily shake off our pursuers, but we must do so before we reach… Ímrelet?" he looked to the old man, who dipped his head in return. "I've had more than my fair share of run-ins with predators in the wild," he continued. "We won't be able to travel much higher into the mountains before the terrain becomes too treacherous for us to safely make our stand."

"Ye mean to fight them?" Skane asked incredulously. "'ow are we to take on a foe that remains hidden?"

Daedrin glared at the blacksmith for his interruption. "We draw them out," he declared. "It's… risky, but so is doing nothing and, we can only go so high up the pass before we lose our opportunity."

Tara nodded. "What should we do?" she asked.

"We move," Hadrîn interjected. "As far as today as the

166

mountain will allow, and then… we defer to Daedrin's skill as a hunter."

"I'm no stranger to defeating a predator," the young man said with a dip of his head. "A few years ago during a hunt I successfully led a wolf that was stalking me into a trap. Catching it off guard was enough to put an arrow into its chest without being harmed myself. I… am hoping that a similar plan will work on the Nasci." He frowned as he looked at Hadrîn.

"There… is a place a several miles further up," the old man said. "A slanted and steep cliff with a great oak at its base and a clearing beyond with steep terrain for even the Nasci to quickly climb. Perhaps such a spot would suffice?" he asked Daedrin.

The young man rubbed his chin for a moment.

"We would be walled in… surrounded," he added. "If we fail there would be no escape."

"It seems there is no escape no matter what we choose," Tara interjected.

"I believe that you are right," the young man said after a brief pause. "If we cannot destroy them, then we are good as dead anyway… this place you have in mind, there is only one way to approach?" he asked with a glance at Hadrîn.

"Yes," the old man replied. "The surrounding cliff is large and would encompass our entire flank."

Daedrin nodded. "Then we would need a fire," he declared as his eyes narrowed and he peered into the forest. "As large as we can build, and as we draw close to the tree we can do our best to kick the dead brush and leaves into piles of kindling; enough to burn bright while not so large as to draw attention." He nodded slowly as the plan began to form in his mind. "I will shoot lit arrows into the brush, see that the forest becomes ablaze and reveals the presence of our enemies… with the proper distraction and surprise, we *will* slaughter those vermin with as much ruthlessness as they slaughtered those we love." His eyes burned with a cold fire, and when he had finished he turned his gaze to Tara, who nodded and tightened the grip around her staff.

"I would rather fight than run," she said, and Daedrin smiled.

"As would I. I've no intention of living out my days as a captive in some dungeon…" His voice trailed off while he stared out into the surrounding timber and rubbed his jaw thoughtfully.

"Let's go," he said finally as he reached for the saddle and mounted Fidelium with a grunt before glancing over to see his companions do the same.

After a few moments the blacksmith had swung up into the saddle behind Hadrîn, who led the way once more as he directed them down the hill in the same manner they had arrived. When they had plunged into the forest again Daedrin looked warily about but, he saw no sign of their pursuer as they turned and continued steadily northwest, trudging on in silence for a few hours before Hadrîn had them pause to give the horses a rest and a drink. While Daedrin moved to stand a few paces away the old man muttered softly to Tara and Skane, handing them each a small piece of parchment before moving to Daedrin as the young man stood still while he peered intently into the forest.

"See anything?" he asked softly.

Daedrin shook his head slightly. "Nay, not a sight nor sound of anything amiss," he replied. "Whatever is following us is quite adept at keeping hidden in the brush… astonishing that I even spotted it last night," he added with a smirk.

"Come," Hadrîn said with a jerk of his head back toward the horses, and Daedrin nodded as he turned and began to move back to his steed when, with a nudge the old man handed him a small piece of folded parchment. "While I kept watch last night I wrote down what little I can remember of the ancient tongue, spoken only by the King and his sons," he said as Daedrin took the piece of paper. "I showed this to Tara and Skane, as well. If the dragons are listening then the use of this language would certainly draw their attention."

Daedrin frowned. "I will commit this to memory," he said while he tucked the parchment into his cloak and mounted his horse; he was quickly followed by the others. They all fell silent once more as each became lost in their own pensive thoughts in light of the encounter that they were rapidly approaching. They pressed forward and wove their way between the trees as quickly as the thick brush would allow while they carefully moved further up the mountain.

Shaking dark thoughts from his mind Daedrin removed the parchment from his cloak with eyes that narrowed as he studied it carefully. While he did not quite understand the strange tongue he thought it to be somehow familiar, though the symbols seemed to him to be out of order. He moved his lips silently while his eyes

169

bounced back and forth and his mind pieced the ancient scribblings together like chips on a puzzle board. Suddenly he blinked, reached for his sword hilt and drew the blade slowly from its sheath just enough to reveal the inscription etched into its length. He took in a sharp breath when he realized that some of the symbols on his own weapon were the same as those written by the old man. His eyes narrowed and his jaw clenched as he sped Fidelium up past Tara to trot beside Skane and Hadrîn.

"You recognized the script on my sword when you first laid eyes on it, didn't you?" Daedrin asked once he had matched their speed.

Hadrîn glanced at him briefly. "Of course not," he replied with some irritation at the accusation. "Whatever is scrawled across your blade is unlike anything my old eyes have seen before."

Daedrin reached out angrily and grabbed the cloak of the old man just above the shoulder. "You expect me to believe that?!" he asked heatedly; Hadrîn jerked his arm away and reined in his horse before turning to face the young man.

"Mind your tone, boy," he ordered as he exchanged his cordial speech for a more level, icy tone.

"The symbols you gave me, some of them are the same as those on my sword!" Daedrin exclaimed while he held the blade up to the light. "See?!"

Hadrîn glowered. "Have you gone mad?" he asked as he glanced at Daedrin with eyes that narrowed in confusion. "Those aren't anything like what I wrote down for you."

Daedrin's brow furrowed. "How," –

"The old man is right," Skane interrupted as he stared at the symbols while they gleamed under a ray of sunlight through the trees. He had pulled a piece of parchment from his cloak which he then studied with a frown while his eyes moved from the blade to the paper. "I can't make 'eads or tails of any of it, whether yer sword there or the scribbles 'adrîn gave me, but I can tell ye they certainly aren't the same."

Daedrin shook his head. "Impossible," he declared. "See these here?" he asked as he pointed one at a time at eight of the symbols on his weapon. "They match those on the parchment," he added as he pulled it from his cloak with his free hand.

"That isn't what I see," Tara, who had come to trot beside Daedrin interjected with a shake of her head. "Although whatever Hadrîn wrote down for you isn't even the same as what he gave to me," she added with a frown after she had looked down at the paper in her own hand.

"What in the blazes…" Skane's voice trailed off while he peered over at Tara. "Yers is different from what I 'ave," he added as he turned to glare at the old man. "Just what kind of game are ye playing at?"

"Impossible," Hadrîn declared as he took the parchment roughly from Skane's grasp and blinked when his eyes scanned the symbols on the page. "I… don't understand," he said slowly. "This… looks nothing like what I wrote down for you yesterday," he added before leaning over to look at the paper in Tara's hand as she held it out for him to see. "Nor does yours…" His voice trailed off and he scratched his chin.

Daedrin sighed. "You've all lost your minds," he declared in irritation while he rubbed his temple with one hand. "I see the same scribblings across all four pages, but..." his voice trailed off as he looked at Tara. "You can't understand it?" he asked, and she shook her head.

"No," she said, and her eyes narrowed while she studied the young man. "But you can, can't you?" she asked softly.

Daedrin frowned, and his eyes darted between all the pieces of parchment. "Yes," he replied slowly. "And, no..." he sighed. "The... symbols, they are... jumbled, like puzzle pieces but, they look... familiar. I... can piece them together, if I concentrate... give me your coal," he added suddenly as he reached out to Hadrîn with one hand. The old man smirked and slowly withdrew a pointed piece of blackened ash from his cloak and handed it to Daedrin. He then watched carefully when the young man scanned the symbols on Hadrîn's parchment before he moved the burnt ember swiftly across the back side of his own page. "There," he declared after a few moments of scribbling before he handed the coal back to the old man and raised his paper to show his companions. "This is how it should read, I think," he added.

Skane shook his head while Tara frowned and Hadrîn's eyes narrowed.

"Those symbols look nothing like what I wrote," the old man said; he was met by a quiet muttered agreement from the healer and blacksmith.

"How is that possible?" Daedrin asked in bewilderment.

"I'm not sure," Hadrîn said as he rubbed his chin and peered into the forest. "I barely remember the script I wrote for each of you from an inscription that was etched across an archway over a spring in the castle courtyard, and I've never known what it meant. Why they all appear different to each of us, except for you..." his voice trailed off as he returned his gaze to the young man.

Daedrin sighed and rubbed his temple before he spurred his horse to a slow trot. The others exchanged uneasy glances while they followed the young man a few paces away before he halted, dismounted and moved to stand roughly a stone's throw away from the rest as they tended to the horses.

Daedrin found that his mind reeled while he stared into the forest with eyes closed while he tried to block the strange flashes that were becoming all too common of late. *What's happening to me?* He thought frantically as he crouched down, placed his head in his hands and took in a deep breath.

"Hey," Daedrin stood up sharply and whirled around when Tara's voice touched his ears from over his shoulder; she stood a few paces away while she eyed him with careful concern. "Are you alright?" she asked softly. After taking in a slow, deep breath Daedrin turned away and shook his head.

"I... can't make sense of what's been happening, lately," he said slowly. He felt a hand on his shoulder and glanced back to see Tara looking at him with narrowed eyes while her left hand rested gently atop his cloak.

"What do you mean?" she asked.

Daedrin stared into the deep green wells of her eyes for a few moments before he averted his gaze and cleared his throat. "I... have been having these... flashes," he explained with a frown as he gathered his thoughts. "They are... strange, yet familiar at the same time... dreams, too," he added with a backward glance at the young woman. "More like nightmares, really," he swallowed hard when the gruesome pictures from his sleep nudged his conscious mind. "This... language that Hadrîn showed us, it should be foreign to us all and yet I feel as if I've seen it before, somewhere other than on my sword, I mean. Which is impossible," he added with a shake of his head.

Tara closed her eyes and muttered quiet prayers. "Let me help you," she said finally.

Daedrin half chuckled, half scoffed. "I don't see how you can," he said despairingly, and Tara felt her lips twitch.

"Perhaps we can start with taking some of the weight off your shoulders," she suggested, for her eyes had turned to Skane as he approached.

"Lad," Daedrin tossed a glance over his shoulder when Skane sheepishly greeted him from a few paces behind. "I... 'oped that we might talk," he continued. "Or rather, that ye would per'aps let me say me piece, and judge for yourself if ye wish to speak with me after."

Daedrin said nothing as he crossed his arms and looked out into the forest; Tara stepped back a few paces to the side and gave the blacksmith a gentle nod.

Skane swallowed hard. "I failed ye, lad," he said finally, and his voice cracked as he spoke. "I know that no apology is enough, for ye trusted me to warn yer family, and truthfully I... I tried but... not soon enough." He fell quiet for a few moments while he built up the courage to finish.

"After Marin and I left ye to recover, we ah, we moved to the village square where many remained still in question. I quickly told them of what 'ad caused yer injuries and o' the danger we likely faced. There was a bit o' debate, but in the end we all decided to prepare for defense, and a few men were sent out as scouts, to return at dawn."

He paused again and waited for a moment for some response from Daedrin, but when he received none he swallowed again and continued.

"I took several men, and we all gathered weapons from my smithy. While they moved to take up defensive positions on the edges of town, I mounted a borrowed 'orse and set out for yer farm." He paused now for several moments, and this time Daedrin turned his attention to the blacksmith; he saw tears staining the man's cheeks while he took in deep, shaky breaths.

"It was on fire," Skane choked, "and I dismounted and moved quickly, shouting their names frantically. I heard screaming from behind the house... rushed toward the sound. As I burst through the brush... they..." He broke down now completely with deep, gut-wrenching sobs that shook his broad shoulders as he fell to one knee and covered his face with his hands. Daedrin swallowed hard, moved over to his old friend and slowly knelt beside him before reaching out to place one hand on the shoulder of the blacksmith as tears welled up in his own eyes.

"I'm sorry, lad," Skane choked out, "so, so sorry. I was too late... too late to save them..." With floodgates unleashed the two men then sobbed together on the ground for several minutes while grief washed over them both and, when the tears slowly subsided Skane reached out and pulled Daedrin into a crushing embrace.

"I'm sorry, I'm sorry..." Skane kept whispering before finally Daedrin pulled away and wiped red eyes.

"I know you loved them, too," he choked out as he swallowed hard the lump in his throat.

Skane shook his head. "I don't expect ye to forgive me, lad," he said. "The Creator knows I've no notion of how to forgive myself." Daedrin's brow furrowed and for a few moments they knelt there in silence until their breathing slowly returned to normal and Daedrin rose to his feet and extended one arm to Skane; he took it fervently and allowed his friend to pull him to his feet.

"I should never have survived," the blacksmith declared as he wiped his face. "Those dreadful beasts were everywhere on your farm, but they all... moved past me, as if I wasn't even there... they even ignored my 'orse," he added with a snort. "I... went back then to the village to get ye, arrived a bit after dawn to find it already under siege. Everyone fell so quickly under the ferocity of those beasts... somehow I made it to my 'ome but found that ye were already gone. I ran through the backdoor and found Tara, seized her by the arm and fled with her into the mountains…"

Silence ensued the conclusion of the story while Daedrin stared off into the forest and took in the fading red and browns as he considered what he had been told. Finally he turned to his friend and, with a short nod at his companion he reached out and grasped Skane's arm in a fervent hand clasp; the blacksmith took in a sharp breath and returned the gesture.

"We need to keep moving."

Hadrîn approached suddenly and interrupted their exchange while he slid his canteen into a pouch on his waist. Daedrin nodded, and Skane patted his friend's shoulder as they turned, moved to the horses and mounted their steeds. As the young man swung into the saddle atop Fidelium he caught the hint of a smile across Tara's lips while she watched him from the back of the mare, and he couldn't help but return the look.

CHAPTER 9

BEST LAID PLANS…

They covered several more miles of thick brush over the next few hours as they moved steadily up the ever steepening mountain range. After a while the terrain became too harsh for them to continue on horseback, and so Hadrîn held up his hand and quietly muttered, "Whoa," and the company halted; the sun was just beginning to dip beneath the horizon. The old man beckoned to Daedrin and Tara and leaned in close when they approached.

"We are nearly to the place I told you of before," Hadrîn said softly while he surveyed their surroundings; his breath turned to vapor when it collided with the chill mountain air. "We must lead the horses on foot from here," he added with a frown as he dismounted. "The climb will only become more difficult."

Daedrin nodded and slid out of the saddle to stand beside Tara and Skane once they had done the same.

"Do your best to arrange the brush," he commanded softly with a glance at each of his companions; they all dipped their heads before continuing to move forward. The going was slow and tedious as they carefully struggled to make their way up the steep slope without losing their footing, all the while kicking the brush into small piles. While they had previously been able to cover several miles in the span of an hour they now traveled little more than one, with legs aching severely while lungs burned until, as the sun exchanged its final dim rays for the first glimmer of moonlight the company beheld their destination.

"There," Tara said softly when the land suddenly cleared to give way to a fairly flat and level surface; she nodded to a large oak a few hundred paces away that rested at the base of a steep, slanted cliff. Quickly they moved to the tree and dismounted before they tied their horses to some low hanging branches and ate a morsel with a drink in silence as each became lost in their own thoughts.

"No doubt whatever is following is watching even now," Hadrîn finally said at length.

Daedrin smirked. "Not for much longer," he declared with a gleam in his eyes before he coughed lightly. "Come," he added. "We need to get the fire built."

"We should move in pairs," Hadrîn suggested. "Just in case," he added with a sidelong glance at the young man.

Daedrin nodded grimly. "Tara," he said her name with a gesture of his head; she eyed him carefully as she moved to his side and, for a few moments they were silent while they poked through the trees and periodically bent down to gather wood from the brush. When arms were full they returned to the flat and dropped their bundles onto a growing pile that was placed at the edge of the slope where it met the steep cliff.

"Did you wish to say something?" she asked finally after several trips through the forest.

Daedrin paused and glanced at her before he stooped to pluck a large limb from the earth. "I... wanted to thank you," he told her, and she smirked.

"Why?"

"For sharing with me the nature of your... past," he replied softly with a quiet glance in her direction; she paused for a moment before turning to meet his gaze.

"Doing so felt... right," she said finally, and Daedrin dipped his head.

"I... before I knew what you've been through it..." he said, "it hardly seemed possible to continue moving forward."

Tara's eyes narrowed as she stooped to grasp a dried log.

"Do you think we will survive tonight?" she asked softly.

Daedrin sighed deeply while he rose with hands full of timber. "I've no intention of leaving this realm behind anytime soon," he declared, and his jaw clenched as he stared into the darkening forest before turning to meet her gaze.

"That isn't an answer," she said with a twist of her mouth, and he chuckled slightly.

"Tara..." his voice trailed off and he averted his eyes. "I wasn't able to protect my family," he said finally. "Nor Marin," he added softly before turning to look once more on her fair face. "I will not let another whom I care for perish, not while I draw breath."

Tara blinked when she met Daedrin's fiery gaze before she nodded slowly.

"We will see these creatures pay with their lives for their pursuit," she said as her eyes became lit with a cold fire.

Daedrin smiled. "I've never know you to be so... fierce," he told her as they moved back toward the pile of lumber with arms full of dead wood.

"I am when I need to be," she replied with a smirk after she had dropped her bundle onto the now large stack before she brushed her hands off on her cloak; Hadrîn and Skane had just returned to add what they had gathered.

"What now?" Skane asked.

"We draw them out," Daedrin said softly while he peered at the massive pile of lumber. "When the fire is blazing I shall let loose several arrows into the forest, try to light as much of the brush as I can. Then..." his voice trailed off as he looked solemnly at his companions. "I will destroy as many as I have time with my bow before they attack us openly, for however many remain will be ours to slay by hand when they approach."

"I imagine there are very few out in the dark," Hadrîn remarked. "The more that follow, the harder to remain concealed."

Daedrin nodded and sighed as he peered into the surrounding darkness.

"Do you still believe we should try to make use of the language you scrawled for us as well, once the fire is lit?" he asked finally, and Hadrîn dipped his head.

"It can only serve to perhaps increase our chances. You said you almost understood the language…" he added as he eyed the young man carefully. "Can you pronounce what was written?"

Daedrin frowned and tilted his head to the side while he brought to mind the words as he remembered them.

"Flumen, vitae, influit, amare," he declared suddenly, and his eyes snapped open to look upon the astonished faces of his companions.

"The words flow from your mouth like water from a spring; natural and smooth," the old man observed with a slow shake of his head.

"I don't understand," the young man said, and he felt his lips twitch slightly when Hadrîn smirked.

"This is beyond my wisdom," he said. "Perhaps the dragons can shed some light on the matter once we reach the safety of their walls. For now I suggest we eat another morsel and take advantage of a brief rest."

Daedrin sighed with a nod as he closed his eyes and rolled his neck. When he lifted his gaze he cast a quick glance at Tara before he bent down and withdrew a piece of flint from his cloak and, as he sent sparks out toward the brush the others gathered the bedrolls and placed them around the modest flame that had begun to burn. When all were settled in with blankets tugged tightly around Skane handed out some bread with the last of the fruit, first to Daedrin who sat on the outer edge and then to Tara who was to the left of the young man; Hadrîn received his own portion with a frown before the blacksmith took a seat himself at the far end of the fire. The meal was a meager one, at best, but it served to sooth well enough the ache within their hungry bellies.

"The moon is lovely at this height," Skane finally broke the somber silence that held them all captive while he looked to the heavens with just a hint of a smile; Daedrin smirked and stared into the roaring flames.

"This peak is something I would like to have enjoyed with Marin," he said mournfully as he lifted his gaze to the stars that glowed brightly in the sky above. "I am glad at least that we reconciled, my friend," he added with a glance at the blacksmith.

His friend smiled. "Aye," he said before swallowing hard. "Should we part ways this night at least it will be as brothers once more," he added softly. "I... know that the last words ye had with your father were not the best for leaving unsettled."

Daedrin's lips twitched and looked to his companion with a somber gaze. "He chose his final words," he declared softly as his jaw clenched and he looked off into the night; Skane and Tara glanced at one another uneasily while they eyed the young man with concern.

"I cannot imagine that he wished any harm to you, Daedrin," the healer interjected after a lengthy silence, but the young man shook his head.

"You weren't there," he told her as he peered into the fire. "He meant every word; even knowing they would be his last would have changed nothing."

At this declaration the company fell into a silence pierced only by the crackling of the roaring flames until finally Daedrin reached into his boot and withdrew the knife that had belonged to Melkai.

"Here," he said as he extended the weapon to Skane, who took it rather timidly, for he recognized its handle.

"Are ye certain, lad?" he asked softly, and Daedrin nodded.

"I... he would have wanted you to have it." After a brief moment of silence he looked up and cleared his throat.

"Tonight we will defeat our enemies, and we will make it to safety," he said forcefully as he peered around at his companions. Hadrîn dipped his head when their eyes met while Skane nodded and Tara smirked with a knowing look beneath fiery eyes; Daedrin felt his lips curl as he looked up at the sky and let his eyes take in the fullness of the moon above the treetops.

"Are we ready?" he asked with a final glance around the fire and, after receiving a nod of assent from each he rose slowly to his feet and moved closer to the flames where he withdrew his bow. Taking the tip of one arrow he plunged it into the heart of the fire with a cringe as the searing heat from the blaze singed his skin ever so slightly even from several feet away. After taking a deep breath he moved swiftly to his left, nocked the arrow and lifted his bow...

The Nasci called Crevan felt his eyes narrow as he watched the nearest human circle the fire with flaming arrow in hand. The miserable wretches had been acting oddly, he thought while he shifted his weight nervously; every impulse in his rigid body told him to attack, attack now! But his orders were clear, leaving no room to fall on the humans just yet. Still, he couldn't fight the terrible feeling that rose inside of him when the human suddenly pulled back on the bowstring and the arrow fly through the air; it plunged into the base of a tree several yards to the right of where Crevan prowled. He let his fangs gleam slightly in the moonlight when he saw the human light another arrow before letting it loose; this struck just to his left and lit some of the brush on the forest floor.

The Nasci jerked away from the light, and a few of the creatures under his command shied away from the flames themselves as they struggled to maintain their hidden position when yet another blazing arrow pierced the night and set fire to more of the forest; Crevan shifted angrily, for the one called Lern shrieked with pain and rage when he was struck by the next fiery projectile. The beast growled, for his Nasci were being steadily revealed while the flames from the arrows grew brighter as they began to light more of the dry twigs and leaves. With a dull thump another was struck when it was suddenly revealed by the warm glow; this one slumped to the ground without so much as a whimper and, with their veil of secrecy having clearly become unraveled the captain turned his head to the side and howled...

Daedrin struggled to keep his breathing steady, for his heart threatened to beat furiously as the Nasci were revealed; one looked to have been slain by the last arrow he'd let fly. Nocking another he aimed it quickly when a hideous shriek pierced the night air and echoed through the trees as he let the bowstring slip from his fingers and smirked with grim satisfaction when the projectile struck its target, for the beast fell to its side.

"Here they come!" he yelled over his shoulder to his companions as his eyes took in the shadows that swiftly began to bound toward them. He let one final arrow fly before slinging sword from sheath and letting out a roar as he swung the blade downward at the nearest Nasci when it came into the light of the blazing fire. The blow connected and sliced cleanly through its forehead and sent the brute crashing hard into the ground with a dull whimper that was quickly drowned out by the wretched howls of the rest as they converged with a vengeance.

Time seemed to slow for Daedrin while he moved, for he spun and stepped around and among the Nasci as if in a dance. Parry, *flumen* – thrust, *vitae* – dodge, *influit* – swing, *amare*; the words of the ancient script flowed through his mind while he whirled his sword with a cold, skilled and calculated vengeance that cut down every foe when it stepped into range of his blade.

His eyes were briefly drawn by one of the creatures as it slipped past him, but the brute was quickly sliced by Hadrîn before Tara plunged her own dagger between the scales on its chest. Another Daedrin cut on the foreleg before it stumbled around him and pounced at the back of the now unsuspecting healer; Skane tackled her out of the way before the pair turned to face it together and slayed it quickly with a thrust from either side. All of this Daedrin noted from his peripherals while he parried an oncoming blow before quickly following through with a thrust that plunged through the eye of the offending beast.

As his foe fell the young man felt his head jerk when a light pain suddenly formed in his temple; it was as if a knife was being slowly driven into his skull. He blinked and grunted when claws just barely clipped one leg and caused him to stumble before he swung his blade wildly to the side and clove the skull of the opposing creature.

His focus he found was slipping while the pain in his head continued to grow; he grimaced and barely dodged a sure to be lethal swipe of claws with a half roll, half stumble to the side. Faintly he was aware of the frantic voice of Tara reaching his ears and he blinked when she appeared suddenly at his side before she slid beneath a Nasci as it thundered toward him; after plunging her blade into its belly she rolled to the side when it fell. Daedrin swallowed hard and struggled to regain his steadily slipping senses when he looked to his left in time to see Skane crack one of the creatures hard over the head with his fist before the blacksmith stuck a knife into the side of its head.

With the pain ever increasing the young man felt his eyes widen when they took in another of the brutes as it pounced suddenly out of the shadows toward the now exposed left side of the blacksmith. Daedrin cried out weakly when red sprayed and his friend fell beneath the extended claws and fangs of the creature that landed on him with a roar. Then, with a noise in his head like a boulder crashing after a long drop from the peak of a mountain all thought was shattered and he fell to the ground, limp...

... Crevan howled with wild eyes as fresh blood filled his open maw from the burly human beneath him. Taking a leap he left his prey where it fell and bounded toward the woman at the edge of the fire before sliding to a stop with his haunches almost skidding into the flames when she whirled to face him with wide, enraged eyes that turned to a look of horror as she looked past him. The Nasci growled with red teeth bared menacingly as he eyed her neck and raised one leg in a motion to the remainder of his Nasci; a low rumble emanated from the throat of the creatures while they gathered to stand several paces behind their captain.

"It pains me that I will not be allowed to end your life here and now," the creature said to Hadrîn in his low, rumbling voice while he and the young woman moved to stand side by side near the other who had fallen earlier of his own accord. The Nasci growled when he looked to the left and right, for he counted only four remaining creatures if he included himself. "You've spilled too much blood to be allowed to leave this mountain…" he added before suddenly baring his fangs once more in a hideous sort of grin. "But you," he declared as his gaze turned to the woman. "My master has no need for you…" The Nasci around him all let their vicious rows of teeth gleam in the light of the fire when Crevan motioned them forward before he paused, for he took note then of a strange sound that began to tickle his ears. It was like that of a rushing wind; gentle at first, but gradually it grew until the trees swayed and the leaves rustled as if caught in a storm.

The creatures under his command exchanged a quick glance with their captain as they held their ground for a moment and awaited further instruction when suddenly a deafening, throaty roar filled the air and the dark night lit up with a blinding fire that consumed the three behind Crevan without them uttering so much as a whimper of pain. The final Nasci howled wildly with rage and terror and pounced toward the now hunched over female while the searing heat sent tingles of agony shooting through his hind legs. Just before his outstretched claws reached their target however he heard a whoosh as some crushing weight pounded him into the ground. Great talons wrapped around his torso before he was lifted suddenly into the air, and the last image he ever saw was of razor sharp fangs as an iron like jaw clamped down on his neck like a vice...

Tara and Hadrîn ducked and cringed briefly with hands covering their faces as the night was suddenly lit by a blinding, searing heat. They blinked when they cast their gaze forward once more and took in the carnage before them with wide eyes, for the Nasci who had previously spoken to them was nowhere to be seen, and the others were nothing more now than three piles of ash. As astonishing as this sudden development was, however, Tara let it give her pause only for a moment before she turned her attention to her fallen companions.

"No, no no..." she muttered softly while her dagger slipped from her grasp as she dropped to her knees at Daedrin's side and flung one arm out toward the fallen form of Skane. "Check him!" she yelled before she placed a hand beneath Daedrin's nose, put an ear to his chest and heaved a sigh of relief when she felt breath touch her fingers while the young man's chest rose and fell in a steady but fevered rhythm.

"Tara…" Hadrîn called out her name softly from where he knelt beside Skane, and she glanced up to see him looking on the blacksmith despairingly. "He… is gone." The old man rubbed his forehead with one hand and swallowed hard at the gruesome sight of the shredded throat and chest before he reached down to close the wide eyes of the fallen man.

Tara closed her eyes as a single tear escaped her lids. "Daedrin still breathes," she choked out. "But I don't know what's wrong with him," she added with a shake of her head when a sudden and dull thud caused her to jump and turn to her right where she beheld the headless torso of a Nasci as it bounced on the ground several paces away.

"His mind has been overwhelmed," a voice rang out from the shadows; deep but clear as it resonated with elegance and grace. Furious orange scales flashed brilliantly when the powerful and beautiful form of a dragon crept slowly into the firelight.

"Stay back!" Tara cried with a quick grasp of her dagger as she moved to stand defensively between Daedrin and the massive creature.

"Stay your blade, lass," the dragon commanded. "I wish no harm on you."

"We have lost one this night already," Tara said with a break in her voice when she glanced at Skane's body with a pang of grief. "I won't lose another," she added fiercely, and to her surprise the mythical beast chuckled with a deep, throaty rumble.

"Your bravery is to be commended," it said, "but it is unnecessary. I... am truly sorry that your friend was slain," it declared with a somber voice while it hung its head. "I am called Mulciber..." the dragon added as it lifted its gaze and raised one scaly claw to point at Daedrin's still form. "In truth, I came for him."

Tara felt lips twitch while her eyes narrowed. "What do you mean, 'came for him'?" she asked furiously. "Do you know what's happened to him?"

The one called Mulciber stooped lower so as to look more closely upon the young man. "I... felt the tongue of old resonating from his thoughts, fueled by some strange power..."

"You forced your mind on his own," Hadrîn declared angrily as he approached with eyes lit by a piercing gaze; his sword he sheathed roughly after wiping it clean.

"Yes," Mulciber said softly. "I am afraid that I pushed too hard when I reached out. He was... unprepared to handle the crossing of my thoughts with his own."

Hadrîn's jaw clenched, and he lifted a finger to point at Mulciber's scaly hide.

"You must take him to Ímrelet, at once."

The dragon reared back at Hadrîn's bold declaration. "What do you know of Ímrelet?!" he asked with a heated snort that sent a tiny burst of flame shooting from one nostril.

"More than you, I should think," the old man said dryly. "Perhaps Crën or Sarin have spoken the name Hadrîn to you?"

Mulciber's eyes narrowed and he leaned forward. "Only when

relaying the certainty of your death as a cautionary tale," he said slowly. "This was a mistake; I cannot bring anyone to the city," he added with an abrupt shift as he rose and extended his wings.

"That is *exactly* what you will do!" Tara exclaimed angrily. "*You* are the one that did this to him! And if he hadn't... if he had continued fighting..." her voice trailed off when she again looked mournfully to Skane's still form before she swallowed the lump in her throat and returned her gaze to the dragon. "Please," her voice cracked and Mulciber sighed as his wings slowly returned to his sides.

"Very well," he consented softly after a beat of silence. "I will let my father decide his fate... and yours," he added solemnly; Tara and Hadrîn moved to the side when the dragon strolled to where Daedrin lay and gently scooped the young man up in his claws. Then, with a great rush of wings that nearly knocked the pair to the ground he leaped up and disappeared into the night sky.

Tara stood in shocked silence for a few moments after the departure of Mulciber before she turned and moved slowly over to the blacksmith. With one hand she reached out to let her palm rest gently on Skane's chest. Her throat tightened when she took in his broken and bloodied form; the dagger that he had been gifted was clutched tightly between his still fingers. "No..." she whispered softly as she hung her head and struggled to maintain her composure when she felt something touch her shoulder.

"I'm sorry..." Hadrîn said with a quiet, downcast voice as he withdrew his hand.

"How did this happen?" she asked mournfully, and the old man frowned.

"We… knew the risks when we chose to attack our pursuers," he said after a moment of quiet contemplation. "His death will certainly not be in vain," he added slowly while his jaw clenched. "Mulciber will answer for his actions."

After giving a grieved nod the healer slowly and carefully reached and out gently removed the knife from Skane's grasp before she tucked it into her boot.

"What happens now?" Tara wiped her face as she looked to the old man with red eyes.

He was silent for a moment while he moved over to the bedrolls and stooped to grasp one of the blankets. Slowly he moved back to the fallen blacksmith where he flung the covering out and pulled it gently over the body. For a moment he knelt there and stared at the wool cloth before he lifted his head to meet Tara's piercing gaze.

"We go to Ímrelet," he said. "Explain to the council what has happened, both this night and of late. Then… we lay our friend to rest before working night and day to see Garrôth suffer for all that has been done in his name."

The words had barely escaped his lips when a great rush of wings turned the heads of the pair as four dragons suddenly landed around their camp.

"Incredible to hear from Mulciber that he has met one who calls himself Hadrîn; a name I have not heard for nearly a hundred years," declared one of the dragons; its dark green scales flashed brilliantly under the gleam of the firelight.

"Alacris," Hadrîn offered the greeting with a low bow. "It is good to see you well."

The dragon dipped his head. "As well as can be in such times as this," he replied with his deep but fair voice. "Tell me, where did this boy come from whom Mulciber tells us possesses knowledge of a language long dead?"

"Is that all he told you?" the old man asked with a twitch of his lips. The statement caused a brief pause during which the dragons all exchanged glances. "Garrôth is pursuing us," he added finally. "It would be better to discuss such matters when we are safely within the walls of your fair city."

Alacris snorted. "While I would not risk bringing you back to Ímrelet, my father has other plans. For now he has ordered us to take you to him… who is your companion?" he added with a wave to Tara.

"Apologies," Hadrîn said. "This is Tara," he added with a nod to the healer. She swallowed hard as she rose to her feet and stepped forward with fingers that tightened around her staff.

"And who is that?" Alacris asked softly with a motion of one scaly claw to the form beneath the blanket.

"His name is Skane," Tara told him after a beat of silence. "He was a good man," she added with angry eyes filled to the brim as she stared at the furious orange scales of the dragon that had appeared earlier that night.

Alacris bowed his head. "Mulciber told us of the… tragic results of his actions. You have my condolences, along with those of my brothers," he added with a wave to the creatures around him, each of whom dipped his head; Tara scoffed at the gesture and turned away to seethe in silence. "We should depart," Alacris continued. "I do not like to tarry so long on the ground," the beast added with a wary glance into the surrounding forest.

Hadrîn nodded and turned to Tara. "Are you ready?" he asked softly, and after a moment she nodded.

"He comes too," she said fiercely as she pointed to the form on the ground.

Alacris frowned but dipped his head. "Of course," he said before motioning to his brother. "Mulciber, will you take his body?" he asked softly.

"Yes, brother," the dragon responded as he moved over to Skane's lifeless form and scooped it up gently before he leapt into the air and disappeared with a rush of wings.

"You may ride on my back, if you wish," Alacris said to Hadrîn with a smirk, and the old man nodded.

"Better than riding between your claws," he remarked. "Don't fear," he added with a glance at Tara. "The ride can be quite unsettling the first time, but I can assure you that you are safer on the backs of these noble creatures than in your own bed."

Tara frowned. "I will believe that when I am safely in this city as you've promised."

"Soon," Alacris promised. "But be warned… if either of you harbor evil in your heart toward my kinsmen… there will be no end to your suffering."

Hadrîn felt his lips curl slightly upward. "You've changed, Alacris," he observed as he approached the dragon, who lowered himself down enough for the old man to clamber up onto his back.

"You will ride on Fortis," Alacris said to Tara who smirked in return when the largest of the dragons stepped forward; his massive shape was covered in deep red scales of a less brilliant hue than she had seen on the rest.

"Absurd to treat ourselves as pack mules," Fortis grumbled as he approached.

Alacris chuckled with a deep, throaty sort of sound. "As the need arises…" he trailed off with a twitch of his dragonish lips as Tara slowly moved toward the now hunched beast and reached up cautiously to find that she could slip her hands between its scales. After pulling herself up with her legs around his neck she took a deep breath and let it out slowly while Fortis lifted his head.

"Always leave me with these four legged creatures…" the remaining dragon said as he strolled over to Liber; his light, feathery blue scales glinted when he moved, and his presence caused all three horses to nicker nervously for a moment before he leaned in and they quieted down.

"Consider yourself lucky that you are not carrying one of these on your back, Saevus," the red dragon said with a glare as he moved forward with Alacris. Quickly the three scooped up the spooked steeds before they cut the ties to the tree with their teeth and bolted quite suddenly into the air.

Tara felt the air leave her lungs in a whoosh when the ground rushed away, and she took in a sharp breath as she watched the land pass, far, far below while the sudden increased pressure blended with the beating of the dragon's wings and caused her ears to ring.

The journey was over almost as soon as it began, though, ending with a sudden rise upward where for a few seconds she felt her skin crawl while frigid air blanketed her body and breathing became difficult before there was a swift drop down out of the sky and into a cluster of trees that lined some sort of wide, deep pit high up the mountain. A few moments more and the light of a city came into view and, the next thing she knew the movement was over and the horses had been placed safely onto the ground. The dragons all landed then gently next to the surprisingly calm steeds before Alacris and Fortis stooped low and allowed Hadrîn and Tara to dismount.

"As promised," Hadrîn declared dryly with a glance at the pale faced healer. "Welcome to Ímrelet."

CHAPTER 10

BROKEN

The pair shivered and clutched their cloaks tightly around them as the chill air from the high valley washed over them while several humans in light armor suddenly moved forward and led the terrified horses away. When Tara looked around her eyes took in a massive oval room; its walls bare save for torches all throughout beneath a massive, open area where a roof would normally rest. In the center sat a very large, high stone table of the same shape as the room. It was polished like marble with steps on one side that led to a raised platform with a dozen chairs rounding one half of the smooth surface.

Her gaze narrowed when she took in a pair of human guards standing off to either side of two large, wooden double doors. They were adorned with heavy cloaks of a deep blue, and the silver glint of mail could just be seen beneath their necks; a sword hung low at each of their sides. Tara turned her eyes slowly around the room in quiet astonishment as they passed over the brilliantly colored scales of the four dragons she had met in the wilderness. She blinked when her gaze came to rest on two more, both quite a bit larger than the others. One she thought to clearly be the oldest, for it was the largest and had deep brown, dull scales with weary, wise eyes above a shriveled snout. The other was a little over half his size yet was still slightly larger than the rest, with fiery blue scales that gleamed beautifully in the light of the torches.

"Here they are, father," Alacris declared with a dip of his head. "Hadrîn, with Tara his companion."

The old man bowed low when his name was mentioned; he tilted his head to the side and gave Tara a look that suggested she do the same. After a pause the healer smirked and curtsied in a half-hearted gesture.

"Hadrîn," the largest dragon greeted the old man with a surprisingly raspy yet still deep voice that was devoid of the elegance and grace of those that Tara had heard thus far. "How is it that you stand before us now, alive and undamaged?"

Hadrîn frowned as he brushed his chin. "It… is a long-winded tale, wise one," he said after a brief pause.

The dragon leaned forward. "When last we saw your face it was to bid you farewell as you embarked on a journey of almost certain doom… do you really expect to return unquestioned after seventy-six years?" he added with a narrowed, piercing gaze, but Hadrîn shook his head.

"Nay, Crën," he said. "Though you may search my thoughts and know that neither myself nor my companions are of any threat to you." The old man sighed. "I beg your forgiveness for being so abrupt but I must ask… the boy who came before us, is he well?"

The one called Crën winced at the mention of Daedrin before he glanced at the blue dragon to his left; he kept quiet as it spoke.

"You mean Daedrin," the fair creature said softly with a voice that radiated warmth and light when it touched Tara's ears; the beast was a female, she realized. "His… mind is recovered but, we were forced to subdue him."

"You restrained him?!" Tara interjected angrily. "Why?!"

"Your companion has spirit," Crën remarked as he eyed the healer. "Careful not to be too brash, young one," he added softly, and Tara glowered at the declaration.

"When he awoke," the female dragon continued, "he became… angry, and violent, shouting for his companions while repeating the name 'Skane', over and over."

Tara felt herself swallow hard as she looked briefly to the covered body on the ground a few paces away.

"There is Skane," she said shakily with a nod to the corpse before she turned her gaze forward once more. "He is… was," she corrected herself with a pang of grief. "He was a good man," she continued softly before her voice began to rise. "He died because Daedrin fell at the field of battle from whatever *he*," she pointed at Mulciber, "did to his mind. So whatever cause you have to question should be put aside. We have a friend to bury…" her voice trailed off and she fought back tears.

The dragons all eyed one another quietly for a while before, as if inaudible words had been exchanged Crën dipped his head.

"Mourn your loss," he said finally with a motion to one of the guards that stood by the doors to the chamber. "Ishail, take them to the healers, and watch them closely," he commanded. The guard nodded, bowed, and motioned for Hadrîn and Tara to follow.

After exiting the oval room they moved in silence through quiet city streets lit only by a few lanterns placed sporadically about until after what seemed like only a few moments they arrived at a small, white stone building. The guard called Ishail pulled the handle of its oak door, stepped to the side and motioned for the pair to enter when they had approached; he followed himself once they had passed.

Tara moved with a swift grace as she passed over the threshold, and her jaw clenched when her eyes took in Daedrin's form, bound with rope to a bed off to the left side of the room; his weapons she saw leaning in one corner. The cloak around his right calf was torn and stained red, and his hair was a disheveled mess above bloodshot eyes that turned to meet her gaze when she entered. She closed the distance between them in three swift steps and reached out to grasp his right hand with her left before turning her head to Ishail.

"Unbind him!" she demanded angrily, but the guard simply shook his head.

"Tara…" the healer turned her attention back to Daedrin when his voice touched her ears. Her throat tightened as she looked into his eyes; the normally deep blue wells were all but masked by the light red veins that surrounded his strained pupils. "Skane…?" his voice trailed off as the look on his face begged the question.

Tara swallowed hard. "He's... gone," her voice came out barely above a whisper, and tears welled up in her eyes while her grip tightened.

Daedrin turned to face the wall as his chin quivered and he closed his eyes. His heart skipped a beat while the color drained from his face and he felt his conscious thought slipping from him. The sound of his unsteady breath pounded in his ears when the image of red spurting from Skane's throat flashed through his mind until gradually he became aware of Tara's voice as it touched his ears but, the sound seemed like an echo that rang out through a mountain range from a great distance. Slowly his senses began to balance and he opened his eyes before turning to meet her tear-filled gaze with narrowed brows.

"Where is he?" he asked hoarsely. Tara took in a deep, shaky breath as she struggled for words before Hadrîn spoke for her.

"His... body was brought to the city," he told him softly.

Daedrin nodded slowly before he turned to the guard. "Please," he said quietly after clearing his throat. "Your people no longer have need to fear me... let me go to him." He hung his head.

Ishail's lips twitched while the guard swallowed sorrowfully and tilted his head to one side. With a dip of his chin he moved to the side of the bed and drew a short knife from his belt, which he used to carefully cut the cords that held Daedrin before stepping back to his post by the door with one hand on the hilt of his sword.

The young man took in a deep breath as Tara released his hand and he lifted his arms to rub the raw areas of his wrists where the bonds had cut into them when he had struggled. Slowly he sat up and swung his legs over the side of the bed where he paused briefly before he rose to his feet; immediately he was pulled into a crushing embrace by Tara as she wrapped her arms tightly around his torso and buried her face in his chest. Daedrin felt his jaw clench when he moved his arms around her shoulders and held her while his thoughts threatened to overwhelm him.

They remained that way for several minutes before the healer slowly pulled away and met his eyes with an agonized gaze before she turned to the guard.

"Take us to him," she ordered; her grieved voice resonated with a quiet tone of command.

Ishail dipped his head. "Follow me," he said as he turned on his heels and exited the room. He was closely followed by the other three while the guard moved swiftly through the city streets.

Daedrin blinked as his eyes half-heartedly took in his surroundings for the first time. The paths and buildings were of unpolished stone, and there was placed sporadically the occasional plant or tree that was either in a corner or next to a door. *Skane will never set his eyes on this place…* the thought caused him to take in a sharp breath as incredible grief pierced his heart and he blinked back the tears that formed behind hazy eyes. He turned his gaze forward then, for they had approached a set of wide, wooden doors with a guard on either side. They gave a short nod to Ishail and swung the doors open when the group had closed the distance between them.

As they entered the room everything seemed to move slowly and with exaggerated motion while Ishail conversed for a few moments with the dragons, whom Daedrin hardly saw when his gaze came to rest on a bloodied blanket draped over a burly form on the ground at the edge of a large stone table. He swallowed hard and felt his jaw tighten as he closed the distance between himself and the hidden figure in a few short strides before he fell to his knees; vaguely he was aware of Hadrîn looking over his shoulder while Tara moved to his side and placed a hand gently on his shoulder.

Pensively he reached out with shaky fingers, grasped a corner of the covering and took in a deep breath as he pulled it back. He blinked when his eyes took in the torn and bloodied form of his friend before he closed them. A strange sensation was rising from within while he struggled to keep his breathing steady; vomit, he realized suddenly as it welled up from the pit in his stomach. He turned his head to the side and retched, emptying the remnants of his last meal onto the ground before hunching over the pool with his knees beneath him as he rocked slowly.

Why... why, why, why...? The single word was all that formed in his mind while his emotions bounced roughly from an agonizing ache, to deep-seated anger, and back again to pain.

Gradually the pounding rhythm of his racing heart began to quiet while his senses steadily oriented once more to his surroundings. He could feel Tara's hand gently rubbing his shoulder and back as he lifted his torso and head and opened his eyes. With a cringe he allowed them to take in the fullness of the injuries that the blacksmith had sustained. After reaching out one hand he let it rest on Skane's shoulder and proceeded to take in deep, shaky breaths while his pulse slowly began to return to normal; he felt his jaw clench as he turned his head and met the gaze of the surrounding dragons.

"Did he suffer long?" he asked, and his hoarse voice trembled slightly when he looked to his companions.

"Nay, lad," Hadrîn said softly and shook his head slowly. "I... moved to him, moments after he fell but... he was already gone."

Daedrin swallowed hard as he shifted his eyes back to his slain friend; with teeth grit he pulled the blanket back over the broken form before he reached out and slid his arms beneath Skane's neck and legs.

"Daedrin..." Tara's voice trailed off while she pulled lightly on the young man's shoulder.

"Let me go," he told her roughly and jerked away with a grunt as he struggled to lift the body of the burly blacksmith.

With a pang of deep sorrow and a blink the healer moved to her right and reached out to grasp the fallen man's legs while Hadrîn stooped to grab his shoulders. Together the three lifted the heavy form and paused for a moment while they each shifted the weight for a better hold.

"Where can I bury him?" Daedrin asked as he turned red eyes to Ishail.

The guard winced at the broken gaze of the young man before he looked to Crën, who dipped his head.

"You may lay him to rest with our own," the guard told him as he moved to the doors and rapped thrice on the wood. After a few moments they swung open and he stepped through, followed by the other three while they stumbled forward with Skane in their arms.

Ishail moved slowly with a heavy eyed glance back every few moments while he led them through the streets in the opposite way they had previously come. The company stumbled on in silence for several minutes, moving from one lane to the next until they came to a path that ended in short stairs before it opened up to a raised garden; trees lined the outer edge. The area was beautiful, despite the once fair green of the open field now being dull in the wake of winter's onset. Several stones could be seen all around, placed on the ground in rows with names carved into the surface of each.

"Here," Ishail directed them as he stopped a few paces from one of the rocks and plunged a long torch he had grasped upon their approach into the ground before waving one hand to the open area of grass beneath him. Daedrin and his companions stumbled forward and let the body of the blacksmith fall as gently as they were able before they all rose to catch their breath.

"Shovels," Daedrin said heavily with a glance at the guard, who motioned to a small lean-to several yards away where crude tools could be seen hanging along its walls. While breathing heavily the young man moved quickly over to the structure, followed by his companions; each grasped one of the wooden handles before returning to the spot near Skane's still form. Taking in a deep breath Daedrin plunged the metal end into the earth and raised it after a moment before he tossed the loose dirt to the side. His motion was copied by Hadrîn and Tara as well as, to his surprise Ishail, for the guard had grasped a shovel of his own and now joined them while they dug.

Less than half an hour later the group stood around a shallow hole where they breathed heavily and wiped away perspiration from foreheads that were damp, despite the cold weather of the mountain top. With a sniffle and a cough Daedrin moved around the mound of fresh dirt and stooped low; he was followed by his friends. Gently they lifted the lifeless form and brought it to the opening in the earth where they awkwardly bent to their knees and carefully laid the blacksmith into the grave. After rising to their feet all merely stood in silence for a few moments before Tara finally knelt and withdrew the knife she had recovered; she silently extended the weapon to Daedrin.

The young man reluctantly took the dagger from her grasp. For a few moments he stared at it with hazy eyes until, with a heavy blink he stooped low and placed the weapon gently onto Skane's chest. After rising once more he took in a deep breath racked with grief before he reached out, grasped his shovel once more and proceeded to cast the dirt onto his fallen friend while he fought to hold back fresh tears. The others followed suit and, after a few minutes there was a raised mound of freshly dug earth at their feet.

"I am sorry, brother," Daedrin choked out while his jaw clenched and his fist tightened around the handle of the shovel, which he had plunged into the ground at the foot of the grave. "I failed you..." The young man hung his head and closed heavy eyes as he took in sharp, labored breaths. After a few moments he blinked and looked up when he felt pressure on his right hand; Tara's gentle gaze met his pain-filled eyes as her fingers became clasped with his own.

"He saved my life," she said softly with a glance down at the raised earth. "Knocked one of those monsters away..." her voice trailed off and she swallowed hard. "If not for him... I would be beside him in that grave... thank you, Skane," she added while her jaw trembled and Daedrin took in a deep breath.

"He was noble, to the very end," he declared with a sharp nod, and as he turned to meet Tara's distraught gaze there with a cold fire burning beneath his narrowed eyes.

"I *will* see your death avenged, my brother." His voice filled with an icy malice while his chest rose and fell steadily and his grip with Tara's fingers tightened. "Garrôth will soon know his error in judgement when he allowed me to leave Cordin with breath still in my lungs..." Slowly he turned away and took in a deep breath. With a hard swallow and a blink he reached up with his free hand to rub weary eyes before he turned his attention to the guard.

"Take me to your masters," he demanded, but Ishail slowly shook his head.

"I... cannot," he said at length. "None go before the council unless granted permission by Crën and Sarin."

"Then you will break that rule," Daedrin said as he drove a piercing gaze into Ishail's eyes, but the guard stood firm.

"Impossible," he said as his lips jerked. "I... am sorry," he added softly with a glance at each of them. "I know your grief but... our caution is what has kept us standing."

Daedrin frowned, and his free hand twitched while he eyed the guard murderously before Hadrîn stepped to his side, placed a hand on his shoulder and gave him a level stare.

"We understand," the old man said as he turned to Ishail, who dipped his head in return.

"It is late. For now I have been granted the authority to see you each to your own quarters," he said with a glance at Tara and Daedrin before he turned to Hadrîn. "You had an apartment here once, I have been told. It is yours still, if you wish to retire there?"

"I think I shall," the old man replied with a short bow of his head.

"Please," Tara interjected. "I... do not wish to be alone," she continued with a glance up at Daedrin; the young man's harsh gaze softened at her pleading eyes.

"She can stay with me," he said as he turned to the guard.

Ishail dipped his head. "Of course; follow me," he said with a wave of his hand while he stepped forward. "I trust you remember the way to your dwelling?" he added with a glance at Hadrîn, who nodded his assent before the guard moved away with Daedrin and Tara close behind; their hands were still clasped as they followed.

Leaving the old man behind the three strolled in silence through the city streets until they came to the building in which Daedrin had been treated and held earlier that night; the young man felt his eyes narrow when they took in the inscription "Domus Sanitatem" burned deeply into the rock above the door.

"You may retrieve your weapons," Ishail told the young man as he paused at the entrance with a light dip of his head and allowed the pair to enter the dwelling. Moments later Daedrin returned fully armed with Tara at his side; he gave a brief nod to the guard when they exited the building.

"Please, honor my decision to grant you access to your armaments," Ishail said with a glance at the intimidating form of Daedrin as he stood before him; he smirked in return.

"None have need for fear save for Garrôth, or those who would dare hinder me from destroying him," he assured the guard.

Ishail's lips curled slightly upwards as he waved one arm in a sweeping gesture.

"Follow me, then," he said before proceeding to lead them to a small dwelling that was only a few minutes' walk from the house of healing. Quietly they bade the guard farewell before they entered the modest structure and took in its plain furnishings. The walls were of a dark blue with white accents, and there was a single bed off to one side; a fireplace in the corner was already lit with a warm glow. Daedrin looked down at Tara and blinked with the realization that their hands were still clasped together. Despite his inner turmoil he felt his cheeks turn slightly hot while a pang of guilt briefly entered his heart before they let their fingers separate as they moved forward to a table that held a pitcher of water; Daedrin filled a glass and passed it to Tara who drained it quickly before extending her arm out and allowing him to refill her cup. While she sipped the cool water

Daedrin then tilted back the pitcher and took several long, deep swigs with eyes closed as the refreshing liquid touched his parched throat.

When he lifted his lids he placed the container back onto the table before he moved slowly over to the bed, removed his weapons and ran one hand over the soft quilt atop the mattress. After placing his sword and bow with its quiver against the wall to his right he turned to sit on the edge of the cushion and bent down to untie the laces of his boots.

"Here," Tara said as she knelt down beside him and reached out with nimble fingers that quickly untied the cords. After tossing a brief glance up at Daedrin's quiet face she first removed one boot and then the other before setting them to the side. She then unlaced her own before rising slowly to her feet and kicking off her footwear.

"Thank you," Daedrin said softly as he stood and stared into her deep green eyes for a moment before he cleared his throat. "Take the bed," he told her finally while he moved past her to the carpet in the center of the room. With a soft grunt he lowered himself down to the floor where he lay on his side with back to the mattress and face toward the fire.

"You don't need to be noble," Tara said softly as she eyed the young man's squared shoulders in the glow of the dancing flames.

Daedrin turned to meet her eyes. "I would never allow a woman to lie on the floor while I rest on comfortable cushions."

Tara smiled lightly. "Of course not," she said. "But I... don't want to sleep alone," she added as she pat the mattress with her left hand. "Please," she added quietly.

Daedrin felt his heart soften at her plea, and so he slowly pushed up to his feet and approached the bed; Tara turned to lie on her side with back to the wall while Daedrin slumped down onto the cushions next to her and eyed the ceiling. With a sigh Tara shifted closer to rest her hand on his shoulder with her head against the pillow as she closed weary eyes and Daedrin pulled the blanket over them both. For a while he simply lay in silence and listened to her breathing as her chest rose and fell with a quiet rhythm.

"I can't believe he's really gone," he whispered finally with a blink when tears sprung to his eyes.

Tara shifted slightly and lifted her head to look on his face; her jaw tightened sorrowfully as she took in his damp pupils before she rested her head once more on the cushions. "You will see him again," she said softly, and her words brought to Daedrin's mind the similar message relayed to him from Hadrîn's lips regarding his family. He took in a deep breath, tilted his head to look at the fire and closed his eyes. Ever so slowly the crackle and pop, mixed with the steady beat of Tara's heart near his own lulled him into a gentle sleep...

Daedrin woke with a short scream as he bolted upright in the bed with chest heaving while he turned frantically from side to side.

"Daedrin," Tara spoke drearily from his side while she reached out to gently grab his arm. With a deep sigh that was almost a choking sob the young man closed his eyes, lowered his head into his hands and breathed heavily while he attempted to calm his racing pulse.

"They're worse now, aren't they?" Tara asked softly.

Daedrin nodded and slowly opened his eyes as he turned to meet her concerned gaze.

Thump, thump, thump! They both jerked their gaze to the door when three loud knocks echoed through the room from the other side.

"Begging your forgiveness," called the muffled and vaguely familiar voice of Ishail, "but the Council has prepared a meal for you."

Daedrin frowned as he glanced at Tara, slid his feet off of the bed and moved to open the door; he blinked in the light of the morning sun when it touched his eyes.

"Greetings," the guard addressed them with a low bow. "I apologize if I woke you, but the Council was... direct. You are to join Hadrîn for breakfast and then be brought before Crën and Sarin."

With a sigh Daedrin waved one hand absently toward Ishail before he moved away, leaving the door open as he slid into his boots. Tara had his sword-belt in one outstretched arm when he stood once more; he thanked her as he took it from her grasp and strapped on the blade before he slung the bow with its quiver over one shoulder.

As they exited the pair pulled their cloaks tighter around them in the wake of the rather frigid morning air. They followed Ishail in silence for a few minutes before they saw Hadrîn up ahead, led by a guard who's face they did not recognize.

"Morning," the old man said as the pair approached; Tara

returned the greeting half-heartedly while Daedrin merely nodded before averting his gaze.

The young man could not help but marvel slightly as he took in the fullness of the surrounding structures for the first time, for he saw that they glowed with a strange, deep green luminesce. The whole city almost seemed to pulse as if some power emanated from within the very stones. He frowned and turned to Tara and had just opened his mouth to speak when they came to a tall doorway wrapped in vines, with the inscription "Victum de Domo" etched into the stone above the opening.

Ishail stopped at the entrance and motioned for them to enter.

"Please, enjoy," he said as they moved past him and entered a large room decorated with several large rectangular wooden tables, all empty save for one laden with dishes; three place settings, to be exact.

"Greetings," a fair voice touched their ears while a middle aged man appeared through a doorway at the far end of the room. His hair was a golden brown that just barely touched the plain brown villager's cloak that covered his shoulders; it moved ever so slightly as he approached.

"I am Lonen," the man continued, "keeper of the house of hospitality. Please, rest your heavy hearts whilst you sit at our table," he added with a motion to the table with the three place settings.

As the company settled into their seats they looked up to see three plainly dressed young men enter the room, each laden with trays of food. Tara, feeling strange at being waited on beseeched

Lonen and his companions to eat with them, but they politely declined.

"This meal is for you and your companions," he said as he motioned to the young men, who distributed a little to each until all were served.

The group ate quietly, for though they seemed to have discovered safety at last they all found it hard to truly enjoy the feast as it was laid out before them in the wake of Skane's passing; and a feast it truly was with fresh, savory grilled meats beneath piles of vegetables paired with crisp spring water that served to cool their parched throats. When at last their stomachs were satisfied, they all exchanged glances with one another as if waiting for someone to break the silence.

"I... know that it is difficult," Hadrîn finally said at length, "for you both are in great mourning." The old man frowned when Daedrin and Tara looked down at the table. "But..." he continued, "there is little time to grieve, I think. Word will soon reach Garrôth of our escape, if indeed it has not already, and while we may rest here in safety I fear it will not be long before he marshals all his forces and seeks to wipe out any resistance. Ishail has informed me that the Council wishes to speak with us... we must decide together what course we should take."

Daedrin frowned and glanced briefly at Tara before turning to meet Hadrîn's gaze.

"We fight," he said simply; his voice was filled with a cold fire.

"At least we now have a chance," Tara added, and the old man dipped his head.

"Indeed," he agreed. "Though that... will not be so easy. Garrôth is... formidable. He is a master of manipulation and strategy, and he possesses an endless degree of patience; it is very likely that after so many years he will have amassed quite the army of followers," he added with a twitch of his lips.

Tara's eyes narrowed. "You've spoken much of... Garrôth." She paused as she stumbled over the name. "How is it you know so much of one who has clearly fought so hard to stay in the shadows?"

Hadrîn glanced briefly at Daedrin before turning once more to the healer. "What knowledge I possess, I have gained first-hand," he told her solemnly, and he then proceeded to relay to Tara all that he had revealed to Daedrin when they had first met. "Though the odds are stacked against us," he said in conclusion, "I know but one truth; we... I, at least, cannot sit idly by. It would seem that with each passing day Garrôth's strength continues to grow as his reach into the realm becomes deeper and more treacherous. Doubtless it cannot be long before he casts off his veil of secrecy and takes the throne of Silmaín in full view of all."

"He must be made to suffer," Daedrin interjected heavily while he absently rubbed the hilt of his sword and met the fiery eyes of Tara. His grief over the recent loss of Skane he felt slowly being replaced by a cold, calculated rage as he leaned forward to meet her gaze with a level, heated look of his own.

"You knew my family well," he said before he moved his eyes from Tara and settled them on Hadrîn, "and while you did not, I

216

believe you would agree with what I am about to say, had you known my father. He... was not the kind of man who would be useful in the times we now find ourselves, as he would not have had the strength to do what was necessary for bringing us safely out of Cordin." He leaned back with jaw clenching as he continued. "I have found that strength. From the ashes of who I once was a purpose has been revealed to me, and with it has come the fortitude to do whatever must be done to see Garrôth brought to a swift and sudden end."

Silence followed his heated monologue, during which Tara's lips could be seen moving silently beneath closed eyes. After a few moments she lifted her lids and directed her gaze to Daedrin.

"I must tell you that I don't agree with how you handled our escape from Cordin," she told him finally. "You stole a horse, assaulted its owner and killed two perhaps innocent men..." she sighed, and her voice trailed off while she shook her head slowly. "But I know that in times of war such things... cannot always be avoided. I am not so naïve as to think that we can hope to defeat Garrôth without sacrifice... perhaps even with pieces of our own hearts," she added softly with a frown as she leaned forward to clasp and rest her hands on the table where she fiddled her thumbs absently.

"I will follow your lead," she said finally, "but I ask that you put as much care into your planning and actions as is reasonable for such a time as this, so as to avoid any reckless loss of life."

Daedrin dipped his head. "None who are innocent have need for fear," he assured her. "Only Garrôth himself with any who serve him will suffer by my hand."

"And fear they shall," Hadrîn declared after a beat of silence. "We will – ."

"If I may." They were interrupted suddenly by Ishail, who made a light bow when they looked his direction. "Apologies for the intrusion, but the council wishes to speak with Daedrin and Hadrîn."

They all exchanged glances as Daedrin rose to his feet. "I will go nowhere without Tara," he said forcefully, and the guard dipped his head.

"If that is your wish, then I am fairly certain she will be allowed to join you. However," he waved a hand to the healer, "as your presence was not requested, you will need to remain outside the council chamber while this query is presented to Crën and Sarin."

Tara sighed with eyes that narrowed as she frowned. "Fine," she said finally with a glance at Daedrin.

"Please, follow me," Ishail said as he exited the room, followed closely by the others. They moved quickly through a few turns before they arrived at the same room that they had briefly visited the night before. Daedrin noticed now yet another inscription that seemed to be burned into the stone arch above the wooden doors; it read "Domus Consilium".

"Please," Ishail motioned to the group as they approached the structure, "wait here," he said while the guards opened the doors and allowed him to pass over the threshold. A few moments later he returned and gestured for them to enter; he followed himself and remained standing with one hand on the hilt of his sword as the latches clinked shut behind him.

Hadrîn couldn't help but smirk at Daedrin's somewhat awed reaction to the council when he beheld the dragons truly for the first time. Seven there were in all with some larger than others; each possessed their own unique shade of colored scales. Formal introductions, filled with snippets of personal anecdotes, were made by Crën, who dipped his head as he greeted them with his deep, raspy voice. He was clearly the largest and oldest, with deep brown scales and weary, wise eyes above a shriveled snout. His mate, Sarin, was a little over half his size yet was still slightly larger than the rest, with fiery blue scales that held Daedrin mesmerized. Next introduced was Fortis, the firstborn son of Crën and Sarin, whose dark red scales shone with a dull hue atop a well-built torso that was the largest compared with the rest of siblings as clear evidence of his age and strength. One called Saevus dipped his head as his name was called; his light feathery blue scales and slender body proved him to be the most agile of the lot.

Then with a low, graceful bow Sharleth stepped forward. Of no relation to Crën, Sarin or their children, she had been rescued while still in her egg when the couple had first gone into hiding. She was truly beautiful to behold, with deep purple scales and brilliant golden eyes. The third son, Mulciber, had a furious orange hide and was barely larger than his brother Saevus. Last but not least was Alacris, the smallest of the family with dark green scales. He could fly farther and faster than all the others, but was weaker than his brothers.

Daedrin glanced at Tara with wide eyes before he returned his gaze to the magnificent forms and proceeded to circle the table slowly while he stared.

"I… know that none of us met on the best of terms," the one called Sarin said softly; her graceful, elegant voice resonated all throughout the room. "You all have my deepest regrets for the loss of your friend," she added sincerely. "Unfortunately there is much that must be answered still before we decide what must be done with each of you."

"You understate, mother." Fortis received a reprimanding glare from Sarin for his rather brash interruption. "We are extremely wary of newcomers – especially you, Hadrîn," he added with narrowed eyes. "Seventy six years now you've been gone, and your return after such a time should not go unquestioned."

"You are right," Hadrîn agreed. "I would have less respect for you all if I was allowed to return without question, and with strangers in tow, no less… I would like to explain."

Crën nodded, and Hadrîn paused while he collected his thoughts.

"I beg your pardon if some of my tale seems… redundant," he began slowly, "but my companions have not yet heard the fullness of my… adventures. You all know why I left the life I had here," he added as he took in the wary looks of those around him. "With the help of Sharleth I learned how to fortify my mind, locking away the nature of my true self in preparation for a truly desperate plan. After a hundred years of hiding and training, I left to seek Garrôth and… I found him." His voice trailed off for a moment while his eyes grew hazy. "After nearly a year of searching I discovered his hiding place, tucked away in great caverns beneath the old castle. There... I spent the next twenty-five years in his dungeons enduring all manner of torture, including Garrôth's scathing goading at the length of my imprisonment," he added quietly while he raised his tunic to gasps from all, for deep scars were revealed all over his chest and back; too numerous to properly count.

"He made full use of the curse placed upon me," he continued as he lowered his tunic, "carving pieces out of me day after day; sometimes with his own hands, other times by the hand of a few of his minions. Always he would stop so that my body could heal, just so that he could start anew. One would think that such torture could not be endured without breaking, but with each cut my resolve only strengthened... however, it became clear to me that I would never gain his trust, nor have the opportunity to end his life. So, I watched carefully for an opening and when it at last presented itself, I fled his dungeons, narrowly escaping and making my way into the wilderness. For years I carefully eluded his Nasci, weaving through the forest until I stumbled on a narrow path that led nearly to the very peak of the Basilicus Mountains. There, safely away from prying eyes I erected a small cabin where I lived for nearly fifty years in seclusion, only daring to venture out with the greatest of caution when supplies were most needed..." his voice trailed off as he looked on the faces of the council.

"How then did you meet your companions, if you have remained hidden since your escape?" Alacris asked, and the old man frowned.

"I… stumbled upon Daedrin," he said with a nod to the young man before he relayed in brief all that had happened since that day, with Daedrin and Tara interjecting here and there until the tale was concluded.

As the story finished Crën suddenly leaned forward to meet Daedrin's eyes with a piercing gaze.

"What is your lineage, young one?" the old dragon asked softly.

Daedrin smirked at the question. "I… come from Kelmîn," he said slowly, "son of Timeal, son of Aristre; farmers, for several generations."

"Aristre?" Sarin said with a blink. "Impossible! How do you even know this name?"

"I… it was…" Daedrin stumbled while his brow furrowed. "I was taught it, I think…" he said finally, "by my father."

"You are certain this was the name of your great grandfather?" Crën asked as all looked on in bewilderment at the encounter unfolding before them.

Daedrin nodded slowly. "Of course."

"His sword!" Sarin exclaimed suddenly while she peered closely at the hilt that hung low on the young man's belt. "How did we not notice it before now?!"

"Impossible…" Crën muttered softly as he leaned forward; his approach caused Daedrin to shy back.

"You carry the very blade of King Vandin himself," the old dragon told him incredulously. "It was said to have been lost or perhaps stolen in the chaos of the assault on the castle; I could never forget its hilt!"

Daedrin scoffed nervously before he cringed as yet more strange flashes assaulted his mind; his senses he found were slipping from him while he struggled to maintain focus in spite of the growing pain in his temple.

"Absurd." He reached up with one hand to rub his forehead. "My father received it from his father, who was gifted it by his as a purchase from a traveling merchant."

"Royal blood!" Mulciber exclaimed suddenly, but the voice of the dragon seemed to come from far off as a steady ringing began to fill the hearing of the young man while the creature continued. "It must course through his veins!"

"Of course!" Hadrîn exclaimed softly.

"You've all gone mad," Daedrin interrupted with a shake of his head as he took a step back and looked around the room with wide eyes.

"Think, boy," Hadrîn declared suddenly while he moved to meet the gaze of the young man. "The ability that surfaced within when you fought the Nasci, and how you were the only one who could recognize the few ancient scribbles I wrote down."

Daedrin continued shaking his head, for his heart now thumped loudly in his ears.

"Peace, young one," Crën urged softly as he leaned forward, and Daedrin suddenly felt… something, touch his mind. A sense of calm washed over him, like the dew on the grass in the first hours of early morning. He closed his eyes, took in a deep breath and let it out slowly; his pounding heart slowed its rhythm and his racing thoughts began to relax. Lifting his lids he found that all eyes were on him but, it didn't seem so unsettling now.

"How could this be possible?" he asked finally as his gaze rested on Hadrîn, who shook his head.

"It shouldn't be," Crën said at length. "Aristre was the king's nephew... I saw him fall." The old dragon shook his head. "Garrôth was merciless... He saw to it that none with royal blood other than himself was left alive before he fled."

"Yet I... can feel the strength within this young man," Sarin interjected in wonder. "You know it to be true, don't you, young one?" she asked while she peered into Daedrin's eyes.

He frowned and let his lids drift closed as yet more images flickered through his mind of strange but familiar people and places; rolling hills and flat plains covered in rocks and trees with a massive structure behind. It was a castle, he realized, covered by great parapets atop vast walls, and as the building filled his vision it was met also by a face he did not recognize; it was a man, running furiously with a young woman in tow. With a blink he opened his eyes and peered at those around him until his gaze settled on Tara's narrowed brow.

"Aristre... he was not slain," he said slowly as he turned to Crën. "I... can't explain how I know but... much that I do not understand has been happening to me of late..." his voice trailed off while he became immersed in thought.

"Does Garrôth know of the existence of this boy?" Saevus asked with a glance at Hadrîn.

"I should think not," the old man replied. "If he possessed any knowledge of Daedrin or his sword then he would have sent his entire force of Nasci against their village, perhaps even coming into the light himself... you would not have escaped," he added when he caught Daedrin's eyes.

A beat of silence followed, during which Sharleth leaned forward and spoke softly.

"You all lost your home," she declared; it wasn't a question, but rather a mournful statement. Tara bowed her head while Daedrin swallowed hard and nodded.

"The Nasci attacked," he told the council, "suddenly and with such a ferocity that we had no hope of defense. Though there were... three, including myself who made it out, to my knowledge Tara and I are all that now remain of what once was hundreds."

The grieved silence that followed was ominous, and Daedrin thought that he could almost feel the pain of the dragons when this knowledge washed over them.

"I am truly sorry for all you have lost," Sarin said softly with a glance at her mate for a few silent moments before she turned once more to the company. "While we cannot bring back those taken from you, our hospitality you shall have. Consider Ímrelet your new home, if you wish it to be so."

"That isn't enough," Daedrin declared forcefully. "I know that I speak truthfully for my companions when I say that we have no purpose now other than to see Garrôth destroyed; a home is the least of our concerns." The vehemence in his voice was not at all lost on those listening while he stepped forward; his voice grew as strength with charisma surfaced from deep within.

"The loyalties of Hadrîn need be questioned no longer. He speaks the truth, I believe; if not, I certainly would be in a dungeon under the knife of Garrôth and not here, with all of you. He brought us here to seek your aid, for I swore an oath at the graves of my family to see that Garrôth pays for what he has done; blood for blood, I swore. Will you help us?"

After a few moments of silence during which the dragons looked all around at one another but said nothing, Crën lifted his head.

"Your arrival with that of the blade you carry I think is a sign that the time is soon coming when we should strike," he declared. "Our aid, you shall have. Let us stand united, and see Garrôth removed from his hidden throne once and for all."

Daedrin felt his heart surge as a smile fueled by hate touched his lips.

"What can we do now?" he asked. "Surely you have some plan after all this time."

Crën looked around at his wife and sons while his eyes narrowed. "We have someone who can be of great help to us, should he be convinced to turn on Garrôth," he said.

Hadrîn nearly choked as he laughed aloud. "You still hold hope for that notion?" he asked incredulously. "If nearly two hundred years has taught us anything it surely has proven that he will not surrender his allegiance."

"Perhaps the lost descendant of the King can convince him of the corruption of Garrôth," Alacris suggested.

"Perhaps," Crën agreed with a dip of his head as he turned to the confused faces of both Daedrin and Tara. "We have locked away here in the city one who aided Garrôth in his uprising so long ago," he told the pair; the narrowed eyes of the young man and woman at this declaration did not go unnoticed. "We have kept him here in the hopes that he would one day see the folly of his ways and use his knowledge and power to lead us to victory against Garrôth. However his mind is unique, and he has proven to be stubborn beyond reason; none here have been able to reach him with the truth."

"What power could this person possibly possess that would stay your hand of vengeance?" Daedrin asked angrily.

"For one, we do not take the life of another unless we must," Sarin said. "Nor do we execute prisoners," she added with a look at Daedrin's fiery eyes. "But he once was an angel, sent by the Creator in ages past to aid in the forging of the blade you now carry. It was crafted with the combined wisdom and might of Garrôth, when once he was still loyal to righteousness, together with myself and Crën, created by and imbued with the power of holiness from an angel turned mortal and given as a gift to King Vandin." She dipped her head. "Perhaps just the sight of this weapon alone will be enough to remind our prisoner of his reason for coming to earth, and break his mind of the illusion of innocence he sees in Garrôth."

Daedrin at first felt a fury that built within him until more images flickered briefly through his mind of a strange man with white hair; he stood with a look of utter horror etched deeply into his features.

"What is his name?" he asked at length.

"Gavron," Alacris replied with a slow, intent look at Daedrin when the young man closed his eyes. "Does this strike you as familiar?"

Yes, Daedrin thought to himself with a frown as he nodded. "Indeed," he said aloud, "though I am finding of late that many things that should be entirely foreign seem almost like a distant memory," he added quietly. "I wish to speak with him." He turned his furious gaze to Crën, who dipped his head after a few moments of quiet contemplation.

"Very well," the old dragon consented. "Ishail can lead you to him, now if you wish." Daedrin nodded and turned to the door as Crën motioned to the guard, who knocked thrice on the wood; a creak and groan was heard when they swung open.

"You're wasting your time, lad," Hadrîn told him as Ishail made a motion for Daedrin to follow.

The young man paused. "Perhaps," he said with a shake of his head. "But if my time with you has taught me nothing else, it's that anything is possible," he added with a glance to the old man's left forearm before he turned to the door; Tara grabbed his arm as he passed.

After a few moments of silent searching she said simply, "Be careful." He nodded before proceeding to follow Ishail when he exited the council chamber; the doors shut soundly behind him as they moved down the street.

CHAPTER 11

THE FALLEN

"What should I expect of this prisoner, Ishail?" Daedrin asked as he took note of the man's dark, short hair and well-built torso while he walked beside him.

The tall guard glanced at him with brown eye's that were level with Daedrin's own.

"He is dangerous, if nothing else," he said, and his gaze narrowed while he continued. "When I was a boy he feigned innocence, and was released. He tried to escape then and was nearly successful, slaying many before he was caught and sealed with more care than ever. I suggest caution, for he will likely try to deceive you. You must fortify your mind," he tapped his temple with one finger, "and do not expect anything beyond his self-deception." They continued in silence past the occasional villager that roamed the streets until they came at last to a stone wall near the edge of the city.

"Are you prepared?" Ishail asked, and Daedrin's brow furrowed.

"What is this?" he asked with a wave at the wall. The guard stepped forward, placed one hand on the stone and pressed hard until his hand broke through the surface with a ripple like that of a pebble entering a pool of murky water.

"Come," he urged with a motion to Daedrin with his free hand, and the lips of the young man parted in astonishment when Ishail stepped forward and disappeared from view. With lips twitching he copied the gesture of the guard, pushing harder until his hand moved through the barrier. Taking in a deep breath Daedrin took one step, then two and found himself quite suddenly in a dark passage, wide enough to fit a dragon even so large as Crën; it was lit dimly by the fire of a blazing torch held by the guard.

"Follow me," Ishail said while he moved slowly down the tunnel. Daedrin kept close behind with eyes that blinked as they took in the strange inscriptions that covered the walls, floor and ceiling. They glowed slightly in the light of the torch, and like the writing shown to him by Hadrîn the scrawled letters felt familiar; they were like a faint memory that was just out of reach. After a few moments they rounded a corner and the tunnel widened into a massive, slightly oval room that was dimly lit by several torches along its walls. Two guards rose from their wooden chairs at the end of the passage and threw a salute to Ishail as the pair entered; the man responded with a wave of one hand.

Five massive cutouts in the stone, large enough to house a dragon lined the curved back wall; each was sealed tightly with slatted steel doors. These glowed slightly as well with etchings of ancient scribblings that spiraled over each section. All but the centermost cell were empty, and in it the strangest of men lay with his back to them on a small cot that was set against the back wall. His hair was brilliant white like fresh winter snow and seemed to be perfectly straight and smooth, for it nearly blended in with his plain bleached cloak.

"Gavron," Ishail called out as he approached the bars and gave a quick rap on the steel with his knuckles. A dull clang rang out in the cavern, however the man made no move nor gave any notion that he had even heard the sound.

The guard sighed and motioned for Daedrin to approach. "Someone wishes to speak with you," he added with a step back when the young man moved closer.

"Why?" Daedrin asked finally after several moments of silence; his throat was tense even as the single word escaped his lips. Simple though it was the power in his voice caused the question to ring out with an echo and even seem to linger in the air a while before the room was plunged into silence once more.

After a few moments Gavron turned, swung his legs over the side of his cot and stood. Daedrin was astonished at the size of the man now before him, for he was a full head taller than the young man with broad, muscular shoulders evident beneath the folds of his snowy cloak and crisp, brilliantly white hair that hung below his shoulders. He looked Daedrin up and down with eyes that narrowed when they came to rest on the hilt of the sword that hung low on his belt.

"How did you come by that?" Gavron finally spoke with a fair voice that echoed despite the tight clench to his jaw; Daedrin moved his hand over the hilt absently before he replied.

"It was given to me by my father, who received it from his father before him."

Gavron sneered. "It does not belong to you," he said as he took a step closer and placed his hands on the bars. The moved caused Daedrin to blink while he ignored the urge to step back and increase the distance between himself and the brilliant golden eyes of the fierce looking man.

"Garrôth forfeit his right to this blade with his betrayal," he declared as he met Gavron's eyes with a level gaze; the knuckles of the prisoner whitened when his grip on the bars tightened.

"Are the lies spread so freely after all this time?" Gavron asked with a fire in his eyes, and Daedrin paused for a few moments as the wheels of his mind turned.

"Much of the history of our realm has been lost," he said finally, "and what remains is chopped; broken and twisted by the countless re-telling…" his voice trailed off while he pondered what little he knew of the prisoner when he suddenly cringed as images and words flashed through his mind; though painful they brought with them a strange idea. "Is it true that none other than yourself can more accurately judge the character of a man, simply from the look in his eyes?" he asked slowly while hiding his own astonishment at the question once it had left his lips.

"I would not be locked away for countless years were it not so."

Daedrin dipped his head and leaned forward while his thoughts brimmed with a quiet clarity.

"Look upon me, then," he challenged, "while I share my story.

Judge then for yourself whether I speak the truth or not." Gavron was silent for a moment before he chuckled and stepped back with a wave of his hand.

"Proceed." His face was lit with amusement when the simple word left his lips.

Daedrin ignored the warning from Ishail behind him as he stepped closer and placed his hands on the bars before he leaned in and locked his gaze with the prisoner.

"I stand before you as one who has lost all that is dearest to me," he began, "and since that time I've found a new purpose in light of my suffering, and I assure you, it is as clear as fresh spring water. I know from the deepest part of me that this path I am on is guided by eyes open, discerning rightly that Garrôth is the one responsible for destroying what I cared for most in this world. I know this because of one simple truth; his creatures, these Nasci are the beasts who carried out the deed, and none with the power and authority that Garrôth does himself possess would allow a subject under his control to commit any act without his consent. Such conduct would lead to a slow but steady loss of control, and Garrôth would be unable to retain power over his minions."

Daedrin kept his eyes locked with Gavron while he spoke with charismatic words that reverberated throughout the cell. When he was finished the fallen angel moved forward to place his hands on the bars once again as he leaned in until he was just inches from the young man's face.

"Who is to say that those destroyed did not deserve the

judgement carried out by the Nasci?" Gavron asked quietly.

Daedrin kept eyes locked, and the intensity of his gaze gave his every utterance a dramatic weight and power.

"I knew every single person needlessly slaughtered by those creatures," he said evenly, "and each one was more innocent than you or I could ever hope to be."

Several beats of silence followed while Ishail anxiously watched the whole encounter unfold before him until finally Gavron stepped back as the fire in his eyes dimmed and he bowed his head.

"I believe you speak the truth," he said quietly while he moved back to sit on the cot.

"It's a trick," Ishail interjected suddenly with eyes ablaze as he stepped forward while Gavron lifted his head to meet the fiery gaze of the guard.

"Nay Ishail," he told the guard softly; his voice was filled with deep sorrow. "I've known in my heart the truth since my recapture... easier to believe the lie," he added quietly as he bowed his head over clasped hands, with elbows that came to rest on his knees. Daedrin looked over with raised brow at Ishail and noted that the two guards at the entrance had risen to approach the cell where they now looked on in utter disbelief at the events unfolding.

"Gavron," Ishail said angrily as moved up to the bars. "Gavron!" he repeated a little louder, and a clang echoed throughout the room when he banged a clenched fist on the door.

"It's a trick," he declared again when he received no reply. Then, with a sudden turn he whirled about and pointed at the two guards.

"Remain at your post!" he commanded as he marched past Daedrin; the men scrambled to stand at the entrance to the room while Ishail exited with the young man close behind. Nothing was said as they moved through the tunnel until they eventually came to the false wall where Ishail hung his torch back in its place in the tunnel before pushing through and disappearing. Daedrin took in a deep breath when he approached the barrier and followed to come out once more into the brilliant sunlight that blanketed the streets of Ímrelet. He hurriedly moved forward to close the distance already between he and Ishail as the guard moved swiftly through the city, and in just a few minutes time they were nearing the entrance to the council chamber. The guards pulled the doors open when they approached and allowed them to enter before they closed the doors tightly behind.

"Ishail?!" Crën exclaimed when he took in the troubled look on the man's face.

"What's happened?!" Fortis added as a tiny burst of flame erupted from one nostril and he leaned forward with eyes ablaze. The guard stood there for a few moments at first and breathed heavily with narrowed gaze before he spoke.

"The prisoner claims to acknowledge his erroneous judgement in aiding Garrôth... 'easier to believe the lie', he said." Ishail's jaw clenched while one hand clutched the pommel of his sword.

Fortis cursed and took off with a sudden leap and rush of wings, quickly followed by his brothers together with Crën; all disappeared in a few moments to leave Daedrin and the others in stunned silence.

With arms raised Daedrin blurted, "Isn't this what you all wanted?!" as he turned to face Ishail, but he found that the man was already exiting the room. Waving for his companions to follow he went after the guard, who was already running briskly away toward the prison. After rushing to keep up they arrived at the hidden wall in just a few moments where Ishail disappeared without slowing his pace; while Tara stumbled to a halt Hadrîn kept moving and plunged through the barrier without hesitation. Daedrin grabbed the hand of the healer and muttered quick words of consolation as he pulled her forward. She moved behind the young man with her free hand outstretched when he pressed forward until first her fingers and then the rest of her body moved past the wall and into the tunnel beyond.

With eyes adjusting to the dark they stood blinking for a few moments until Daedrin took note of faint torchlight up ahead.

"This way," he said as he walked toward the modest flames. They crept down the passageway until they rounded the bend that brought the oval room into view. The sight that greeted their eyes was truly strange to behold, for both Alacris and Saevus had their brutish forelegs wrapped around those of Fortis, who lay pinned on his side beneath his brothers while a low, angry rumble emanated deep from within his chest, and his lethal fangs were bared in a monstrous growl. Mulciber stood next to his father, both of whom had prison cells at their backs while they faced the subdued dragon. Ishail stood off to the side near the other two human guards; each had a hand on their sword hilts as they stood and tensely watched the situation unfold. Tara and Daedrin moved to join Hadrîn, who stood a few paces behind the confrontation with one hand resting on the pommel of his own blade.

"Be still, my son!" Crën commanded. "Peace!" he added as he bent his head down to look Fortis in the eyes. After a few moments the breathing of the pinned dragon slowed and he let his head move down to rest on the cold stone. At a nod from their father Alacris and Saevus then released the hold over their brother and allowed him to rise slowly.

Fortis shook his massive torso and craned his neck to the side in a stretching motion before he spoke.

"Why does he still draw breath?" he asked with one scaly claw directed at Gavron. "It isn't enough that he kills several of our people in a failed attempt to escape after feigning to have changed," he continued heatedly, "but now he mocks us, openly putting on display our shame for our failure?"

"He's right," Ishail agreed as he took a step forward. "He breaks his silence after so many years, only to speak the very lies he once used to prey on our hopes before?" The guard shook his head. "He is a fool if he believes we will fall for his schemes a second time."

"I say we put an end to him," Fortis declared angrily, "place his head in a crate and – ,"

"Enough!" Alacris interrupted his brother with a stamp of his foot on the floor. "Execution has never been considered by our race," he added with a glare.

"Perhaps it is time to start!" Fortis roared as he turned to give his brother a level stare. "Why do we even bother with the resources to keep such a dangerous creature alive?" he added with a wave in Gavron's direction.

"Because," Saevus interjected, "as it has always been, we have no other choice."

"Maybe in ages past," Fortis replied, "but now real hope has been brought to us; this human!" He pointed at Daedrin. "The return of the royal bloodline brings with it more of a chance for victory than the notion of redeeming the traitor ever has!"

"The arrival of the boy is more reason than ever to keep him alive, treacherous or no," Mulciber argued as he looked to his father, who dipped his head in agreement.

"Mulciber speaks rightly," Crën said. "But the choice is not ours alone, I feel," he added with a look at Daedrin.

"What say you, young one?" he asked softly. "It was your ancestors as well as ours who were slain as a result of Gavron's treachery."

Fortis snorted. "What relevance can this human —,"

"Silence!" Crën commanded as he cast a level stare at his son before turning again to Daedrin.

After a beat of quiet the young man let one hand fiddle absently with his sword before he moved slowly toward Gavron's cell; Crën and Mulciber stepped aside and allowed him to approach.

All watched intently as he continued forward and stopped just a pace away from the bars while he looked upon the alert man who now stood before him.

"Words from a language that should be entirely unknown to me somehow feel... familiar," he said, "and fighting... has become a natural instinct, with more ability than my father ever granted to me through his teaching." Daedrin frowned and turned slightly to look at all of the faces in the room before he let his gaze settle again on the prisoner. "I should want nothing more than to remove your head from your shoulders after what you've done, and yet when I look on your face I... do not feel anger as I expected I would when I first laid eyes on you. What do you see when you look at my face?" He asked suddenly, and he stood firm when Gavron moved forward to place his hands on the steel cage.

"Strength," he replied, "akin to that observed of Garrôth, with his father and brother."

"Convenient lies!" Fortis declared heatedly. "We have alluded to as much here in his presence!"

"Take my power," Gavron exclaimed suddenly.

"Take it?" Saevus asked incredulously. "How?"

"My magical strength comes from the angelic spirit residing within this human skin. It can be separated, leaving behind the weak spirit of my mortal body."

All were quiet for a few moments while they pondered this idea, until at last Alacris smirked and said, "What harm can there be in trying?"

Ishail however shook his head.

"How are we to know it isn't another trick?" he asked. "We have no way to discern whether his power is truly gone."

"Daedrin should be able," Hadrîn said with a nod in the young man's direction. "The ancestral blood would grant him the strength to feel the magic inside another." He turned then, approached Daedrin and placed one hand on his arm.

"Focus," the old man told him as he pointed at Gavron, "let your instinct guide you as it did with the language I scrawled back in the wilderness."

With a sigh Daedrin looked intently at Gavron and, after a moment he found that he was reaching out with his mind to touch the essence of thought in the prisoner, though how he knew that was what he was doing was beyond his reckoning. Slowly he felt... something; deep and loud it was, like the rumbling of a rushing river as it poured over a high ridge before crashing down onto the surface of the water far below. He stepped back and blinked.

"I... can feel it," he exclaimed softly, "something... powerful. I... can't explain it," he added with a frown.

"Incredible," Hadrîn declared as he glanced at Crën, and the old dragon dipped his chin.

"What do you need?" he asked when he turned his gaze to the prisoner, who responded with a slow shake of his head.

"Nothing on this earth can contain the essence of my spirit," Gavron said while he slowly bent to one knee and clasped his two hands together with one crossed over the other.

As he took in a deep breath a red light began to emanate and escape from beneath the tight grip of his fingers. Sweat began to bead on his forehead, a curious thing to behold for the dragons who had never before seen any such sign of weakness or exertion from the angel. Slowly they noticed that his form began to change, for his hair gently turned from the brilliant shade of white to a faded blonde, and the muscular shoulders became diminished beneath a cloak that now fit loosely over a figure that stood at the same height as Daedrin.

After a few moments more the light faded and Gavron released the air from his lungs slowly and swayed slightly as if struggling to maintain his balance. Finally he opened his eyes, shakily rose to his feet and moved toward the bars; he stumbled when he reached them. With one hand clinging tightly to the steel he extended the other out and opened his palm to reveal some sort of gemstone. It was deep red; a ruby, Daedrin realized once he had moved closer to inspect the faintly glowing object.

"Take it," Gavron said weakly while his hand trembled. "But be careful not to let anyone other than yourself touch the stone," he added as he locked eyes with Daedrin. "None but those with angelic blood can handle the power contained within this gem without being utterly destroyed."

The young man nodded as he slowly reached out and gently plucked the object from the palm of the prisoner's hand. He inhaled sharply when it touched his skin, and he closed his eyes and stepped back while his fist clenched tightly around the stone. His whole body seemed to tingle as the power of the object pulsed through him, for it seemed to reach deep into the core of his being and activate some great strength that up until that moment had remained subdued. After a few moments that felt like an eternity he opened his eyes and breathed slowly, and it seemed to him that the gem pulsed in rhythm to his own heartbeat. He lifted wide eyes to meet Gavron's weak stare and reached out easily now with his mind to find... nothing.

"He is... weak," Daedrin said finally with a slight shake of his head. "I... can no longer feel the strength within," he broke his stare to look upon the gem in his hand. "But this... I feel the power within this stone." *It's... intoxicating,* he thought to himself while his lips curled with a gentle grin. "How he has done it I cannot say but... I believe that he has indeed relinquished his power."

"Lies," Fortis declared with a snort. "He means to entice us with this illusion so that we will release him from his cell."

"Don't release me," Gavron said from his place against the bars. "Leave me here. I can teach the boy much from within my confinement."

"I would like to learn." Daedrin drew the attention of all in the room with his sudden declaration. *If he can teach me how to harness the power within this gem...* his thoughts trailed off and his lips twitched. "These past days have been filled with confusion," he said aloud, "raising more questions than I care to admit. If Gavron can unravel some of the mystery then I shall entertain the notion of his newfound remorse."

For a while the room was silent while Crën looked around at all of his sons, each of whom dipped his head after a time.

"Use caution, young one," he said finally. "The actions of this traitor can neither be undone nor forgotten through one act, no matter how great the gesture may appear."

"Time should tell whether Gavron speaks the truth," Hadrîn

interjected with narrowed eyes. "In the days of old even he in the fullness of his power could hold no advantage over the focused might of King Vandin."

Daedrin looked once more to Gavron as the prisoner dipped his head.

"I will prove myself by my knowledge and instruction, I swear…" the voice of the angel-turned-mortal trailed off and his face scrunched up in a look of discomfort; he closed his eyes and slid down to his knees while still clutching the bars.

"Another ruse?" Ishail asked as he warily stepped forward; he was careful to keep one hand ever ready on the hilt of his sword.

Gavron shook his head and looked up.

"I… am weak," he said shakily. "Without my angelic spirit giving me strength, this mortal form is… well, mortal," he added with a light chuckle.

Ishail's lips twitched. "Grendal," he said with a motion to one of the other guards, "see to it that the prisoner receives a meal; bread only," he added, "with water."

The one called Grendal nodded as he grasped a torch with his right hand and quickly exited the room.

"Come," Crën urged with a motion of one scaly claw. "We will leave the prisoner to his rest. There… is much to discuss…" he paused as his eyes narrowed. "Ishail, will you remain here?" he asked with a look to the guard, who nodded and gave a light bow.

CHAPTER 12

GIFTS

As the dragons moved single file out of the room and into the tunnel beyond Daedrin backed slowly away from the cell and passed his companions before he removed a torch from the wall and entered the passage himself; he was followed closely by both Tara and Hadrîn. A few moments took them to the barrier where the torch was placed onto an empty mount before they pressed through and found themselves standing in the brilliant glow of the sun as it hung directly over the city. A quick glance upward showed the dragons flying overhead with a course that looked to be carrying them to the council chamber.

"What will you do with it?" Tara asked as she looked to Daedrin's tightly clenched fist that still held the stone he had been given be the fallen angel. He shook his head slowly while he opened his hand and allowed his eyes to take in the remarkable object that rested in his palm before he tucked it securely into a pouch on his belt. The strange heated sensation in his veins dissipated the moment the gem left its contact with his skin, leaving Daedrin to feel almost weak in comparison to the few moments he had held the stone; he found then that he had to resist the urge to immediately retrieve the device and feel that intoxicating power once more.

"I'm not sure," he said slowly as they began to make their way through the city. His imagination ran wild while he pondered the possibilities that arose in light of this newfound power. "Gavron made it quite clear that none but I must touch it, which I can understand after..." he blinked and shook his head. "None of this makes any sense but then... it serves to explain everything." He glanced at Tara's narrowed gaze. "The... dreams, the bizarre familiarity of a language I'd never before laid eyes on... except for the inscription on my sword..." his voice trailed off as he looked away and his eyes narrowed. "Angelic blood," he smirked. "Perhaps the power within the stone will help to see my oaths fulfilled... even if it means that I must draw my final breath as the fatal stroke is dealt, I will see it done," he added solemnly.

Tara frowned while she eyed the man beside her and reached out to take his hand in her own. They continued in an ominous silence for the remainder of the journey until the doors of the council chamber came into view. As the three approached the guards dipped their heads, swung open the doors and allowed them to pass unhindered. Once they had crossed the threshold they were greeted by the wonderful aroma of beef stew; Daedrin smiled lightly when he beheld Lonen and his compatriots with bowls in hand. When the vittles had been distributed the company all took a seat around the large stone table where they ate and listened to the dragons.

"I still believe that this is a foolish decision," Fortis was saying with a sneer. "Gavron has played on our hopes before, and we suffered as a result."

"You may very well be right," Sharleth told him as she nuzzled her neck against the deep red of the eldest brother's neck. "But there is always room for redemption," she added. "Is that not what we have always believed?"

Fortis huffed while Crën dipped his head.

"This is the very reason we have held Gavron all these years," the old dragon said. "We have kept our faith in the Creator revealed to us by King Vandin so long ago, and it has never led us astray."

"Hasn't it?" Mulciber asked with a frown. "Look where we are today… for nearly two hundred years our race has been forced to remain hidden away while the rest of the world suffers at the hand of Garrôth. Why would the Creator you have always spoken so highly of allow such fell deeds to occur for so many long years?"

"Our present state is one of our own making," Sarin interjected; her elegant voice radiated throughout the room as she spoke. "It was Crën and I who abandoned the search for Garrôth after he had destroyed the kingdom. We followed our own code instead of the one established by King Vandin, and as a result Garrôth was allowed to be set free to rain destruction down upon all."

Fortis snorted. "So the Creator allows all in the land to suffer for generations because of one failure? It was he who sent Gavron to our realm in the first place, as one who was meant to aid us, not see our land destroyed under a tyrant! Why does he not claim responsibility?"

"He has," Alacris cut in as he lifted his head. "He has sent us Daedrin. Don't you see? Mother and father have shared with us how they saw with their own eyes all of the royals slain under Garrôth's cruelty and yet here before us is one of royal blood, carrying even the very sword of the King."

"What kind of benevolent Creator would allow so many years of death to pass before setting things right?" Daedrin, having finished his meal stood now as he spoke angrily. "Even if I truly am descended of this... Vandin, then I cannot say I have any desire to serve his Creator."

"And has everyone forgotten Sharleth?" Saevus asked quietly; his question was met with an ominous silence while Daedrin and his companions looked around at the forlorn faces before Tara asked, "What's wrong with Sharleth?"

Hadrîn sighed and spoke after a few moments.

"She is barren," he said softly; Tara and Daedrin blinked as this profound information sunk in.

"Can you no longer bear children, either?" the healer asked Sarin, who shook her head.

"Sadly my time has passed," she said mournfully. "Our hopes for preserving our race lay with Sharleth, but it seems that such is not the way of the Creator..." her voice trailed off as she closed her eyes and a rather large tear slid down her cheek; Crën cleared his throat after a beat of silence.

"We still must do all in our power to free Silmaín," he declared. "This has always been our duty; we failed before, and yet the Creator has given us hope in spite of it. Even if it is the last act of our race we must see it done."

Fortis huffed angrily and with a rush of wings leapt into the air and disappeared from view, with Sharleth quickly following.

"Maybe you can help her," Tara suggested softly as she leaned in to whisper in Daedrin's ear. "Using the power within the stone."

Why would I help those who abandoned the realm when they were needed most? The thought drifted through his mind before he frowned and nodded slowly. "I… cannot fathom the grief you all must be facing in light of this," Daedrin said. "It was my ancestor, it seems who brought your species to this ruin, so in light of this I would like to make another vow…" He paused and waited for those in the room to turn their full attention to him before he continued. "I know not the full power of the blood that courses through my veins, but if there is ever a way to restore Sharleth, I swear to you that I will find it and make certain that the dragons live on for many ages to come."

"A most humbling and worthy sentiment, Daedrin," Crën said with a low bow that was copied by the others. "But our time on this earth has taught us nothing if we believe that any other than the Creator himself can bring such healing."

Daedrin smirked but said no more as he sunk into deep thought and allowed the chamber to fall into silence for a while.

"What more can you tell me of Gavron?" he asked finally.

Crën frowned. "What little we know has already been shared with you," he said.

Daedrin nodded slowly before he glanced at Tara. "I wish to return to him," he said. "Perhaps he can shed some light on whatever has caused Sharleth to become barren."

Crën dipped his head. "You need not seek permission," he told him. "While trust ought be earned, I believe our faith is rightly placed in you, young one."

Daedrin dipped his head and turned; he paused when Tara grabbed his hand.

"I'm coming with you," she said firmly as she locked her gaze with his heavy eyes. With a short nod to her he moved to the doors and knocked thrice as Ishail had done before. The wood creaked when the hinges swung open and they pair quickly left the oval room behind as they made their way down the street.

Daedrin grimaced, for his temple began to throb while flashes touched his mind; brief glimpses of strange scenes and faces. Some only felt familiar while others he realized belonged to Crën and Sarin, though the shapes in his vision were much smaller and more brilliant than those of the dragons he had met. He shook his head and banishing the flickering images as he continued forward with Tara watching quietly by his side. After a few minutes they came to the barrier, and this time neither hesitated but pressed through and immediately plunged into the dimly lit tunnel where Daedrin grasped a lit torch from the wall and led the way down the passage.

Ishail rose to greet them when they entered the oval room, a sentiment that Daedrin responded to with a nod before moving past the guard as he approached the cell containing Gavron.

"You never answered my question before," he said, casting aside for the moment all thoughts of his promise to restore Sharleth while he stopped just a few paces away from the bars; his eyes caught briefly an empty dish and cup off to the side.

The former angel rose to his feet. "You wish to know why I supported Garrôth," he said softly; his fair voice resonated quietly throughout the room. Daedrin nodded while the eyes of the prisoner narrowed.

"I was a fool," he muttered with a light shake of his head. "Garrôth befriended me, and over the course of time I saw how he was mistreated by Candrin, his older brother... beheld the spell that his father, King Vandin, seemed to be under whenever it came to Candrin. It wasn't long before Garrôth began to convince me that his father had become corrupt, and he implored me to aid him in a peaceful coup."

"How was he able to deceive you?"

Gavron huffed and moved to sit with head hung low while he continued.

"Instead of seeking the counsel of my Creator, I took matters into my own hands," he replied quietly, "operating by my own wisdom. In an image similar to that of the Grenleth I created the creatures that now plague the land... the Nasci. I meant for them to have only instinct but Garrôth convinced me that it would be well for them to possess intelligence, able to think and speak while branding into their core complete subservience to him and myself." He paused for a few moments and shook his head while he absently rubbed his jaw with one hand. "I created one hundred and fifty of the beasts, for that was all we needed for our plan to invade the castle quickly by force, taking the inhabitants along with the royal guard prisoner as we went."

Gavron chuckled then with a low, sad sound as he continued. "Garrôth changed the plan at the last moment, urging me to keep my involvement hidden, in case the coup did not go as smoothly as we had hoped. So, I moved ahead of him and our army to the royal chambers and conversed with the King, together with Candrin his eldest son, as well as Aristre, the King's nephew. It wasn't long before there were screams from the castle streets, joined by the angry cries of those being taken. I urged the King to remain with his family in the royal chambers, where they were safe. Garrôth himself entered soon after, challenging his father and urging him to lay down his arms and surrender the throne. King Vandin was... displeased. He used his magic to subdue Garrôth, who then pleaded with me to come to his aid..." His voice trailed off as a single tear slid down one cheek before he cleared his throat.

"While the King was distracted I intervened with my own angelic might, intending only to force him to give up but... I misjudged, and Vandin was slain, by my own hand..." Gavron shook his head. "Everything fell apart so quickly after that," he said softly, "for Candrin took up the sword of his father; that blade," he added as he pointed at the sword hanging low on Daedrin's belt. "He fought with his brother while I stood back, horrified at my own actions..." Gavron stood now and turned his back to Daedrin while he walked slowly to the back wall of his cell where he reached out to rest both hands flat against the cold surface.

"The battle was over in moments, ending with Garrôth piercing his own brothers heart before quickly turning to Aristre, slaying him as well with a quick blow... though, it seems clear to me now that somehow both our eyes were deceived and one at least was not slain, for here you stand."

Daedrin swallowed hard as he ran one hand over the hilt of his blade, for his thoughts with their questions were interrupted when a brief and searing pain suddenly shot through his chest while a blurred image flashed through his mind; merciless eyes full of hate filled his vision for a moment and he looked down with a grimace before he blinked as it faded when he felt a hand touch his shoulder. He looked up to see Tara's worried gaze meet his own while her fingers rested on his cloak; with a deep breath he turned his eyes back to Gavron and was met by a piercing stare.

"You felt something, didn't you?" the fallen angel asked as his eyes narrowed.

Daedrin's lips curled slightly and he nodded. "Pain," he replied slowly, "in my chest, and... eyes, full of malice seemed to fill my vision for a moment."

Gavron's cheeks twitched with a curve that looked almost like a smirk as he moved closer.

"Have you experienced such things in the past?"

After a few moments Daedrin dipped his head. "These... flashes, they could perhaps be called have been occurring more and more frequently... you know something of what I've been experiencing, don't you?" he asked pensively, and Gavron nodded.

"The blood coursing through your veins is... special," he said.

"You have… gifts, granted by the Creator to King Vandin for his righteousness, and by extension his descendants."

Daedrin moved up to grasp the bars with both hands.

"What can you tell me of these 'gifts'"?

Gavron shrugged as he moved to sit on the cot. "What would you like to know?"

"I've been experiencing… familiarity," Daedrin began slowly while he collected his thoughts. "Things that should be foreign to me seem almost like a distant memory, and the skills my father taught me with a blade have been surpassed by a sort of… instinct that takes hold when the need arises."

Gavron nodded as the young man spoke.

"You are experiencing what your ancestors called 'epegenetic haereditatem'," he said.

Daedrin's brow furrowed when again the sense of familiarity combined with the foreign sound of the language that was spoken by the fallen angel.

"It would best mean in the common tongue 'inheritance of memory'," Gavron explained. "It's a sort of… imprint, you could say. The past experiences of your ancestors are branded into the very core of who you are, allowing you to learn from their success or failures; even so far as to grant the knowledge to harness abilities that had been learned by the previous generations."

Daedrin couldn't help but marvel as this reality sunk in, for he somehow knew from deep within that what Gavron said was indeed true. He took in a deep breath when the full implications of this ability drifted through his mind.

"I have the very knowledge of my ancestors…"

Gavron shook his head slightly. "Not quite," he said, "though that is near the mark. A more accurate way to think of it would be to say that you have the ability to harness their knowledge to supplement your own."

Daedrin shook his head as his eyes gleamed ever so slightly.

"Can you teach me to fully use this… inheritance of memory?" he asked, and Gavron dipped his head.

"Epigenetic haereditatem," he said. "Yes, I indeed can. I have the same ability, or at least I once did when I lived with the Creator in his palace."

Daedrin tilted his head to one side. "The King was given an ability of the angels?"

Gavron smiled lightly. "Indeed," he said. "This was but one of the gifts with which he was so graced by the Creator, who marked the blood of your ancestors with that of his angels, thus granting to the King and his descendants some of the power he had already bestowed to the servants of creation. He meant these gifts to be used as tools for righteousness across the land."

Daedrin huffed. "It would seem he failed in that regard."

"Who failed?" the fallen angel asked with a frown.

"The Creator," Daedrin said, and Gavron blinked while the young man continued. "His 'gift' has caused the turmoil our land now faces."

Gavron shook his head. "You are wrong. The Creator makes no

mistakes. It is his creation that sometimes falls short of the mark."

Daedrin's felt his eyes turn cold at this declaration as he pushed away from the bars and backed away a few paces. With teeth grinding he turned slowly and started to move while the voice of Tara barely reached his ears and his pace quickened. He exited the prison and entered the passageway beyond before quickly coming out into the now dim light of a sun whose rays could just barely be seen over the edge of the city. Taking a deep breath he moved forward and made his way through the streets while ignoring the nod and wave of the occasional villager that he passed before he soon came to the room he had been assigned.

After swinging open the solid oak door and stepping inside he jerked his hand with the intention of slamming it shut behind him but was instead stopped by Tara, who caught it with one outstretched arm as she met his eyes with a mixed gaze of worry and anger. He stared at her for a few moments while his jaw clenched and furious thoughts filled his mind before he turned and moved across the plainly furnished room to the pitcher of water on the table in the corner; ignoring the glass he raised the entire container to his lips and took several long, deep swigs. He set it down hard in frustration at his racing thoughts and moved to the bed in the corner where he unstrapped his sword and withdrew his bow before removing his boots and lying down with one arm behind his head. As he closed his eyes he let out a long sigh of irritation in an attempt to calm his mind and, after a few moments he became aware of Tara as she slid onto the mattress; she placed an arm across his chest and eyed him carefully while she mouthed silent prayers.

"What are you thinking?" she finally asked softly with a frown at the tight jaw of the man beside her. Daedrin remained quiet for a while as he wrestled with the turmoil in his heart, for he couldn't fight the feeling that the Creator was real, and yet in light of this he could not help but harbor nothing but a steadily growing resentment. Dark images flashed through his mind, first of his family brutally slain, followed by the horrifying sight with the recollection of the putrid smell of those that lay dead in Linull before culminating in the torn and bloodied form of Skane as his friend lay lifeless on the ground.

He sighed heavily and turned to look at the bare wall. "I... cannot question the existence of the Creator," he told her with a quiet frown. "But..." his voice trailed off while his jaw clenched. "He is cruel; one whom I have no intention of following. One I cannot follow..." he added softly as he closed his eyes briefly before opening them and turning to face Tara's narrowed gaze while she looked down at his chest.

"What if... the Creator is bound, by the actions of those he has created?" she asked finally as she lifted her eyes.

Daedrin's lip twitched. "What do you mean?"

Tara's head tilted to the side as she slowly collected her thoughts. "You heard Gavron," she began. "It was righteousness that granted this... Vandin the abilities that are beginning to surface within you. We know that the dragons fled instead of remaining to fight... what if they had stood firm? Perhaps our land would be free." She paused and averted her gaze.

"This realm… it has a certain… order, I think," she reasoned. "We are free to choose our path," she added with narrowed eyes.

"I still don't understand," Daedrin told her as he tried to follow the direction of her reasoning.

"We all breathe," she replied. "We live by working the ground, consuming what we sow. We love," she added while she lifted soulful eyes to meet Daedrin's piercing gaze. "With love comes commitment, and the creating of new life…" her voice trailed off and she cleared her throat as she looked away. "What I mean is, if our lives only progress as far as we are willing to take them, then perhaps the Creator can only move as far as we are willing to go."

Daedrin lay quietly for a while and pondered what she had said before he shook his head. "Perhaps," he said softly. "Though I am not convinced."

Tara smiled. "You have me for that," she declared with a light-hearted twinkle in her eyes. Daedrin returned the look with a brief smile before he averted his gaze as a pang of guilt nudged his heart and he closed weary eyes.

He allowed the room to fall into silence while his heart struggled in somber turmoil. The sun now barely cast it's dim rays through the glass of the window while they remained in silence as its glow slowly faded to leave the room in near total darkness. As the last beam of light slipped away it took with it Daedrin's conscious thought, and he fell into a light sleep…

CHAPTER 13

DREAMS & VISIONS

The young man tossed and turned in a restless slumber as images flowed through his mind while his unconscious thought was carried from memory to memory. After a while it seemed that a voice was reaching out to him, urging him gently awake; he rose suddenly and his eyes took in Tara's familiar face smiling down at him from where she stood by the side of the bed.

"Good morning," Daedrin said with a smile as he swung his legs over the side of the bed and quickly moved to embrace her. She was oddly quiet, he thought, and she was grinning rather foolishly.

"What is it?" he asked, bewildered by her expression while she gave him a mischievous look before moving to the side. Time seemed to slow as Daedrin's heart skipped several beats, for before his eyes was one whose loss he had before mourned bitterly; she now stood in the open doorway, alive and well.

"Marin," he cried weakly, nearly falling to his knees as he stumbled toward her and pulled her into a crushing embrace. They held each other there for several minutes, unmoving as both wept with joy. Finally they pulled away just slightly to let their foreheads touch, and Marin smiled at him with tears streaming down her face as she gently placed a hand on Daedrin's cheek.

The young man breathed deeply and laughed aloud, unable to contain the wonder in his heart as he beheld the beauty before him, for she had exchanged her plain garments for a more elegant dress of a deep, fair blue, like the sky in summertime; its sleeves were short, just covering her slender shoulders. She appeared more lovely to Daedrin's eyes than ever before and, without pausing to consider anything other than his joy and immense relief at finding her well he pulled her close and kissed her gently. When their lips parted they both smiled sheepishly and Marin blushed as she took hold of Daedrin's hands before she led him out of the room where they found Hadrîn waiting for them outside.

"Hadrîn!" Daedrin exclaimed and greeted the old man with a fervent hand-clasp. "This is Marin." He was unable to contain a huge grin when he said the name, a gesture that Hadrîn returned as he took Marin's hand, kissed it gently and caused her to blush fiercely.

"It is an honor to make your acquaintance," he said, "though I can hardly believe my eyes, seeing you alive and well." Daedrin's brow furrowed.

"What do you mean?" he asked, and Hadrîn turned to meet his gaze with a level stare.

"You know as well as I that she perished with the rest of those you once knew from Linull," the old man told him with a frown. Daedrin blinked and took a step back with his lips quivering when

Marin's beautiful face twisted briefly to become covered for a moment in dirt, grime and blood over pale flesh before returning to its flawless state.

"No..." he said softly as tears welled up behind now red eyes and his heart seemed to pound in his chest like mighty thunder.

"Daedrin, what is it?" Marin's voice touched his ears while she approached, but he took a step back, then two; continuing until his back rested against the stone wall behind.

"This is a dream," he whispered as he closed his eyes. Marin smiled, closed the gap between them with four quick strides and pressed her lips against his. When they parted Daedrin opened his eyes to behold her fair face just inches from his own. He leaned in to touch her lips once more, but just before they collided she suddenly was pulled away from him like a wave of the sea as it crashes against the shore before rolling back out to the depths...

"Nnnh!" Daedrin jerked upright and choked back a sob as reality crashed over him.

"Marin..." he whispered softly while his chest heaved with one grieved breath after another. He swung his legs over the side of the bed and let his head fall into his hands while he struggled to hold back the river of tears that threatened to burst forth. After a while he became vaguely aware of Tara's hand on his back as he remained that way for several minutes, taking in deep, shaky breaths until his breathing began to relax. Slowly he opened red eyes, lifted his head and blinked as his vision adjusted to the dark, for the room was lit only by dim moonlight that shone through the single window. After rising to his feet he shuffled over to the container of water and poured some of the clear liquid into a shallow basin that was built into the table.

After putting the pitcher back in its place he scooped up some of the water with his hands and splashed the cool liquid onto his face with a sharp inhalation of breath when it touched his skin. He leaned on the table for a few moments before he turned to see Tara eyeing him from the mattress where she lay propped up on one elbow. The all too familiar guilt at having her in his room, innocent though it was filled his heart once more as an image of Marin's fair face flickered through his mind. With a quick blink he shook the notion away as he moved to sit on the edge of the bed where he grabbed his boots from their place on the floor, slid his feet into them and proceeded to tie the laces while Tara rubbed his shoulders gently. Slowly he lifted his head, craned his neck to one side and closed his eyes for a moment before he looked around the room once more. With a glance backward he reached over his shoulder, placed his right hand atop Tara's left and cast a brief smile her direction.

"I... think I shall go out," he said softly. "Perhaps a walk will serve to clear my head."

After a moment Tara nodded. "Would you like me to walk with you?"

Daedrin sighed and shook his head slowly. "It's alright," he told her. "Get some rest," he added as he turned without thinking and kissed her forehead gently. She closed her eyes and let her hands fall to the mattress when he pulled away and rose to his feet.

In a few moments he was armed once more and had exited the room; his cloak he tugged tightly around himself as the cool night air caressed his skin. He made his way through the dimly lit city streets while he sought to keep his thoughts from wandering, though despite his best efforts that is exactly what they did. *Marin…* her name gently drifted through his mind and caused him to wince while his heart skipped a beat. He missed her; this he knew with absolute certainty, and yet the time he had been spending with Tara was serving to quickly replace his feelings for Marin by those of affection toward the healer. *Am I really beginning to love Tara, or is my heart merely exchanging its love for Marin with feelings for another…* he scowled at the thought and sighed as he paused and turned to the building nearest him. With arms outstretched he leaned against the cool stone and closed his eyes while the fair face of Tara briefly filled his vision with her gentle smile, touched by an elegant grace. He took in a deep breath and let it out slowly before he pushed himself away from the wall in frustration and continued to make his way down the street.

Soon he found that he had come to the false wall of the hidden prison and paused for a moment with a blink as he wondered why his subconscious mind had brought him to this place, out of every area in the city. He frowned for a moment before deciding to push through the barrier where he found himself in the dim light of the torches beyond. After grasping one from the wall he moved forward slowly until he came to the oval room where he was greeted by two guards whose faces he did not recognize; despite them being foreign to him, they knew his name and allowed him to pass. He walked slowly toward the bars of Gavron's cell and paused at the edge as he beheld the former angel lying on his side with back to the bars in deep slumber. After a few moments the young man cleared his throat and rapped on the iron with his knuckles; the dull clang as a result echoed throughout the chamber. With a start Gavron rolled over, and his eyes narrowed when he beheld Daedrin standing before him.

"What do you know of dreams?" the young man asked while he fought off the horrific images that threated to fill his mind.

With a sigh Gavron swung his legs over the side of the cot and rolled his neck from side to side.

"I certainly hope you don't intend to make a habit of waking me at your every whim," he said as his jaws widened in a deep yawn. After heaving a second quick sigh he frowned when he lifted his gaze to meet Daedrin's own troubled stare.

"Tell me what you have seen," the prisoner said softly.

For a few moments Daedrin was quiet before he began to relate to Gavron the flashes that had haunted his sleep of late, beginning with a hazy description of the field surrounded by swirls of darkness and concluding with his persistent nightmares regarding Marin. He interjected here and there bits of his own story as the need arose, and when he had finished the fallen angel remained in quiet thought for several minutes.

"These... dreams," he said slowly, "did they begin before or... after you lost those you love?"

Daedrin lips twitched while his eyes narrowed. "Before," he answered finally with a harrumph as he cleared his throat.

"Though... I can never quite remember exactly what I saw in my earliest dreams. Only the faint image of perhaps a blade, with a sense of foreboding... darkness swirling, like a vision of some impending doom."

Gavron sighed. "There are dreams," he said, "and there are what seem to be dreams but are far more intricate by nature."

"What do you mean?" Daedrin asked as he reached out to rest his hands on the bars.

"Visions," Gavron replied. "Often they are a brief glimpse of something to come."

Daedrin blinked and was quiet for a moment while he pondered this statement.

"The future?" he asked, and Gavron dipped his head.

"Very rarely do your kind, humans I mean, see such things. But, visions increasing were a... side effect of sorts, resulting from the power the Creator incorporated into your blood."

Daedrin took in a deep breath and shook his head. "How can I tell the difference?"

Gavron frowned and rubbed his jaw. "At the core, I believe that you must already know which is a dream and which is a vision," he replied. "The differences are subtle, but look deep enough and you can find them. Dreams, for instance, that are intense enough to sometimes seem like a vision are often brought on by something truly traumatic... like the agony you no doubt experience from your loss."

Daedrin hung his head and fought with some irritation tears that suddenly threatened to spring up from the grief in his heart.

"How can I make them stop?" his voice was hoarse as his throat tightened.

"The images you've described... they are of the woman you loved, Marin, or sometimes of your other companions?"

Daedrin nodded, and his jaw clenched while the prisoner continued.

"Yet you do not have such dreams of your family."

The young man shook his head after a moment of silence.

"Nay," he said. "I have seen nothing of my own family during the late hours," he added shamefully.

Gavron leaned forward. "Daedrin," he uttered the name and then waited to continue until he was met by the eyes of the grieving soul. "You need not feel regret or shame."

Daedrin scoffed. "Why should I not?"

"Because," Gavron replied, "as you said before, you laid them to rest. As harsh as such a matter might be, there is a semblance of relief in burying those we have lost that allows the heart to move forward despite the pain of them being gone."

Daedrin pondered this quietly for a few moments.

"You think I should find Marin and..." he choked as his voice trailed off.

Gavron's jaw clenched when he took in the turmoil of the young man before him.

"As difficult as it certainly shall be, that is indeed what I would suggest," he declared solemnly. "I fear you will be haunted by these dark images until your spirit is allowed to leave behind those whom you have lost."

After a beat of silence Daedrin nodded slowly and sniffled for a moment as he pushed away from the cage.

"I... will leave you be," he said while he turned and shuffled past the guards. Quickly he moved through the tunnel and placed the torch back in its place before he pushed through the wall with a frown as his face was caressed by the first dim rays of the morning sun. He heaved a sigh and rubbed weary eyes before he turned to left and blinked, for he beheld Tara watching him quietly from where she leaned against the stone wall.

"This is where your early morning walk took you?" she asked as he approached.

He nodded slowly. "It wasn't intentional," he said. "I... was lost in my own thoughts at first, until I found myself outside the barrier... why are you here?"

Tara smirked as she pushed off of the wall. "I was worried, so I followed you while I took a walk of my own and prayed in the stillness of the night... did our illustrious fallen angel have any insight into the cause of your nightmares?"

Daedrin sighed as he closed the distance between them and nodded lightly. "Yes but... I don't think I'm quite ready to talk of it," he replied softly.

Tara frowned but nodded and turned to walk beside the young man when he strolled slowly past her. They moved in silence through the quiet city streets, and Daedrin found that the faint pulsing glow that surrounded them served to distract his weary mind from the burdens it carried until, as they rounded a corner he stumbled when he ran right into Hadrîn.

"Well good morning," the old man exclaimed with a chuckle as he pushed the young man away.

"Apologies," Daedrin said with a glance at to Tara.

"Where are you headed?" she asked.

"To find a hot meal," Hadrîn replied. "What are the two of you up to?" he added with a smirk.

"Same as you," she told him after a brief glance at the man beside her. "Out for a stroll this fair morning, hoping that Lonen will perhaps be gracious enough to show his hospitality once more."

"After you, then," the old man said with a sweeping gesture.

"Astonishing how wonderful the air is here," Tara said as she absently pulled her cloak tighter around her while they moved down the street.

"How so?" Hadrîn asked with a sideways glance her direction.

"We should be frozen to death at such a height as this place sits, and yet it feels no worse than the onset of winter following a mild year."

"Perhaps it's the glow," Daedrin interjected with an absent shrug. "It certainly seems to radiate some warmth." Both of his companions were silent following this remark as they each gave him a bewildered look after turning their eyes to and fro.

"What glow?" Tara asked finally, and Daedrin's brow furrowed.

"The… glow," he said with a wave of his arms at the surrounding stone. "You can't tell me that you don't see it; the way the city seems to pulse with a faint green light."

Tara looked around once more before she shook her head. "I see plain white stones," she said while Hadrîn chuckled.

"What else do you see, lad?" he asked as he looked at Daedrin with a twinkle in his eyes.

"Well," the young man responded after a beat of silence before clicking his tongue, "the prison. The writing across the stone and metal pulses with a similar emanation."

Tara blinked as her eyes narrowed while Hadrîn's lips curled in a twisted grin.

"Neither of you can see the inscriptions, can you?" Daedrin asked, and they both shook their heads while Tara eyed him carefully.

"I wonder what other strange abilities rest within those veins," Hadrîn mused as he rubbed his jaw absently with one hand.

Daedrin remained quiet when Gavron's words regarding his dreams of late trickled through his mind while they walked. After a few minutes more the now familiar arch that led to the 'house of hospitality' as Lonen had called it came into view, and a few paces more took them over the threshold and into the building.

They were greeted by the steady hum of voices and found that the room was nearly full of others of their own race, each with plates before them while all chattered; most took no note at all of the company when the entered and moved to sit at a table in the corner. Quickly there were plates before them filled with bacon and eggs, and the three remained silent at first while each scarfed down the food in from of him.

Finally Daedrin leaned forward and crossed his arms as he rested them on the table.

"Do you ever think of home?" he asked softly with a glance at Tara.

"Every day," she replied, and Daedrin winced.

"Marin keeps me from sleep at night," he added in a voice so low that the others barely could hear him over the chatter of voices around them; Tara blinked at the sudden declaration while the young man continued.

"She visits me in my dreams," he said, slightly louder this time as he sighed. "Vivid images that feel so... real. She... I miss her," his voice cracked toward the end and he tilted his head to one side to hide his quivering lips.

"You're not alone," Tara interjected. "The faces of those left behind haunt me..." her voice trailed off and she looked down. "To think that they just... lay where they fell." Her voice was tense and hoarse when she had finished speaking.

Daedrin took in a deep breath as he looked up. "I... spoke to Gavron." His declaration drew attentive stares from his companions while he continued. "Late last night or... early this morning, it must have been." He paused and cleared his throat. "Gavron... he urged me to go back to Linull, to find..." his eyes closed as he took in a deep, shaky breath. "To find Marin and... lay her to rest." He looked around at the forlorn faces of his companions. "She certainly deserves more than to lie in the dirt for the wolves to find," he added softly.

"They all do," Tara remarked as her eyes narrowed.

"Are you certain you wish to take this course?" Hadrîn asked softly while he eyed the young man. "It... would be most unpleasant. You saw as well as I the... state of decay, after just a single day. It has been well over a week, now..." his voice trailed off and Daedrin frowned as he swallowed hard the lump rising in his throat.

"It would be right to see them all buried," he said pensively, and his jaw clenched while he closed his eyes and let his fingers tighten around Tara's own when she grasped his hand with hers.

"If this is truly what you desire to do then I would like to join you," Hadrîn said slowly. "Such a task should not be taken by the two of you alone."

"We all go, then," Tara replied with a dip of her head. "Before anything is done for the land, we return to bury our dead."

They all fell silent again as each drifted into his own quiet thought, and Daedrin frowned when like a band of leather under the hand of the tanner tries to keep itself from being stretched a wave of sudden resistance to the notion of this new plan touched his mind.

"Perhaps the council will transport us there," Hadrîn interrupted the strange sensation Daedrin felt as the silence was finally broken. He and Tara nodded and let their hands part as all rose to their feet and they proceeded to exit the banquet hall with a quiet *"thank you"* to those who had served them.

CHAPTER 14

BETRAYED

After passing through the door Daedrin took the lead as he moved toward the council chamber while the others followed quietly beside in a somber silence while they all pondered the request they were about to make.

"Ishail," Daedrin said in greeting when they approached the door; he found himself pleased to see the familiar face of the guard.

"Greetings," Ishail responded with a dip of his head. "The council awaits your presence." His declaration caused the company to look at another in confusion. "It seems they expected your arrival," Ishail added with a smirk. "Something you become accustomed to after a while…" he finished with a waving gesture as the doors were pulled open. The company passed over the threshold into the room beyond, followed by Ishail and, to their surprise they were greeted by a somber look from the dragons, all of whom were present.

"Please, sit," Crën directed them with a gesture to the chairs at the table; he waited while all settled in nervously. "As you all are doubtless aware," he said once all were seated, "we possess the ability to sense the thought and emotion of the sentient life around us."

Daedrin felt his cheeks grow hot while his eyes narrowed, and he interrupted the old dragon by rising slowly to his feet as the realization of the source of his earlier trepidation dawned on him.

"You dare to press your thoughts onto my own again," he said with a cold, level malice. "Do not, *ever* encroach upon my mind," he added forcefully while his jaw clenched. "I lost my best friend because one of your own had the audacity to force himself onto my thoughts," his voice steadily rose and he finished with a clenched, shaking fist that hung in the air as his words echoed throughout the chamber.

Crën and Sarin exchanged somber glances with one another while they cast their eyes over the dejected face of Mulciber before returning their attention the ferocious gaze of the man before them.

"That… was a tragic accident," Sarin said softly; her elegant voice rang out mournfully. "Mulciber is young, and he broke one of our most sacred rules when he reached out to you that fateful night. I assure you, he has and will continue to face the repercussions for his actions, for we only use this ability to monitor those under our charge; nothing more."

I will show him the true meaning of repercussions! The furious, hate-filled thought flashed through the mind of the young man while his fingers started to slide into the pouch on his waist. Moments before his skin touched the gem that was his target however he felt a hand on his shoulder and turned to see Tara as she beckoned him to sit, and when his brash attitude began to calm he did so slowly.

"We know that you all wish to return to your home to lay to rest those you have lost," Crën said with a stern, knowing gaze at the young man once his mate had finished. "This is a notion that while admirable and to be commended is something we cannot allow."

"Allow?" Daedrin said levelly. "What right have you to keep us from burying our dead?" While Crën and Fortis remained still the others on the council shifted uncomfortably as Sarin interjected.

"Please, don't be angry," she implored. "Times are growing ever more perilous with each passing day, and the four of you leaving the city would not only put us at risk, but would also serve to expose each of you to unnecessary danger."

Daedrin took a deep breath and resisted the urge to feel the cold of his sword hilt beneath his fingers as he closed his eyes.

"I will scout ahead," Alacris interjected suddenly; he ignored the glare from his father for his interruption. "They should be allowed to mourn their loss according to their own custom," he continued as he leaned forward. "I will make sure the path before them is secure, and will keep watch while they do what they feel must be done, and when all is accomplished I shall see that they are returned safely."

"I will fly with you, brother," Saevus remarked with a dip of his head, a sentiment that was quickly echoed by Mulciber. A beat of silence followed, during which Sharleth turned her gaze to Fortis who rolled his eyes.

"If you all must go then so shall I," he said.

Crën heaved a heavy sigh as he dipped and shook his head. "Be careful, my sons," he urged while he cast a stern gaze around the room, and each of his children bowed their chin when his eyes were met.

"Of course, father," Alacris replied. "We all know that this is the right course to take," he added, "for you raised us each with the will to never let fear cause us to abandon seeing that which is just prevail."

Sarin chuckled. "Well, he is certainly your son," she mused with a smile that was weakly returned by her husband.

"Ishail will see to it that you have the provisions required for the journey," the old dragon told them with a gesture to the guard, who dipped his head and motioned for the group to follow before he rapped thrice on the doors. The company rose to their feet with Hadrîn bowing low before following the others as they left the council chamber behind them.

"If I may be so bold, I wish to accompany you," Ishail declared as they walked, to the surprise of the company.

"Why?" Daedrin asked.

The guard turned to give him a sidelong glance. "The more hands you have, the quicker your journey will be completed and all of you will return safely here to Ímrelet. Your arrival has brought with it the first real hope of salvation for our land; I do not wish to see that chance destroyed before it ever truly begins."

"Thank you, Ishail," Daedrin said as he absently looked around while they moved down the street and rounded a corner where they came to a wooden door that was guarded by two fully armored men who stood on either side. They gave a crisp salute when Ishail approached; he grasped the handle and allowed the door to swing open to reveal a storeroom. Casks of water were stacked from the floor to the roughly eight foot high ceiling along two walls while dried fruits and meats in baskets lined the remaining space. Hanging from the ceiling were several leather packs, two of which Daedrin recognized as their own from the journey through the wilderness; his he removed from its hook while Ishail grasped another.

"Be sparing," the guard told him. "Pack only what is needed for three days journey. If we must linger more outside the city we will gather our own provisions from the wild."

Daedrin nodded and put a few handfuls of the dried foods into his leather bag as the others each grabbed a pack of their own and did the same. When all were ready with provisions and full water skins Ishail led them out and proceeded back the way they had come.

"It will not take long for Alacris to return," he said as they walked, "for he is swift."

Daedrin nodded slowly. "He is already here..." he replied with a troubled look on his face. "I... can feel him," he added with as he shook his head. "Something is wrong..."

He cast a glance to Ishail, whose eyes narrowed while his pace quickened. A few hurried steps later took them to the entrance to the council chamber and after a few paces more they all were passing through the doorway.

"What is it?" Ishail asked when he took in the disturbed looks across the faces of those on the council.

"Alacris has discovered something... troubling," Crën said, and

Daedrin's eyes narrowed while he looked around at his companions.

"What?!" he asked with some irritation.

The deep green dragon shook his head. "Your village is... rebuilt," he told him with an expression that looked truly odd on his elegant features; it could perhaps have been called a frown.

Daedrin blinked while Tara's jaw clenched. "What do you mean, rebuilt?" she asked quietly.

"Your former home is bustling with life," the powerful beast replied softly, "and I saw no sign of the destruction you all have described."

Daedrin closed his eyes and took in a deep breath as he struggled to contain the rage rising within like a mighty rushing wind before a destructive storm. He felt his jaw tighten while his teeth began to grind and the sound of his breath filled all of his senses as the voices continuing in the room became like dim and faint echoes from afar. Suddenly he felt pressure on his shoulder that caused him to open his eyes and blink when his mind returned to the present situation; he turned his head to see Hadrîn looking at him through narrowed eyes.

"Peace, lad," he said before removing his hand and returning his attention once more to the council, all of whom were now becoming engrossed in a heated argument.

"This changes everything!" Saevus was saying. "Who knows the depths of Garrôth's schemes if he is able to reach out his arm and replace an entire village!"

"He could be baiting us," Mulciber added.

"It doesn't matter," Tara interjected with a shake of her head as she took a step forward. "An entire people have been wiped from existence, yet a new society has taken *our* homes? Surely this can't have gone unnoticed! We may have been a small community but we had many who came to trade with us. Someone will have answers," she added with a cold fire.

"She's right," Fortis agreed, to the surprise of all. "I certainly made my objections to the venture clear before, but I can only guess that Garrôth is somehow behind this, and if that is the case then we should move with a sense of urgency to discover what plan he has set into motion." He shook his head. "We have been diligent to record to the best of our ability every move he has made out in the wide world, and yet this incredible undertaking has somehow escaped attention." A moment of silence followed the eldest son's dark declarations before Ishail stepped forward with a calculated fire burning in his eyes.

"We should leave at once," he declared, but Alacris shook his head.

"We should not risk being seen in open daylight," he replied solemnly.

"Ordinarily I would agree," the guard argued, "but you heard the words of Fortis; this can only be a scheme of Garrôth, and to have so large a venture go unnoticed is truly troubling…" he shook his head before he turned his attention to Crën.

"My instincts tell me to leave, now; to waste another moment could mean the end of all our plans after so many years."

The wise old dragon frowned, but nodded slowly. "I cannot

shake the terrible feeling that something is very much amiss," he said softly. "Go," he added, "and may the Creator shroud you all with security and wisdom as you embark on this venture."

All gave a quick bow while Alacris lifted his head.

"Fly low," he commanded as he cast a stern glance at each of his brothers. "We should skirt the mountain; land several miles out to avoid being seen."

All nodded while Ishail moved to climb onto the back of Saevus as the other brothers moved to scoop up the remaining three in their claws with only the most brief of pauses to ensure that the humans granted their permission.

Daedrin inhaled sharply when the ground fell swiftly away beneath him and the air in his lungs grew cold. His chest tightened in the midst of the frigid air before the dragons crested the edge of the peak and plunged downward, all the while keeping their flight low and quick, just above the blurred treetops below. After only a few minutes they had rounded the pass and were circling a clearing in the trees where they slowed to hover above the ground and place the company gently onto the earth; they all took in deep, shaky breaths as their bodies adjusted once more to the climate at the base of the mountain.

Ishail quickly dismounted and moved over to the group. "Move quickly," he said softly, "but go with as much stealth as you are able. It would be tragic indeed if we are discovered here in the wild," he added with a wary glance into the surrounding forest.

"We shall keep watch from above," Alacris promised. "Be

vigilant!" he added when he leapt into the air; he was quickly followed by his brothers as all disappeared around the edge of the pass. Daedrin stepped forward with a deep breath while the others followed him into the trees.

They moved cautiously and took great care not to disturb the brush as they moved through the forest. Daedrin and Ishail left everything completely undisturbed, showing plainly their ability as master huntsmen while Tara and Hadrîn did their best to follow in the footsteps of the pair in front. They had traveled in this manner for just over an hour before the sounds of life from a bustling village began to touch their ears; the ringing of hammer on steel echoed first through the trees, followed soon by the sound of voices carried faintly by the wind.

The company exchanged wary glances while they pressed forward, and soon the trees began to thin as Daedrin led them further to their right when familiar trees and other landmarks filled his vision. After a few moments more he held up his hand as he stopped and motioned for the others to move closer.

"The village is just over that ridge," he whispered while he pointed to a gentle slope roughly a stone's throw ahead; he winced as memories of that spot touched his mind.

"Some of us should remain here," Ishail said. "Watch for danger behind," he added with a glance at Daedrin, who nodded before motioning for the guard to follow as he turned to move toward the hill; he paused when he felt something grasp his arm and tilted his head to see Tara looking upon him with eyes ablaze.

"If you think I'm staying behind, you're a fool," she said.

Daedrin's lips twitched in a smirk as he dipped his head. "Come with me, then," he told her with a motion then for Ishail to remain with Hadrîn.

Quietly the pair moved to the base of the hill where they crept cautiously up the mound and fell to their stomachs just before they reached the top and crawled the last few paces until they peeked over the edge with eyes that narrowed when they took in the sight before them.

Linull looked exactly as they remembered it before its destruction; every home and building was in pristine condition, and it was clear that the streets had been cleaned and paved with fresh dirt that was now lightly trampled under the feet of the bustling villagers. Skane's smithy could be seen from where they lay, with a large, burly man swinging a hammer at the glowing surface of a scythe. Daedrin and Tara exchanged dark glances while the young man's hand crept to his sword hilt, but the healer quickly grabbed his wrist and shook her head as she crept silently back down the hill; she was followed shortly by Daedrin.

"Well, what did you see?" Ishail asked when the pair had returned.

"Exactly what Alacris said we would find," Daedrin replied with an angry shake of his head.

"The village shows no sign that it was ever attacked," Tara added with a scowl. "Even Skane's smithy is up and running…" She cast a cold glance at Daedrin's furious gaze.

"I swear, I'll rip the throat out of the man stealing his tools!" the young man declared with eyes ablaze.

"Don't be a fool," Ishail said; he received a sharp look for his warning. "We've no notion of who those people might be, or what their purpose is here. They might very well each be trained soldiers under orders from Garrôth," he added softly. The company fell silent for a while as all pondered what this could mean.

"My farm…" Daedrin suddenly exclaimed softly as his eyes narrowed and turned cold. "If it has been taken by strangers…" his voice trailed off while his jaw clenched and his hand tightened around the hilt of his sword.

"You had a farm?" Ishail asked, but Daedrin gave no sign that he had even heard the guard.

"Yes," Tara spoke for the young man while she eyed him carefully before she turned to the guard. "It's a few miles to the northeast, near the edge of the forest beneath the mountains."

The guard rubbed his jaw beneath narrowed eyes. "We should visit this place," he said with a slow nod of his head as he continued. "If it has indeed been taken in the same manner as your village then it will be occupied, but likely by only a few. We can perhaps take them by surprise and bring them back to Ímrelet for proper questioning."

Hadrîn nodded. "Sound counsel," he agreed, and Ishail dipped his head before he turned to look at Daedrin.

"Lead the way," he commanded softly.

The young man rolled his jaw before he turned to the side and quickly moved deeper into the trees with the others close behind. While still moving more quietly than most his stealth was not nearly as sound as their initial journey, for each step was fueled by a growing apprehension and anger with a sense of dread. In just under an hours' time they had completed the silent journey; Daedrin stopped at the edge of the trees just before they opened up into the vast clearing where his home lay spread out before him.

He felt his chest tighten as he took in the sight before him, for the barn which had been a heap of rubble and charred flesh when last he had laid eyes on it was now a cleared space, with a large pile of lumber off to one side. Three men could be seen with woodworking tools in hand while they moved together to place timber around in the beginning stages of the erection of a new structure. One was older, with two younger men beside him; they appeared to be the approximate ages of Daedrin's slain father and brother while one seemed to be much like Daedrin himself. The three talked and laughed while they worked; chatter that couldn't quite be made out as the voices echoed faintly across the field.

Daedrin felt an overwhelming fury surface within as his eyes scanned the yard behind his home where he looked for markers that were nowhere to be seen. His jaw tightened while the sight of desecrated graves washed over him and filled him with a hate that far surpassed even the deep seated resentment he harbored toward Garrôth. The voices of his companions whispering behind him seemed to come from far off as he drew sword from sheath and took a step forward before he was grabbed from behind by strong arms.

He struggled to break free, and his eyes were wide and red as his anger consumed him while his mouth opened to cry out before a hand clamped over his lips and jaw to muffle the sound when it escaped. He felt his sword being pulled from his grip as his own body was yanked backward by Ishail, who dragged him further into the forest before tripping and falling to land hard with the young man atop him.

"Peace," Tara's voice touched his ears, and he turned to see her on one knee by his side. Her gaze was filled with sympathy as she reached out to rest a hand on his shoulder; his naked blade was clutched tightly within Hadrîn's grip.

"Peace," she repeated more softly this time, and slowly, ever so slowly Daedrin felt his chest relax while his breathing began to slow. At a nod from the healer Ishail slowly released his hold and let the young man collapse to his side on the ground.

"They will answer for this," Tara said; her eyes were ablaze with fury and compassion as Daedrin reach out to grasp the hilt of his sword. He stuck the blade into the earth and used it to push himself to his feet.

"Yes," he agreed shakily. "I will see them *burn* for this atrocity!"

"I see only four," Ishail observed as he peered into the clearing. "A woman through the window, with two men and a child outside."

"We should take them now!" Daedrin said a little too loudly; his voice carried through the trees and caused the group by the farmhouse to tilt their heads toward where the company stood in the forest.

"Down!" Tara exclaimed softly as she yanked Daedrin by the arm and fell to her hands in a motion that was quickly copied by the others. They all nearly held their breath while the three in the clearing scanned the woods quietly for a few moments before returning to their chatter and work. Slowly the company rose slightly with each coming to rest on either one knee or the balls of their feet as they took up a crouching stance.

"We will never take them by surprise at this hour," Ishail whispered. "The cover of darkness will be our ally if we truly wish to capture them unawares."

Daedrin ground his teeth. "Very well," he conceded as he backed slowly away to increase the distance between himself and the farm while he slunk deeper into the forest with the others following closely. He led them to a tighter cluster of trees a few hundred paces away where he settled in with his back to a great oak while the rest followed suit.

None spoke while the hours passed and the sun moved across the sky. Ishail passed the time by absently running a whetstone quietly across the edge of his sword as he stared into the wilderness, while Tara and Hadrîn exchanged whispered conversation off to one side and Daedrin closed his eyes for a brief rest; all waited for night to fall. When at last the final rays of sunlight were replaced by a gentle glow from the moon Ishail moved over to Daedrin and reached out a hand that was snatched out of the air as Daedrin's eyes snapped open.

"Time to move," the guard smirked at the hand of the young

man as it clutched his wrist. With a frown Daedrin released his grip and rose to his feet, and in a few moments all were crouched at the edge of the forest once more where they peered at the now quiet farmhouse.

"They are asleep," Hadrîn observed as he took note of the darkened windows.

Ishail nodded. "So it would seem," he said and, with a wave of his hand for the others to follow he took a step forward but remained crouched while he closed the distance between them and the silent structure with several quick, soft paces. He placed his back against the nearest outer wall and turned to see the rest of the company copy the position when they had all caught up to him. Slowly he slid quietly to the edge of the building that faced the rear of the dwelling and peered warily around the corner. Seeing no sign of immediate danger he motioned once more for all to follow as he crouched and moved quickly to the back door of the home where he tossed a look over to Daedrin and gestured for him to move closer.

"You know the terrain from here," he said in a barely audible whisper whenever Daedrin was inches from his own face. "Remember," he added with a stern gaze, "we take them alive."

Daedrin narrowed his eyes and nodded as he moved past the guard to the door where he reached out one hand and slowly turned the handle. The latch made a light pop when it released and the hinges creaked slightly while the door swung open; the sound caused all to cringe. With a soft but deep breath Daedrin stepped through the doorway, taking great care that his footfalls remained completely silent. As his eyes adjusted to the dark he scanned the structure, and his jaw clenched ever so slightly when he took in its pristine condition. He waved the others in and stepped to the side while all moved through the doorway; they each lined the hallway after they had entered.

Daedrin motioned to a closed door down the hall to his left and held up two fingers before pointing at Ishail and Tara who each nodded as they crept toward the room. He began himself to move to an entryway with no door to his immediate right with a motion for Hadrîn to follow. The old man nodded as he moved to stand beside the young man with one hand on his sword hilt before they moved slowly into the nearest room. The sleeping form of two young men met their eyes when they entered; each lay on his own small bed on opposite walls.

Daedrin felt the overwhelming urge rise with him to take his sword and slit each of the throats of those who would dare lie in the very beds that he and his brother had rested their weary bodies after a day of hard labor. His dark thoughts however were interrupted by Hadrîn as the old man placed a hand gently on his shoulder and gave him a gentle yet stern gaze. Taking in a quiet, shaky breath Daedrin moved closer to the slumbering form to his right and watched for a moment the chest of the boy rise and fall before he locked eyes with Hadrîn and nodded to the other figure. The old man dipped his head and moved to kneel down as he closed the distance between himself and the young man to his left. When they both were in place the former farmer held up his fingers and counted down slowly from three. As he reached "one" he and Hadrîn jerked with a quick motion to tightly cover the mouth of each of the sleeping forms; their screams were muffled when they awoke.

With a sharp follow-through the pair pulled the two young men from their beds and grappled them as the strangers struggled and screamed beneath the hands of their captors. Hadrîn moved backward first while he dragged his kicking and jerking captive through the doorway and out of the home before he spun the young man and threw him down face-first onto the dirt. Quickly the old man dropped one knee into the back of the form that was now pinned beneath him while with his hands he grasped one of the flailing arms, jerked it back and held it tightly twisted across the squared shoulders of his captive. Daedrin moved through the doorway shortly after with the younger of the two boys held tightly in his strong arms as he moved beside Hadrîn.

"Be still!" Daedrin commanded sharply, "or I will not hesitate to relieve your brothers' shoulders of his head!" The struggling slowed before it finally ceased while the boy's screams turned to whimpers. With a scowl Daedrin watched the form beneath Hadrîn continue to resist for a moment before the young man kicked him roughly on the side of the head.

"The same goes for you with this runt," he said with a cold malice as he roughly jerked the boy in his arms.

Hadrîn smirked at the remark when the shuffling of feet behind them caused the pair to turn and see the raised hands of a man and women approaching; the glint of steel under the moonlight could be seen shining off of the naked edge of a dagger at each of their throats. Tara stood behind the women while Ishail held the tall man as they pushed the captives forward.

"Please, don't hurt my babies!" the women wailed when she saw the subdued forms under Hadrîn and Daedrin.

"If you hurt them, I swear…" the man said with teeth grinding when he jerked for a moment. Daedrin threw the child hard onto the dirt and drew his blade slowly as he moved closer to the man in front of Ishail.

"Daedrin…" the guard warned while he warily eyed the naked blade before him.

"Relax Ishail," the young man told him. "You wanted someone alive to question and I have no intention of taking that from you. But I have the right to my own answers before you are allowed your turn!" His jaw tightened and he moved closer to the eldest of the children; his blade he placed gently against the side of the captive's throat. "Who's to say we need to bring them all back?" he added coldly.

"Enough!" Tara exclaimed while she forced the women in front of her to her knees; the healer's eyes burned with a curious sort of fury.

"This is not the way," she added, and her voice broke as her eyes connected with Daedrin. The young man swallowed when took in her desperate gaze, for his mind wandered briefly back to the story she had relayed to him of her tragic past. He backed away slowly with a blink as he heaved several deep breaths and sheathed his sword.

"There is rope in my pack," Ishail said with a nod at Daedrin who moved slowly over to the guard, reached into his satchel and withdrew a coil of threaded twine. With a kick Ishail forced the man whose throat was close to his own dagger down to his knees, and Daedrin quickly proceeded to cross the man's hands before he cinched them tight with a coil of rope. After cutting off a section long enough for another binding the young man passed the rest to the guard before he himself approached the woman held by Tara. When she was securely bound the young man turned to see that Ishail with Hadrîn had restrained the remaining two, and in a few moments more the prisoners were standing in a line as Ishail cinched all of the bindings together in one long train with a lead rope in his own hand.

"Let's go," the guard commanded as he moved forward with a tug that forced the captives to follow when he began to take quick steps toward the forest. The rest of the company surrounded the prisoners while they walked together and came into the cover of the trees after a few moments.

"Why are you doing this?" the woman wailed while they moved; her breathing was labored as tears spilled down her cheeks. Ishail only glanced back with a glare and a frown.

"Daedrin," he said once they had come to a slight clearing in the forest, "it's time to call our ride."

The young man nodded and took in a deep breath as he closed his eyes, concentrated and reached out with his mind when… *Snap!* His eyes jerked suddenly open when his ears took in the sound of a twig breaking in the brush ahead of them. He locked eyes with Ishail as the guard moved the lead to his off hand and drew his blade with the other while his eyes scanned the dark trees beyond.

Silver gleamed under the pale moonlight after Daedrin quickly pulled his own sword from its sheath and warily looked around. More noise reached his ears, like the footfalls of something perhaps heavy disturbing the forest as it moved through the bramble; Hadrîn quickly drew his own weapon while Tara brandished her staff defensively. The cracking sounds grew louder as the unknown something drew nearer until suddenly a slender, two-legged figure stumbled out of the forest and into the clearing. Its eyes glinted briefly before the form collapsed face first onto the ground where it then remained still and unmoving.

The group all exchanged wary glances before Daedrin started to move toward the shape on the ground with Tara close behind. He closed the distance cautiously with blade extended as he knelt down next to what he now saw was a form veiled by a dark, dirty and torn cloak. Slowly he reached out one hand when, with a sudden twist the figure kicked the sword from his hand, grabbed his other arm and pulled him close as a short knife was placed against his throat.

"Stay back!" said a strained feminine voice that was light and fair beneath the panic. "I'll cut his throat, I swear!"

Tara held up her hands. "Please, don't," she pleaded in her raspy, elegant voice as she slowly lowered herself to one knee and placed her staff carefully on the ground. The breathing of the slender figure began to slow slightly while the hand which held the knife relaxed somewhat.

"Tara?" the voice said, and the healer blinked with sudden recognition.

"Marin?" she replied softly, and at the sound of that name the village girl lowered the dagger and released Daedrin as she burst suddenly into deep sobs.

The young man rolled to his knees and stared in complete shock and wonder that turned to pain when he took in the tattered, torn and scarred appearance of the woman before him. Slowly he reached out one shaky hand to rest on her dirty face for a moment before he wrapped it around the back of her neck and pulled her into a crushing embrace. Tears began to well up within his own eyes as he held her trembling form, for she wept so intensely that the cloth against his shoulder began to grow damp. Tara moved to kneel beside them as she placed one hand on Marin's shoulder while Hadrîn sheathed his sword and made a motion to Ishail that all was well.

After several minutes Marin's sobs began to slow and she pulled away to meet Daedrin's intense gaze with an entirely wild look of her own. He took in the fullness of her appearance with a hard swallow as he reached out and gently ran one hand over the scars that now covered the left side of her once-fair face. Marin took in a trembling breath and looked down in shame before Daedrin pulled her into another embrace and turned to stare at Tara with wide eyes.

"Is she alright?" Hadrîn's voice caused Marin to flinch. She looked up and took in a sudden sharp breath when her gaze fell on the old man before her lips parted and she let loose ear piercing wail that caused those listening to cringe.

"Stay away, stay away!" she screamed as she recovered her dagger and frantically pulled away from Daedrin. She scrambled backwards before Tara rushed to her side, pulled her into an embrace and wrapped concerned hands around Marin's head while the frightened girl rested her face on the healer's chest and sobbed.

"What is it?" Tara asked while Daedrin half crawled, half stumbled over to the pair where they knelt on the ground.

"Why is he with you?" Marin whispered frantically between shaky breaths as she lifted her gaze to meet Daedrin's.

"Why is he with you?!" she repeated, and her voice rose to a near screech while her chest heaved from her labored breathing.

"He's... a friend," Daedrin told her. "Do you know him?" he added as he bent lower to look her in the eyes.

After a beat of silence interrupted only by Marin's choked gasps for air her breathing began to settle and her gaze slowly lit up with a fire while her jaw clenched.

"He... had me taken!" she declared with slow forcefulness as she pointed her finger toward the wide-eyed face of the old man. "He handed me over to... to Garrôth..." she stumbled while her voice broke and several tears spilled down her cheeks.

"Daedrin..." she turned her gaze to the young man when he blinked with confusion. "He had our village destroyed..." her voice was barely more than a whisper as she looked upon him with wide eyes.

Daedrin felt as if his blood turned while this knowledge coursed through his mind and he once again took in Marin's battered form. He met Tara's eyes and saw within them the same shock and anger that was beginning to fill his own heart as he reached out to the grass and felt the hilt of his sword fill his hand. Slowly he rose to his feet and turned to face Hadrîn with chest heaving while the lifted blade trembled in his furious grasp.

The old man raised both hands and backed away a step. "This is a trick," he said slowly.

Daedrin shook his head as he took a step forward. "You were tortured by Garrôth..." he said, and his was voice tense while he steadily closed the distance between them. "Lived... in seclusion, above *my* farm... the 'chance' meeting of you and I... and the horse...." Daedrin's eyes slowly began to burn with a cold fury as he moved to within a few paces of the old man. "Back in Cordin... the man whose horse we stole bore the same mark as your own, this horse you supposedly bought... you *did* kill those men on the mountain."

"I assure you," Hadrîn said while he shook his head slowly. "I did not."

"His loyalties may have been compromised," Ishail interjected as his eyes moved between the old man and the prisoners. "Restrain him." He removed the remaining coil of rope from his pack and tossed it to the young man.

Daedrin snatched the bindings from the air with his free hand before he returned his attention to the man before him.

"On your knees," he commanded slowly as he eyed Hadrîn's hands while they twitched above his sword hilt.

"You cannot kill me, boy," the old man warned. "We both know as much."

"I know," Daedrin said as with sudden brashness he dropped the rope and swung his blade outward and down.

The piercing sound of metal on metal rang out through the night when his blade connected with Hadrîn's swiftly drawn weapon. With a cold focus the young man pushed forward a step and slung his arms to the side before he let them fly forward with such tremendous force that the blow nearly knocked the old man over as it collided with the steel of his sword. Letting slip a fell cry Daedrin whirled, and as he spun the night was lit up with a brilliant, gleaming white light that suddenly radiated from his blade. His eyes widened as his third blow connected and sliced cleanly through Hadrîn's own sword like a hot knife through butter before it struck the old man in the chest and clove a deep wound from his right shoulder down to the lower left part of his ribcage.

With lips parting in bewilderment at the white hot glow emanating from his weapon Daedrin let his grip relax and his blade fell to the ground. He watched in astonishment as the light vanished the moment the sword left his grip before it hit the earth hilt-first, bounced and settled flat on the grass; the inscription etched into its length burned with a faint orange tint that slowly faded to its usual black. With a blink he swallowed and turned to Hadrîn in time to witness the old man fall to his knees while he clutched at the deep gash on his chest; smoke rose slightly, and the smell of burnt flesh touched the nostrils of the two men.

For a few moments Hadrîn only knelt there clutching the wound before he looked up to meet Daedrin's shocked gaze. The old man opened his mouth to speak but only groaned instead with a kind of raspy moaning as he blinked and his breath grew shallow while his eyes widened in confusion, for the wound was not healing itself. His body swayed for a moment before he collapsed sideways to the ground with a final moan.

Daedrin's heart began to pound in his chest while he knelt slowly to the ground beside the fallen man and reached out to place one hand on his neck.

"No…" he whispered to himself as the realization of Hadrîn's death washed over him, carrying with it his only chance to know what the old man had been planning.

His thoughts were interrupted suddenly by a painful crashing sensation upon his mind that caused him to fold forward with body convulsing as his muscles grew taut before he fell to the earth. The voices of his companions seemed to come from afar when Tara rushed to his side, but her tone of concern was overwhelmed by a sudden furious wind that filled the clearing for a moment before a loud crash caused those in the field to cover their heads as first one dragon and then two others landed hard onto the earth around them with a horrendous roar.

Daedrin groaned and slowly rolled to his knees with the help of the healer. It seemed as if the world around him was moving at half its normal speed while he blinked and clutched his chest, for his heart pounded and became filled with a terribly painful burning sensation.

"Ímrelet!" he exclaimed suddenly as he turned to grab Tara by both her shoulders while he met her wide eyes. "Ímrelet," he said again more softly, and tears suddenly welled up in his eyes before they spilled down both cheeks as he cast his gaze to the top of the mountain. *Ímrelet...*

The End

ABOUT THE AUTHOR

I started writing when I was just 12 years old and now as an adult, I haven't stopped. With the constant support of my loving wife creative writing is without a doubt more than just a hobby; it's a passion that has led to a career. I find the most fulfillment from life when I enter the created world of my works of fiction, seeing through the eyes of the characters as they are brought to life. Through this I am able to manifest some of the issues that I deal with in my own life and walk with God, so as you are reading you will find a few parallels of my personal story, some of which I imagine you will be able to identify with, as well. In The Redemptive Chronicles: Retribution, as well as with the rest of the series going forward I hope that you as the reader are able to connect with the characters as I have, perhaps even learning something about yourself by the end of the story.

- *D.M. Kurtz*

Made in the USA
San Bernardino, CA
25 July 2017